Working Through It

Kasha Thompson

WEBSTER AVENUE PUBLISHING
LINCOLN, CA

WORKING THROUGH IT

WORKING THROUGH IT © 2021 Kasha Thompson

Paperback ISBN: 978-0-578-97667-9

Published by Webster Avenue Publishing
Lincoln, CA

Printed in the United States of America
First Edition February, 2022

Cover Art by: Beka Giorgadze
Cover Design by: Make Your Mark Publishing Solutions
Interior Layout by: Make Your Mark Publishing Solutions
Editing: Make Your Mark Publishing Solutions

ACKNOWLEDGEMENTS

To my husband, Michael, you make me happy. When we first started dating, I remember driving home from work with a smile on my face and realizing it was because being with you made me happy. I am a strong personality, and you have never been intimidated or asked that I water myself down. With you I can be exactly who I am. You love my son as your own and have been a true example for our son on how a man should love a woman. I am not into mushy expressions of love, but thank you for allowing me to love you and for loving me.

To my son Xavier, you are the best thing I've ever created. You are a curious, smart, funny young man, and you get that all from me. It has been such an honor to be your guide on this journey called life. Thank you for keeping me young and allowing me to say things like "No cap" and other slang. My dream for you is that you live the life you want, finding happiness in all that you do. You are the dopest person I've ever met. My love for you is vast and never ending.

To my mother, from you I learned the importance of hard work. You worked hard to support us, oftentimes pushing aside your dreams so your daughters could realize their own. You taught me to be independent and believe in my abilities. I am a strong, educated, confident woman because I watched you. I love you.

Twana, I could not ask for a better big sister. Growing up, you were my role model and my guide. You're my best friend, and even when we were on opposite sides of the country, I knew if I ever needed anything that my sister would be there for me. I cannot express what it has meant to have you by my side during this process. Thank you for allowing me to vent my frustrations or ramble with excitement. Thanks for your feedback, hyping me up when warranted, and keeping it real when necessary.

To my father, the storyteller, I will always appreciate the times when I was allowed to listen to you reminisce about the past. You provided an oral history of our family that included culture, family dynamics, and a bit of juicy gossip.

To my friends, thank you for always being there for me. I am a private person, but when I shared my dream of writing a book, you supported me and encouraged me even before one word was on the page. Thank you for always supporting my dream, even when I had doubts.

Thank you to Monique Mensah and the team at Make Your Mark Publishing Solutions for your editing expertise, insight, and guidance while helping to polish my manuscript.

Beka Giorgadze for creating the character illustration for my book cover. You listened to my ideas and created an image that represented my characters perfectly.

M. Ross Photography, the last time I took professional photos was on my wedding day, so it had been a minute. Your photographs captured the start of my journey as I embark on this new adventure. Thank you.

For Beverly and Twana, my day ones.

Chapter 1

"Are you getting nervous?" Phor Thomas asked.

Travis Holmes checked his watch. He was meeting with Senior Pastor Eugene Randolph in thirty minutes.

"A little bit." Travis pinched the brim of his nose. As the business administration manager, Travis had meetings with the pastor often, but something about this felt different.

Phor scratched at his thick beard. "Any ideas what it's about?"

Knowing Pastor Randolph, it could be any number of things. For all Travis knew, they could end up talking about fly fishing for an hour. He made a mental note to Google quick facts about the sport so he wouldn't be caught off guard.

Travis bounced his shoulder. "Your guess is as good as mine. But he had Tami call me to schedule the meeting, which was odd because, usually, he just shoots me a text."

His phone alarm began to chime; he had set it to go off twenty minutes before the meeting. He wanted to give himself ample time to make it to the main building.

Tossing his laptop and notebook into his backpack, he gave Phor a dap. "All right, I'm out."

"Give 'em hell," Phor teased.

Travis had been a member of Life Church since he was twenty-two years old, which was now almost ten years. If you told him years ago he would end up working full-time at a church, he would have asked to take a puff of what you were smoking. Growing up in Oakland, California, his mother would drag him and his sister, Aisha, to church every Sunday. She was a faithful member at their little Baptist church, offering to volunteer at every opportunity. Aside from preacher, there wasn't a church position she hadn't held. Much like his mother, ever since he could remember, Travis found particular interest in "church business," which is what they called it back in the day. So, there he was, business administration manager at one of the most progressive mega churches in the Metro Atlanta area.

Exiting one of the annex buildings on the ten-acre campus, Travis took hurried steps toward the main structure. The rain was coming down in heavy sheets as he crossed under a covered walkway, narrowly missing a puddle. He entered the main building through a side door that led to the lobby. It was a Tuesday afternoon, so the lobby was virtually empty, with a few members of the church staff milling about. Wiping the raindrops from his tapered fade, he once again scanned his watch. He'd made good time; he still had fourteen minutes to spare.

Eyeing the church café, he wagered that he could grab a coffee before he headed to the wing of the building that housed the administrative offices. Much like the lobby, the café was virtually empty, and Travis made it in and out with ten minutes still on the clock. Back in the lobby, he raised the cup to his mouth, stopping mid-sip as the glass doors of the front entrance swung open, the wind so fierce it caused the door to bang against its frame. In rushed the lead pastor's youngest daughter, Makayla Randolph. Struggling to close the door, she fought against the wind as her long black curls circled her head like a tornado. The black-and-white polka dot umbrella she was attempting to balance between her neck and chin was caught by the wind and drifted into the center of the church lobby.

"Need help?" Travis yelled as he surveilled from the café entrance.

Makayla ejected a tight-lipped huff. "I got it," she said, giving the glass door another pull.

The lobby was now empty, except for the two of them. Travis took slow sips from his coffee, taking special interest in Makayla's fight with nature. Her Michael Kors tote bag slipped from her shoulders, scattering its contents to the floor.

"Son of a bit … biscuit," Makayla muttered as she tried to brush her voluminous hair from her face.

With a grunted breath, he decided it was time to put her out of her misery. Placing his cup and backpack on a café table, he hopped across the lobby and tugged on the door, but it didn't budge.

"I tried that already. It's stuck or something." She scooped up her items, cramming them back into her purse. Bending, Travis pulled onto a clasp, which released the door and allowed him to close it successfully. He waved his arms up and down like a game show model in the direction of the door. Makayla swung her tote bag back across her shoulder and walked away.

"You're welcome," Travis shouted after her, sucking his lower lip between his teeth. Makayla didn't respond; she just made her way through the spacious modern lobby, only stopping to grab her rogue umbrella. "Thank you" wasn't a phrase he ever heard her say, at least not to him. With her, no good deed went unpunished. *I should have just let her pull at the door in vain*, he thought.

Returning to his coffee, he took another sip. The nutty, chocolate medium-dark roast helped soothe his grumpy mood. With his coffee in one hand and his backpack slung across his shoulder, he headed down the long hallway that led to the administrative offices.

"Good afternoon, Tami," Makayla greeted Pastor Randolph's assistant. Tami was a petite woman in her early thirties, a year older than Makayla, who sported large dimples on both cheeks.

Flipping through the pages of a magazine, Tami returned a bright smile. "Hey, girl. You here to see your father?"

"Yeah, I have a four thirty meeting."

"OK, well, just take a seat. He's finishing up a conference call. It shouldn't be long."

Makayla sunk into the oversized leather armchair. The waiting room was contemporary with pops of gemstone-colored accent pieces and a glass chandelier making it look more like the Cosmopolitan hotel in Las Vegas than the waiting area of a house of worship. Grabbing her tote bag, she searched for a hair tie. The rain and wind had done a number on her hair, and she didn't want to look like a puff ball in her meeting. She took pride in her appearance; her nails and toes were always freshly manicured, hair perfectly coiffed, never an errant curl. Examining her image in her silver compact, she was surprised Tami hadn't commented on her appearance. Her long, twisted curls were a frizzy mess, which always happened anytime her hair got wet.

Finally making his way to the administrative office, Travis approached the receptionist desk.

"Hey, Tami, how are you?" he asked.

Makayla raised her head slightly, eyelids at half-mast.

"I'm doing good. The pastor is finishing up a meeting. You staying dry?" Tami replied, her dimples emerging as she subtly flirted with him.

"It's crazy out there. I heard it was supposed to rain the rest of the week." Travis leaned on her desk.

"I hate the rain. Prefer feeling the sun on my skin."

"Rainy days can be nice when you have nowhere to go and you can just chill on the sofa and watch old movies."

Makayla rolled her eyes and let out a soft cough to remind them she was in the room, catching the not-so-subtle frown he threw in her direction.

"Talk later." He tapped his knuckle on Tami's desk, sauntering over to the waiting area. Reaching down, he organized the magazines scattered on the large wooden coffee table so they were displayed in a neat stack before taking a seat opposite Makayla. She stared at the magazines, fighting the urge to scatter them across the table. Pulling her long hair through the hair tie, she twisted it into a neat bun, purposely choosing not to look at or engage in small talk with Travis.

"Are you meeting with your dad?" he asked as he flipped open a *Fast Company* magazine.

"No, I just really like the ambiance."

Travis's mouth spread into a bright, toothy grin.

She liked Travis in small doses, and she had already passed her threshold. Looking at her reflection in her compact mirror, Makayla reapplied her plum lipstick to her full lips, running a finger across her rich brown skin. She tried to ignore the constant rhythm from Travis patting his thigh with his hand. Her knee bounced, giving away her battle with the increasing nervous energy she was experiencing. She'd visited her father's office many times, but this was the first time she could remember being summoned. Her father founded Life Church before she was born, and it had grown exponentially over the years, especially the past ten. With an established career at a private foundation, Makayla made the tough decision to leave her job and assist her father as an administrative leader in the teen ministry. With more than twelve thousand parishioners, there was no question about whether her father could match her salary. He did that and more.

Finally, when she'd had enough of Travis's noise, she blurted out, "Can you stop that? Geez!"

"What?" Travis asked, cocking an eyebrow in surprise.

"The rapping on your knees. It's annoying." Makayla waved her hand back and forth.

"It's not bothering me." Travis picked up the tempo. She rolled her chestnut eyes, which made him hum along softly to the beat, a slight smile spreading across his face.

A loud buzz rang out from Tami's desk.

"Yes," Tami said as she adjusted the earpiece in her ear. "Yes, they're both here." She paused before continuing. "Yes, will do." Tami cleared her throat. "Pastor Randolph will see you now."

"Me?" Makayla asked, pointing at her chest.

"Both of you."

Makayla snorted, dumbfounded as to why she and Travis would be called to a meeting with her father. She and Travis didn't exactly share the same social circles. Draping her raincoat across her arm, she grabbed her purse and headed for her father's office. Travis followed closely. Tami's long fingernails frantically typed on the keyboard, but she glanced up long enough to give Travis a quick smile.

"Good luck," she whispered before they disappeared behind the office door.

Chapter 2

Makayla walked into her father's outstretched arms and planted a soft peck on his cheek.

"How are you?" she asked, setting her coat, umbrella, and purse in a paisley armchair in the corner of the room.

"I can't complain . . . no one would listen," Pastor Randolph joked.

Travis's low-pitched laugh filled the room. Makayla shook her head, settling into the chair directly in front of the massive desk. Her father had quoted that same line since forever. It had stopped being funny years ago. What Travis found in her father's age-old cliché she would never understand. Rolling her eyes, she wondered whether he was going to suck up to her dad the entire time. As part of the staff, he had spent plenty of time with her father. Travis attended family dinners, backyard pool parties, and birthdays. He even spent a couple of holidays at her folks' house when he couldn't make it home to be with his family for Thanksgiving or Christmas. So why he chose to be a first-class ass kisser was beyond her.

"Can I offer you some coffee or tea?" Pastor Randolph asked.

"No, thank you." Travis held up his nearly empty cup of coffee.

"I'm good. Meeting friends for dinner afterward," Makayla said, crossing her legs.

"Sit down." The pastor tapped Travis lightly on the arm. He claimed a seat next to Makayla.

As she waited for her father to return to his leather office chair, she surveyed the walls of his office, which were lined with plaques and photographs of her father with celebrities and other well-known pastors, such as Oprah, Joel Osteen, and former President Barack Obama. Behind his desk were family photos with her mother and sisters. Makayla's eyes came to rest on a framed picture of her with her parents at her college graduation, all smiles.

"I hope I didn't keep you both waiting for too long," the pastor said, scribbling on his notepad.

"No, not at all. Why are we here?" Makayla asked, never one to mince words. She knew that if she let him, her father would ramble on for fifteen minutes before getting to the reason he'd called them together. Eugene Randolph loved the sound of his own voice and thought every moment was a teachable one.

Pastor Randolph chuckled at his daughter's impatience. "Well, I've been thinking a lot about making some changes here at the church. You know . . . shuffling some pieces and adding a few new ones to the board." Pastor Randolph looked up from the notepad, surveying their anxious facial expressions.

Travis squinted his hazel eyes, trying to grasp where this was going.

"I think change keeps people on their toes. Don't you agree?" Pastor Randolph asked, gesturing toward Makayla.

"Ah . . . yeah, I guess so. You definitely like surprising people." She could think of more than one occasion when her father had come home excited about a new change or appointment he was about to make at the church.

"I was thinking about the singles ministry." Pastor Randolph directed his gaze toward Travis. "I know we've talked in the past about your path here. Helping to manage a church this size is no small feat. You remind me a lot of myself when I was your age."

Makayla rolled her eyes. She had not come here to witness the never-ending bromance between her father and Travis.

"Well, thank you, sir. I appreciate that."

"So, tell me, Travis, how would you feel about leading the singles ministry full-time?" Pastor Randolph asked.

Makayla's mouth went slack, turning toward Travis, who appeared more surprised than she did. He had always been a hard worker, valedictorian in high school, top of his class in college, and as quiet as it was kept, he was secretly doing everything in his power to eventually become the director of operations at Life Church. But ministry leader? Travis was more of a facts-and-figures guy not the praise-and-worship guy.

"What about Jason?" Travis asked.

"Brother Jason is moving on. Remember what I said about mixing up the game pieces." Pastor Randolph grinned.

To Makayla's dismay, her father had always had an affinity toward Travis. He served as a mentor, taking Travis under his wing, slowly sharing the inner workings of the church. Why he couldn't share these things with his more-than-capable daughters was beyond her.

"So, would I work with Raeann?" Raeann being Jason's wife and co-leader of the singles ministry.

"The McPhersons are going to lead the married ministry," Pastor Randolph said. "Since you're a bit of an outsider when it comes to ministry work, you can bring a fresh new approach to how we do things.

If Travis is being placed in another ministry, will I be moved too? The breath left her chest as her mind raced. The one thing she didn't want was to be tossed from ministry to ministry. If she'd known that was what her father had in store for her, she would have stayed at the non-profit organization. She recalled the day her father asked her to come work for the church. Although her mother didn't believe Makayla would leave her job as an outreach director for at-risk teens, her father was certain she would. As a natural-born salesman, he could sell water to a drowning man. Life Church was a family business, with both of her older sisters also working in the administrative office.

9

"I get that you're more of a behind-the-scenes type of guy, but that's where Makayla comes in," her father casually announced. "I want you two to lead together." He smiled from ear to ear, clearly tickled pink by the revelation of the plan he had sprung on the two.

Makayla cackled so loudly it seemed to vibrate the glass figurines on the desk. "You can't be serious." She waited for her father to say April Fools', even though it was March.

"The both of you are exactly what the singles ministry needs. Two go-getters, eager to put your stamp on things and make it your own. Don't you agree, Travis?"

Travis hitched his shoulders. "I'm not really sure this is the best fit." He moved his hands between them.

"I agree with him." Makayla ignored Travis, who was eyeing her with disbelief. They were never on the same page, but on this, they were united.

Clearly sensing their apprehension, Pastor Randolph offered, "I know it's a lot to take in. I want to give you some time to think about it. Pray about it. I'll expect a decision in a few days."

"But . . ." Makayla paused, not knowing what to say.

"All right, get out of here. I have to start working on this sermon." The pastor stood, signaling the end of the meeting. Both Makayla and Travis rose, vacant expressions settling on their faces as they walked toward the door. Travis turned on his heels, abruptly bumping into Makayla, who was close behind. Grabbing her hand, he reached for her waist to help her maintain her balance. Makayla snatched her hand from his, retreating backward.

"Have a good evening," Travis addressed the pastor. Opening the office door, he glanced back to see Makayla scowling in his direction before slamming the door in his face.

"What are you doing?" Makayla asked.

"I am growing our leadership."

"I am not going to work with him." Makayla drew a thoughtful breath and checked her tone. "I'm not saying he wouldn't make a good leader, but—"

The pastor pinched the brim of his nose. "Then, what are you saying?"

"He's my ex-boyfriend. Don't you think that would be a tiny bit awkward." Furrowing her brow, she wondered why he couldn't get this.

"I thought you two had moved past that."

Her right eye started to twitch. A throbbing pressure was creeping in the base of her skull. "We have, but that doesn't mean I want to work with him every single day," Makayla lied. She and Travis had not moved past it; they were at an impasse.

He walked over to his daughter, placing his hands on her shoulders. "Just think it over before you make a rash decision. Can you do that for me, baby girl?" Her father pulled her into a hug, kissing the top of her head.

"I'll try," she whispered through gritted teeth.

Making his way back to the lobby, Travis stood in front of the doors, staring into the virtually empty parking lot. The gears in his head were whirling and buzzing at a hundred miles per hour. He was definitely looking for promotion opportunities, but leadership wasn't exactly what he had in mind. During their mentoring sessions, Pastor Randolph had mentioned that if he wanted to run a church, he had to understand what the church did, from maintenance to the final amen on Sunday. Travis assumed he meant volunteering, not running one of the largest groups on campus. But if he wanted to end up as director of operations one day, he needed to learn all aspects of the church, and the ministries were the heartbeat of the organization.

"Hey!" Makayla yelled, entering the lobby.

The muscles around Travis's jawline tightened as she advanced. He was in no mood for her attitude. Hurriedly exiting the building, he was immediately hit in the face by the chill of the air. Fortunately, the rain had stopped. Tugging at his jacket, he hurried toward the parking lot.

"Wait! We need to talk about this," Makayla said.

Travis halted his advance. If she wanted to do this now, they could do it now.

"What did you say to your father?" He whipped around to face her.

"What are you talking about?"

"Come on. Don't act like you weren't just in there calling me everything but a child of God," Travis shot back. Makayla was a daddy's girl, so the fact that she was able to speak privately with her father left him uneasy.

"Your name never came up. News flash, not everything is about you."

"You've always been a bad liar," Travis said, with an impatient sneer.

Without missing a beat, she said, "I think you should decline the offer."

"Wait a minute. What? Why should *I* decline?" Travis's nostrils flared.

"Because this is my church." She threw her hands in the air. "Leadership is in my blood. If anyone should walk away from this opportunity, it shouldn't be me."

"OK, see, that's not how this works. You should decline the offer because you're already in a leadership role." Travis crossed his arms in front of his chest. *After all these years nothing has changed. She's still selfish and greedy.*

"So, I should just put my dreams on hold for you?" She snickered.

"Isn't that exactly what you're asking me to do? And if memory serves me correctly, you are far from passionate about church leadership." The veins in his neck twitched. *She's not interested in leadership; she only wants to prevent me from getting the opportunity.*

"I was raised in this church, so of course I have a passion for it."

"Makayla, you could do anything, go anywhere. You don't need this."

"And you don't deserve it." Her face bore a sour expression.

Flinching, Travis shook his head. *That was low, even for her.* He moved closer until he was inches from her face. "I've busted my tail every single day for this. I haven't taken a real vacation in over two years. I'm at this church more than I'm at my apartment. So, don't pull that sanctimonious crap on me. Acting like this is your fucking birthright like you're Queen Elizabeth or something." He was able to keep his tone measured, but she was pushing it.

"Hmm, sounds like poor time management to me." She rolled her eyes. "You're not the only one whose put in work. I work just as hard as you. I spend—"

"No, you don't!" Travis yelled, cutting her off before continuing. "No, you absolutely do not. Everything you have has been given to you. Your car, your townhouse, this job. That's not hard work. That's privilege." It was hypocritical of her to stand there and claim she was deserving for doing the bare minimum.

"You're not going to shame me because of how I grew up. I'm not privileged; I'm fortunate."

"Yeah, fortunate enough to have grown up privileged." He was raised by a single mother, whom he'd watched struggle to keep the lights on. She grew up in a McMansion in an affluent, gated community. For his sixteenth birthday, he got a Timex watch and dinner at Applebee's. On her sixteenth birthday, her parents threw her a huge party and gifted her a brand-new BMW. In Travis's opinion, they were not the same.

"This is getting us nowhere. You and I both know that leading the singles ministry together would be a disaster."

"Yeah, it would because you like to turn everything into an argument," he said, partially agreeing.

Rubbing her eyes, she breathed a mirthless laugh. "I don't know what my father was thinking. But this has to be a joke. I can't even have a civil conversation with you."

"I'm willing to talk this through."

"There's nothing to talk about." She released a shuddery breath, which could have been caused by the gust of wind or her brewing anger. "You know what, do what you want. You always have."

He watched as Makayla tromped across the parking lot to her car. That conversation had gone exactly how he'd expected. He hated to admit it, but he agreed with her, questioning the pastor's judgement. Pastor Randolph believed pressure made diamonds. But by suggesting this appointment, he was underestimating just how fractured their relationship was. This wasn't going to work. Travis believed in the impossible. He fully accepted that a guy built a huge boat and loaded it with wild animals. He wholeheartedly believed that a man could walk on water or turn said water into wine. Miracles happened every day. But working with Makayla would require more than a miracle. This request could come from God Himself, and she would still find a way to object.

Chapter 3

"I'm going to decline," Travis said, tossing his napkin on his plate.

"Wait . . . what?" Regina asked, running her hand across her curly auburn hair.

Travis and Regina Beaumont had been dating a little over a year, recently becoming engaged. They met at the Atlanta Breakfast Club one Saturday as Travis was nursing a hangover. Even with his head pounding in his ears, he knew right away that Regina was beautiful, smart, and easy to talk to. He learned later she was also predictable, which he loved because he knew exactly what to expect with her. To some, Travis's life may have seemed boring, but he preferred routine: daily devotional every morning at 5:30; hit the gym by 6:15. Every Tuesday night, he and Regina cooked dinner together and watched an old '90s movie afterward.

"I just think it's more trouble than it's worth." He rubbed his hand across her light, golden-hued cheek before grabbing her plate. Dishes clanged as he washed their plates and utensils.

He wanted to learn all that he could, but having to do that alongside Makayla would be corrosive. The one thing he hated was messy, overdramatic, know-it-alls. Even though he worked at a church, he tried to ignore gossip, which was difficult when rumors spread like wildfire through the congregation. Most importantly, he did his best not to create, invite, or associate with drama. There were always stories circulating about Brother So-and-So or Sister What's-Her-Name.

Travis believed in minding the business that paid him and distancing himself from people who seemed to revel in others' plight.

"Because of Makayla? I get it may be weird at first, but if you set the tone early, she'll fall in line," Regina said, wrapping her arms around his neck.

Travis scoffed. "Maybe, but I highly doubt it." Regina didn't know Makayla like he did. She wasn't the type of woman who would just "fall in line." She was the type of woman who would listen to his plan then present a thirty-page PowerPoint presentation explaining all the ways his plan sucked and why he was an idiot for even suggesting it.

"Look at me." Regina grabbed his chin, forcing it downward. "Pastor Randolph said you needed more ministry experience, and here he is laying it at your feet. This promotion could be really big for you. You do have a fiancée you'll eventually need to support," she teased.

"You're right. I have to keep you laced with expensive bottled water." He shook an empty bottle of Smartwater in her face.

"It tastes better."

"It really doesn't. The filtered water from the fridge—"

"We are not doing this. Stop trying to change the subject." Regina snatched the bottle from his hand and tossed it in the trash. "Pastor Randolph chose you because he trusts you can get stuff done."

"He didn't just choose me. He chose me *and* Makayla. He has to know that's not going to work." Truth be told, Travis hadn't had a productive conversation with that woman in years, so expecting them to somehow come together and lead was asking a lot.

Regina plopped onto the tweed gray sectional with a stubborn fold to her arms.

She didn't understand how deep the acrimony between him and Makayla ran. How could she, when he had always been so cryptic about their past. *Their* being Travis and Makayla. The most he would ever tell her was that they dated, and, ultimately, it didn't work out. He knew she would eventually hear the stories from loose lips at church about just how serious his six-year relationship with Makayla had been.

She would hear about the way his eyes would come to life when Makayla entered the room. Or the way his hands instinctively found hers whenever she was near. How, mid-sentence, he would be rendered speechless, dumbfounded by the little dimple that would appear at the corner of her mouth when he made her smile. Everyone had a past; he just hoped Regina couldn't tell how his past still affected him.

Sitting next to Regina, he rubbed her knee. "Look, there will be other opportunities. I just don't think this one's for me." It hurt him to admit this, but he wasn't going to willingly bring this kind of chaos into his life.

"Why does Makayla Randolph always get to win?" Regina asked, pouting.

"I'm taking this job. I just need to figure out how to get Travis to walk away." It hadn't even been twenty-four hours, and the wheels in Makayla's head were already spinning.

"How exactly are you going to do that?" Porsha Dankworth, Makayla's older sister and best friend, asked.

"I'm still figuring that part out," Makayla said, taking a sip of her water.

"Last month, you were seriously considering leaving the church and going to work at that digital media company," Porsha reminded her.

"Yeah, but clearly, God had bigger plans for me." She stretched her hands to the heavens. The only reason she started job hunting was because her father threatened to cut the financial purse strings on her extra-curricular activities. Makayla loved what she did at Life Church. She loved the teens, and she made good money. Her father wanted her to be independent, and she wanted that too, but she believed in baby steps, and her father was ready to throw her in the deep end, hoping she could swim. Makayla wasn't the best with money. When she ran out of her own, she just went to her personal ATM machine: Pastor Eugene Randolph. Yes, she toyed with the idea of leaving, but she prayed to God and asked him to show her a sign. What bigger sign could there be than a promotion with increased responsibility and a bump in pay.

"See, now you sound petty," Porsha said, stabbing her fork into her Cobb salad.

Porsha was right; when it came to Travis Holmes, Makayla was Petty Labelle. Like that time at the church bake sale when Travis ordered a slice of their mom's lemon meringue pie. Makayla accidentally on purpose dropped the entire pie on the ground because she didn't want him savoring her mother's baking skills.

"I'm not petty. My career is in flux. Leading the singles ministry is a viable option. I can't just walk away from something I really want," Makayla countered.

"Do you really want this?" Porsha pressed her lips in a fine line.

"Yes." She examined her garlic fries so she wouldn't have to look Porsha in the eyes. Running the singles ministry was a big deal. It would be a high-profile position within the church. It could also lead to bigger opportunities. If she was being honest, seventy-five percent of her interest in this job was getting the chance to leave a tangible mark on the church, and twenty-five percent was having the opportunity to stick it to Travis.

"I know ministry leadership isn't his ultimate goal, but I don't think Travis is just going to walk away from this. He just got engaged and that extra cash could help pay for his wedding. Weddings aren't cheap," Porsha reminded her sister.

Makayla did not want to talk about Travis's pending nuptials. "They can have peanut butter and jelly sandwiches at their reception. I don't really care. I'm not going to step aside so he can fund his dream wedding." She pinned her arms across her chest.

"What if he decides to take it?" Porsha asked, shoving half an egg in her mouth.

"Why would he do that? He just cares about the business. He couldn't care less about the people. He wouldn't do that. It wouldn't work." She shifted in her seat. Porsha's words ignited Makayla's over-active imagination. *What if he calls my bluff and says yes? What if he's on the phone with my father at this very moment, accepting his offer?* "I think we should take this to go." Makayla signaled the waiter.

"But I'm not even done." Porsha pouted with her hand over her mouth.

"OK, you can stay, but I just remembered I have an important appointment I need to get to, so we gotta wrap this up." Makayla needed to strike first. She was going to talk to her father and accept the offer, and when Travis found out, he would have no choice but to back down.

Standing in the foyer of her childhood home, Makayla rehearsed what she planned to say to her father. *I'm super excited for this new opportunity. I thought about it, and you're right; I am willing to move past my differences and work with Travis.* Makayla frowned. *You were right, that stuff between Travis and me is water under the bridge. I'd love to work with him.* Chewing on her lip, she decided to tone down the enthusiasm. Her father wasn't a fool, and he could smell bullshit from a mile away.

With her acceptance, Travis would have no choice but to decline, making him look small and bitter. Maybe that would be just what she needed to help her father get over his obsession with that man. He still believed there was a possibility the two could get back together. Travis was engaged, and Makayla, well, she had all kinds of options. She had a date this Thursday with a man who could end up being the love of her life. So a reconciliation between her and Travis was unlikely.

"Hello," Makayla called. The house was silent. Heading toward her father's study, which was more like a mini library stacked floor to ceiling with books, she found the room empty. Making her way back to the foyer, she headed up one of the dual staircases, stopping on the landing. "Hello! Are you guys home?" Makayla shouted a little louder.

"In here," a muffled voice yelled back. Makayla found her mother in the master closet. Patricia Randolph was the matriarch of the Randolph family, a southern belle with a thick accent. Like her daughters, she had golden-brown skin and wore her black hair in loose waves that stopped at her shoulder. "Well, this is an unexpected surprise. What do you want?" her mother teased.

Makayla knitted her brow. "You act like I only come over when I want something. What's up with all the wigs?" Makayla asked, running her hands over several wigs spread out on the marble island in the middle of the closet—a short tight bob, a chestnut wet and wavy, and a bold blonde her mother wore when on tropical vacations.

"I'm just sorting through some stuff. I think it's time to lay some of these out to pasture." Patricia sighed, holding up a frizzy, curly wig.

Makayla reached for an auburn wig with loose, beachy waves. "Well, if you don't want this one, I'll take it off your hands."

"Put it back," her mother instructed.

Setting the wig down, Makayla asked, "Is Daddy here?"

"No, he went to visit a parishioner who just had surgery. But he should be back any minute now."

Eyeing the designer clothes in her mother's closet, Makayla grabbed a fitted brown leather jacket, admiring herself in the full-length mirror. "Did he talk to you about the leadership changes?"

"Are you referring to his plans for the singles ministry?" her mother asked, throwing the frizzy wig in the trash.

"Yeah, it's a bit absurd. Travis, a ministry leader?" Makayla threw her arms in the air.

"You know your father, and I don't think it's all that far fetched," Patricia said, ignoring her daughter's eye roll. "Travis is charismatic, ambitious, and good looking. He would be an exciting new face and could help energize the ministry."

"And me?" Makayla asked, fishing for a compliment.

"You're outgoing, spontaneous, and calculated."

Makayla frowned, uncertain if that last point was a compliment. "That may all be true, but I think you're forgetting one important fact. We're like orange juice and toothpaste. We don't see eye to eye on anything. He hates my guts," Makayla confessed to her mother.

"Sweetie, he doesn't hate you."

"No, I'm pretty sure he does."

"Why? Hm, what did you do to make him hate you?"

Makayla's shoulders inched toward her ears as she bit her lip. She didn't want to get into that.

"Patty, I'm back. Where you at?" her father called out.

"I'm in here," her mother yelled back.

Makayla hung the blazer back on the rack. It was showtime.

Upon entering the closet, Pastor Randolph did a double take. "Ah, I thought that was your car I saw in the driveway. I didn't know you were coming over," he said, acknowledging Makayla and giving his wife a quick peck on the cheek simultaneously.

"Yeah, I was here to see you, actually. I was hoping we could talk."

"Well, let's not have a mini conference in your momma's closet. Come on and join me in the kitchen. I'm thirsty."

Staring into the double-wide stainless-steel refrigerator, Makayla asked, "Ginger ale?"

"Baby, I'll just take some ice-cold water." He pulled out a chair from the table.

Removing a twenty-ounce bottle of water from the side door, she wasted no time delivering the speech she'd practiced on the drive over. "I thought about what you said. I prayed about it. It means so much that you thought of me for such an important role in the church, so I came over here to officially say yes, I'm in. I wanna lead the singles ministry."

"Now, that's my baby girl," Pastor Randolph congratulated, slapping his knee. "I knew you'd come around. This is going to be great."

"Uh huh," Makayla said, not sharing her father's enthusiasm.

"So, have you heard back from Travis yet?" She poured water over a glass of ice.

"Not yet. But I have faith he'll be on board."

"I sure hope so," she lied. Her *hope* was that news would travel fast about her acceptance, and Travis would respectfully decline. But of course, she knew she had to play the opposite role and act as though she was hopeful Travis was all in. "I sure hope so," she repeated. Handing her father a glass of water, she sat next to him, staring out the large bay window that looked out toward her mother's rose bushes in the backyard.

"Well, if I have to, I'll talk some sense into him."

"Yeah, uh . . . you should. But I would just caution you not to force it. I know he respects you, and he may feel pressured to say yes. If he and I are going to work together, he needs to really want it or it won't work." Looking her father directly in the eyes, she tilted her head slightly. She needed to walk a fine line, showing her willingness to extend an olive branch while also suggesting Travis may not be interested in the job.

"You know as well as anyone else that no one can get that man to do anything he doesn't want to do. If he doesn't want it, he'll be plain about it and let me know." The pastor smiled, tapping his hand on the kitchen table, delighted his plan was coming together.

"So what's your plan for him exactly?"

"Travis? Well he wants to run Life Church, and to do that he needs to know how the church runs. Throwing him into the singles ministry, he'll either sink or swim."

"He's crafty. He'll probably build a raft and float."

"He doesn't take no as the final answer. That's something you two share."

What her dad really wanted was for Travis to become a pastor, but his head was filled with statistics instead of scripture. It was best not to press her luck. She didn't want to harp on the issue and give her father any reason to question her motivations.

"So now that you have this new job and you'll be making all this extra money, maybe it's time for you to start making payments on the townhouse." Her father took a big sip from his water.

Makayla raised her eyebrows, smiling sweetly in his direction. "Daddy, you know I couldn't afford the monthly mortgage on that townhouse alone. I would have to move out and find a cheaper place in a less safe neighborhood." Her voice dripped maple-syrup sweet. Makayla lived rent-free in a townhouse owned by her parents. All she was responsible for were the utilities. She wasn't trying to take advantage of her parents, but she hadn't paid rent in over four years. In her opinion, her father was trying to go from zero to sixty, something he hadn't done with her older sisters, Summer and Porsha.

Makayla stood, returning the water bottle to the fridge.

"It's important you learn to take care of yourself. I fear your momma and I did you girls a disservice by giving you the world."

Makayla emerged from the refrigerator with an unopened carton of berry-flavored juice. "I appreciate everything you two do for me. I'm lucky to have parents who are able to help me the way you can." She wrapped her arms around him, giving him a hug from behind his chair. Makayla meant what she said, and she was making strides toward independence. Last year, she financed her new car all on her own. Yes, her parents provided a substantial down payment, but she was responsible for the monthly installments. "I don't want to take up any more of your time," she said.

"Thanks for stopping by, sweetheart. I'm excited to see what you and Travis will get up to in your new roles."

Grabbing the juice, Makayla headed for the door. "Tell Momma I said bye."

"Makayla, where are you going with my juice?" he yelled after her.

"Bye, Daddy. Love you!" she called back, shutting the door behind her.

Back in her car, she released a stifled breath. She had pulled out her wild card. Now, all she was waiting for was to see whether Travis would hit her with the draw four.

Chapter 4

Since he'd made his decision to decline the position, Regina had been noticeably irritated. She hadn't questioned him any further, but he could definitely sense a chill in her demeanor. He didn't take it personally; he knew she just wanted the best for him. And she wasn't wrong; this job and the raise that came with it could help pay for their wedding and place a down payment on their first home. Travis wasn't struggling—far from it. He had always been frugal, saving more money than he spent. Regina didn't know this, but he had a comfortable nest egg squirreled away. If she knew, the wedding budget would probably increase by twenty-five percent. He was already suffering heartburn just thinking about the money they were going to waste on this wedding.

"What do you think about these colors?" Regina pointed at her laptop.

"For what, exactly?" He leaned in to get a better look.

"Our wedding colors, silly."

"Orange?" His head slid left and right.

"It's not orange; it's burnt sienna. Perfect for a winter event." She tapped the screen.

"I don't get it." Travis cocked a half-opened eye at the laptop. They'd gotten engaged two months ago, and Regina had wasted no time planning the upcoming nuptials. They hadn't even set a date yet, and he was up to his eyeballs in color swatches, invitation samples, and guest spreadsheets. Was one night off from wedding talk too much to ask? He just wanted to spend time with his fiancée without having to look at tablescapes or flower girl dresses.

She tried to sell him on it. "Burnt sienna would be one of the secondary colors, not a primary one."

Sitting next to her on the sofa, he grabbed a chip from the bowl on the coffee table, shoving it in his mouth. "I don't know, baby," he mumbled between chews. "Can we just give it a rest for the night? I'm not really in the mood to deal with this stuff right now."

The smile slipped from her face as she closed her laptop, tossing it aside. "Did you speak with Pastor Randolph yet?"

"No," Travis said, pressing play on the remote.

"What are you waiting for? Are you having second thoughts?"

"No. He's just been busy, and I owe it to him to tell him in person." He didn't want to talk about this either. His mind was made up.

"Maybe this is God giving you a chance to reconsider." She poked him in the ribs.

He hoisted his chin with a heavy sigh. "Can we just watch the movie? Seriously, it's been a crazy week, and I just want to hang with my favorite girl."

"Sure, sorry." Regina leaned back into his arms.

Usually, they were on the same page, but he saw this job offer very differently from her. Leading a ministry group was like night and day when compared to finance and administrative work. Travis was good at reading contracts, balancing budgets and hiring staff, but interpersonal skills... not so much. Those people he'd always tried to avoid would now be looking to him for guidance. Saying no to this position wasn't just about having to work with his ex; there was also a real likelihood that he could fail.

Pushing the thoughts from his head, he looked to Regina for a distraction, leaning in to kiss her.

She placed her finger over his lips, stopping his momentum. "I thought you wanted to watch the movie?" she said playfully.

His mouth parted into a wicked smile. "Why watch a movie when we can make our own?" Travis pressed the record button on his phone, capturing the length of Regina's body in the camera lens.

Using her hands to cover his view, she chuckled. "Absolutely not. Turn it off."

Tossing his phone aside, he grabbed her waist, pulling her onto his lap. "Is this better?"

"Much better." She smirked before he consumed her lips with his.

Makayla was on a first date with Hosea Wright, a man she'd met during a business trip to Texas a few months back. Hosea was the lead pastor of a large church in Houston, Texas called Brook Willow. It was a miracle the two exchanged phone numbers, let alone agreed to go out on a date. Ever since she could remember, Makayla vowed she'd never date or marry a pastor.

She learned early on that the wife and family of a pastor had to share them with the congregation: the late-night calls summoning her father to the hospital to pray for church members when they were gravely ill or had been involved in tragic accidents; her mother ripping up inappropriate letters sent to her father and lighting a match to gifts his many female admirers had given him over the years. Makayla remembered all of that and didn't want any part of it. Well, you know what they say about "Never say never." Because here she was, seated across from Pastor Hosea Wright, enjoying her favorite seafood dish.

Being a pastor was one strike on her list, and the fact that Hosea lived in Houston was strike two. Makayla didn't invest in long-distance relationships because she didn't believe they worked. But despite those two strikes, she'd made an exception for Hosea. He was down to earth and easy to talk to. Unlike other pastors, he wasn't praying for her eternal soul when she slipped up and blurted out a four-letter word. Maybe it was because he was young, at thirty-four, and he didn't take himself too seriously, understanding that people were flawed, including himself. The fact that he was attractive and tall with a muscular physique and beautiful mahogany skin a few shades darker than her own also didn't hurt.

"Listen, you're talking crazy right now. *Love Jones* is not better than *Love and Basketball*," Hosea protested.

"What! Dude from *Love and Basketball* was a straight-up user. He did Sanaa so dirty." She shook her fist.

"But in the end, he realized he had a real one." Hosea took a sip of iced tea.

"Yeah, after he was washed up and nobody wanted him anymore. You know, typical man." She brushed her shiny, straight hair from her face. Makayla had spent hours on her hair—washing, conditioning, drying, and straightening it. It had been a while since she'd been on a date, so she was excited about getting dressed up to spend time with someone of the opposite sex.

"Listen, sometimes God has to yell to get your attention." He smirked, following her fingers with his eyes as she ran them across her collarbone.

Taking one last mouthful of her bowl of shrimp and pasta, her head fell back in delight and her shoulders appeared to dance. The shrimp was sweet and tender, and the pasta was cooked perfectly with lemony, garlicky, parmesan-y goodness.

"This was so good." She released a satisfied moan.

"I can tell from your shoulder shimmy."

"Oh, you know it's good when the shoulders start to shimmy," Makayla said, biting her full lips.

"So, tell me this ..." He laid his knife and fork on his empty plate. "What made you finally say yes?"

"To a date?"

"Yeah. I asked you out a bunch of times. It's actually kinda embarrassing."

Makayla didn't readily respond. Her breakup with Travis had left her gun shy. She'd trusted him, only to end up hurt and alone. After their breakup, she vowed to never fall, trip, or stumble into love again, and for the past five years, she'd held true to that. No other man had ever gotten close to her, and even when they tried or when she felt her resolve growing weak, she found a reason to push them away. Her focus was on Makayla and getting all the things she wanted, and heartbreak wasn't one of them.

She knew exactly what she was doing when she turned Hosea down the first four times he'd asked her out on a date. But how Hosea lucked up getting Makayla to finally go on a date had everything to do with Travis. It had always been easier to pretend her ex didn't exist, but when he announced his engagement two months ago, everything changed. She realized she'd been stuck in suspended animation for far too long and if she wasn't careful, life would pass her by. So when Hosea asked her out again, she said yes.

Hosea looked Makayla square in the eyes. "But I'm on a date with you now, and that's all that really matters."

"Yep. That's really all that matters." She fidgeted with the top of her off-the-shoulder little black dress that clung to her curvaceous frame. Logic told her that a perfect man didn't exist, but Hosea Wright checked almost all the boxes on her list. God-focused man with leadership aspirations, check. A commanding presence, check. A charismatic personality, check. A man who was tall, check. A good kisser, unknown.

"So where do you stand on dessert?" he asked, perusing the dessert menu.

"Yes to dessert. Always. I have a pretty intense sweet tooth. The key to my heart is through baked goods."

"Noted. So, do you wanna share something?"

Makayla served a long, blank stare. She could think of a few things she would like to share with the good pastor. "I don't share dessert, sorry." She cringed, hoping she wasn't being rude. "That's not breaking some first-date etiquette is it?"

"No, I think date etiquette is kind of overrated." A smile spread across his face as the waiter returned, ready to take their order.

"I'll have the peach cobbler. Thanks," Hosea said, handing the waiter his menu.

"And the lady?"

"I'll take the strawberry shortcake. Can I get extra whipped cream, extra strawberries, and extra powdered sugar?"

After dessert, Hosea drove her home in his rented Toyota Camry, their conversation occasionally interrupted by the British-accented Siri feeding him directions. As they walked to her porch, the faint sounds of Anita Baker could be heard playing in the distance from a neighboring townhouse.

"Well, thank you. I had a really good time," Makayla said, tugging at the belt on her mauve-colored coat.

"So did I." He shuffled from one foot to the other. "If you want, maybe we could do it again?"

"Yeah, I'd like that." She wondered why she'd waited so long to say yes.

Hosea stepped forward, causing her heart rate to spike. With a quick squeeze to her shoulders, he said, "Well, goodnight." Stepping off the porch, he stopped short, pivoting on the balls of his feet. "You know what? I wanted to kiss you, but I wasn't sure if that would be breaking first-date etiquette."

"I don't normally kiss on the first date," Makayla bashfully confessed. She was attracted to Hosea, which she knew would make it hard for her to stick to her "Makayla's Dating Rules" playbook.

"Oh. Yeah, I totally get that. That makes . . . yeah." He dropped his gaze, suddenly interested in the hairline cracks on the stairs.

"Normally I don't, but . . . exceptions," Makayla whispered. Her stomach tingled with anticipation. She'd thought about it. Following the acceptable dating rules all these years had gotten her nowhere. She was still as single as a dollar bill.

"Exceptions," Hosea repeated, stepping back onto the porch.

As she stood inches away, goosebumps pebbled her legs and she exhaled. Hosea gazed down at her with a crooked grin as he placed his hands on her waist and pulled her against his chest. The world went silent, and all she could hear was the sound of her heart attempting to beat its way out of her chest. Hosea's mouth met hers, his kiss firm yet soft. As she slid her arms around his neck she thought, *Good kisser, check.*

Chapter 5

"Do you know what would make this paint night better? Wine. Red, white, rosé," Porsha said, answering her own question.

Makayla smirked. Truth be told, she could go for a tall glass herself. You see, when they were handing out artistic ability, she must have been M.I.A. She had beauty and brains but not a lick of creative genius. But that didn't keep her from attending this month's women's ministry event being held at Margolis Wine and Design, a popular paint-and-sip spot located near Perimeter Mall on the outskirts of Atlanta Metro. It had taken lots of arm twisting to get Porsha to agree to accompany her to the event. Makayla may have left out the part about the sips being nonalcoholic.

"You owe me a bottle of wine, and I'm not talking generic grocery-store wine. I'm talking top-of-the-line, like a 2016 Cabernet Sauvignon from Opus One," Porsha demanded.

"Rich-people wine?" Makayla raised an eyebrow.

"Yes, rich-people wine." Porsha knew all about the finer things in life after marrying attorney Colin Dankworth a few months earlier. The son of a prominent Atlanta judge, I guess you could say Colin came from money. The Randolphs were rich, but the Dankworths were wealthy. Although he'd never admit it openly, her father always steered his girls in the direction of dating with a purpose—and that purpose was financial stability. The last thing he wanted to do was support the lifestyle of another grown man.

Makayla grimaced. "I mean, I could put something on it. Maybe lay it away and pay for it in installments."

"See, that's why you need to learn to be better with your money."

"Oh, so because I can't afford a five-hundred-dollar bottle of wine, I'm bad with money?"

"Can you afford a fifty-dollar bottle of wine?"

"Shut up," Makayla said, lifting herself out of her chair to grab brushes and paint. Wine was a luxury item, and whether it was ten dollars or a thousand, it still got you drunk all the same. Money should be spent on things that were useful, like food, and trips, or sexy outfits that would render Hosea speechless. Makayla squeezed red, orange, green, and purple paints onto a plate. They were painting an owl, and she was looking forward to bringing her masterpiece into the world. She poured water into a bowl when the bell, attached to the studio door, chimed. Makayla looked up to see Regina enter the crowded studio space.

Makayla was distracted by the unexpected entrance, letting the bowl overflow, water racing across the table. "No, no, no," Makayla muttered. Pulling at the roll of paper towels, she grabbed far too many in an effort to soak up the mess. "Sorry," Makayla said to the lanky instructor, who threw her a peeved look. It was a balancing act trying to make it back to her table. Her brushes were tucked in her back pocket with a plate filled with paint in one hand and a water bowl in the other, dripping with every step. "Excuse me. Pardon me," Makayla said as she tried to squeeze her curvy backside between the chairs.

"You good?"

"Great," Makayla said, spilling more water onto their table.

"Did you notice Regina's here?" Porsha whispered as she handed Makayla a paper towel.

"Really?" Makayla asked, rolling her eyes.

"I will never understand what he sees in her." Porsha leaned back in her chair to get a better look.

"Stop staring," Makayla whispered, struggling to tie her apron.

"Turn around. Let me help," Porsha directed as she grabbed the plastic apron strings and tied them into a lopsided bow. "I'm not saying she's ugly, but her personality is such a drag. I will never get how he went from you—vivacious, fun loving, smart, and, may I add, with a body to die for—to her, unimaginative, monotone, and dry like a saltine cracker."

"I'm sure he had his reasons." She glanced over at Regina, who was looking in her direction. Averting her eyes, Makayla pretended to inspect her canvas.

"All right, ladies, welcome to our paint-and-sip party. My name is Morgan, and I'll be your instructor." Morgan gathered her frizzy red hair into a ponytail.

"Paint and sip. Someone needs to be smacked for false advertising," Porsha complained, taking a swig of the nonalcoholic raspberry sparkletini.

"Shhh," Makayla said, trying to remain discreet. But she could still feel Regina's eyes on her. And if those eyes could emit fire, the nape of Makayla's neck would have been burned to a crisp.

"Tonight, we are going to paint an owl. There is no right or wrong way to do this, so just let your creative juices flow," Morgan said.

Makayla stole another quick glance at Regina. She was pretty, slight, and delicate. Regina seemed like the type of girl who needed to be protected. Makayla wondered what that felt like. Most people assumed she could handle anything because she was outspoken and confident, so they never offered to help. But that didn't mean she wanted to fix every problem on her own. If she had a dollar for every time she heard the words "You're smart; you'll figure it out," she could buy a house in the South of France, full cash offer.

Picking up the smallest brush, she started on the outline of her owl. "Do you think I'm hard to love?" she asked.

"Do you want my honest opinion?" Porsha said, her tone signaling to Makayla that she needed to brace herself for her sister's reply.

"Of course, I do." She tried to hide her embarrassment.

"Yes. Yes, I think you're a hard woman to love." Without making too much eye contact with Makayla, Porsha continued to swirl her brush in her water bowl, making the clear water murky.

"What makes you say that?" Makayla probed.

Softening the blow a bit, Porsha replied, "You're an acquired taste. Some men's palettes aren't sophisticated enough to handle you."

"So, what does that mean . . . I'm just alone forever?"

"Maybe. You know, guys just tend to like women who need them." Porsha flicked her wet brush.

"I need them." Makayla pouted, dipping her medium-sized brush in the red paint.

"No, you don't. You change your own tires and kill the creepy crawlers."

"So? You know how to change a tire."

"Yeah, I know how, but I don't ever do it. Guys like to have a purpose. If you take that stuff away from them, then why are they there?" She tapped her finger to her temple.

"So, I should pretend to be scared when I see a bug?"

"You should pretend to be afraid of bugs; you should ask them to open jars, even when you don't need them to. Get them to get the serving bowl from the high shelf instead of pulling out the step stool. You know, a modern-day damsel in distress," Porsha said, adding a glob of blue paint to her canvas.

With slow, deliberate strokes, Makayla added purple to her owl to represent the feathers. Maybe Porsha was right; maybe she did need to tone it down and allow men to take care of her. She'd tried everything else, and it wasn't working. Why not try this? Going forward, she was going to try to be sweeter, more docile.

"OK, ladies, let's take a ten-minute stretch break then come back and finish your works of art," Morgan said in a sing-song tone.

"I'm gonna run to the restroom. These sparkletinis are just running through me."

"I didn't need to know that," Makayla said, watching her sister's slender physique disappear from view. Porsha's painting resembled a realistic owl. Makayla's owl, however, had wide eyes and a hooked nose. Standing back, she tried to find some beauty or inquisitiveness about the creature she had drawn.

A dainty voice called her name from behind, interrupting her thoughts. "Makayla."

Swinging around, her eyes doubled in size.

"Can I talk to you for a minute?" Regina asked, her tone rather matter of fact.

"Ah, yeah, Regina, sure." She squared her posture, bracing herself for the foolishness that was bound to come out of Regina's mouth. Beyond passing pleasantries, the two women had never had a conversation. Makayla's intuition told her the request was centered around Travis, but she accepted, nonetheless. "How can I help you?" Her lips pitched upward in a forced smile.

"I know this is not really the place to talk about this subject, so I'll try to keep this brief."

Makayla felt an attitude coming on. "Yeah, that's probably best."

Regina let out a curt chuckle. "As you know, Travis was offered a chance to lead the singles ministry. But because of you, he isn't going to take the job."

"Because of me?" Makayla snickered behind closed lips, trying to mask the excitement in her voice.

"Yeah, I just think it sucks because he worked so hard, and this opportunity, while unexpected, means a lot to him."

"With all due respect, I'm still not seeing what any of this has to do with me." Makayla was stupefied, silently questioning Regina's gall to blame her for Travis not taking the position. Although Makayla would have loved to take full credit for him standing down, she knew she didn't have that kind of control over him. If she did, they would probably still be an item.

"He knows that working with you would be a nightmare . . . a complete catastrophe. And by the way, those were his exact words." Regina gave her a smug, angled grin.

"Yes, it would be difficult, but not because of anything I did. I appreciate you coming over here to defend your boyfriend—"

"Fiancé," Regina interrupted, flashing her ring finger.

Makayla turned up her nose, sniffing dismissively. "Whatever. I've known Travis a long time, and his turning down the position has nothing to do with me and everything to do with his guilty conscience." She'd had enough of this conversation. *Who the hell is Regina to accuse me of anything?* she thought.

"Guilty for what? Falling out of love with you?"

Makayla snorted. "Is that what he told you? Sweetie, I was the love of his life, and you're just, like . . . you know . . . a consolation prize."

Regina's jaw fell slack as she folded her arms over her chest. Makayla could tell she'd struck a nerve.

"I am not a . . ."

"Runner up, silver medal winner, second-place loser." She finished Regina's sentence and simultaneously drove her point home.

Regina's nostrils flared and her hands were balled into fists. Makayla suspected she would be sporting a black eye right about now if this wasn't a church event.

"Oh, my God! That bathroom had one of those skinny mirrors in it. You know, the kind that makes you look, like, ten pounds thinner. It was weird," Porsha said, placing her purse on the table, unaware that she had shown up just in time to referee the fight that seemed to be brewing. After detecting the friction between Makayla and Regina, Porsha offered a seemingly warm pleasantry. "Hi, Regina. Enjoying paint night?"

"Oh, Regina was just leaving." Makayla made an about face, turning her back on her without giving her a chance to respond. Regina stood stone still, her eyes like hot embers aimed in Makayla's direction. After what seemed like an eternity, she retreated and made her way back to her table.

"OK, why do I feel like you're gonna get jumped in the parking lot?" Porsha said in jest.

"She started it." Makayla pointed in the direction of Regina's table.

"Well, knowing you, I'm sure you finished it." Porsha glanced over at Makayla's canvas. "What is that? We were supposed to paint an owl."

Makayla eyed her colorful canvas. If she closed one eye, she could make out a little owl energy. "It's abstract like my love life," she joked.

Chapter 6

Scrolling through her playlist, Makayla selected oldies-but-goodies, and the melodic sounds of Roy Ayers' "Everybody Loves the Sunshine" began to play. It was Saturday, and Saturday mornings were always dedicated to house cleaning. A routine Makayla had grown up with, it had become a habit in her adult life. Crouched under the sink, pulling out gloves and cleaning supplies, she was still pretty pissed about the incident with Regina the night before.

All she'd wanted to do was enjoy a night out with her sister, whom she didn't hang out with as much anymore since she'd married Colin. But no, Regina had to poke the bear. Even when she tried to be low-key, drama always seemed to follow. The two ladies weren't friends, but Regina had to know Makayla wasn't just going to roll over and show her belly. She knew Travis would never ask his girlfriend to fight his battles for him, so she was certain Regina came up with this hair-brained idea to confront her on her own.

Midway through wiping down her oven range, the doorbell rang. *Must be one of my Amazon packages*, Makayla assumed, knowing she wasn't expecting any company. One of the side effects of being single was having too much time on your hands. Last night, instead of somebody's son making her legs quiver, she was scrolling through Amazon, purchasing a mug shaped like a llama and flavored sugar for her coffee.

She glanced at the clock on the range; it read 9:42 a.m. She tossed her sponge in the sink and removed her purple floral-patterned rubber gloves. After peering through the peephole, she could see Travis on the other side of the door, pacing. Makayla removed her head scarf, smoothing her hair.

"I guess this is supposed to be round two," Makayla sarcastically chimed as she swung the front door open.

"We need to talk." He brushed past her, inviting himself inside.

"Yeah, sure. Come on in." Makayla stuffed her head scarf in the pocket of her tie dye Nike sweatpants. "I have a feeling I know what this is about. But before we get into that, I'd just like to know what the hell makes you think you can just show up at my door without calling first?"

"Look, Makayla, I'm only going to say this once. Stay away from Regina."

"And how do you suppose I do that? She came up to me," she barked, pointing at her chest.

"Makayla, please. I know you. Don't forget that. You were probably staring her down all night long; she had no other choice but to approach you."

"Approach me, huh? Is that what she told you, that I was mad-dogging her?"

"Doesn't matter. You hurt her feelings, and it was totally unwarranted. Why can't you just let us be? You—"

"If you think you're going to come to my home, barge your way in, then threaten me, and I'm supposed to back down, you have another thing coming. And just like you know me, I know you. And I know this ain't about the few cross words between Regina and me. This is about Travis Holmes, the man who wants everyone to think he's so perfect, even his girlfriend. And you're mad because I just told the truth. Listen, she's gonna figure out you're an asshole one of these days. And that's why you're here. You're here for you, not Regina."

Travis coughed out a laugh. "You don't know what you're talking about. You know what your problem is? You're too stuck in the past. You can't move on, let go. I've moved on, and I'm really happy. And maybe if you weren't so obsessed with me, you could be happy too. I can guarantee that bullying Regina will get you nowhere."

"If this is what happy looks like, I don't want it." She wrinkled her nose at him. "I don't know, Travis, maybe you shouldn't date women who are so easily intimidated."

"Well, I'll take intimidated over spoiled and entitled any day."

"OK, are you finished? You done? You got to paint me as the villain while continuing to pretend you are completely blameless. You've said your piece, now can you please leave?" She hit him with a fierce look.

"No, I'm not done. You know, Makayla, you hold people to standards that you're not willing to hold yourself to. You think you're supposed to get everything you've ever wanted in life, but that's not the way the world works."

A surge of heat crept up on the sides of her neck. "How dare you come over here with this self-righteous crap? Don't you ever talk about someone expecting to get what they want. I want what I want when I want it. Who doesn't? You do. Take a good look in the mirror, baby; we are not that different. As long as I've known you, you've been plotting your next career move. So what, you get to be ambitious, but I can't? Sounds like you're afraid of a little competition. And that's the real reason you don't want to accept the position with the singles ministry."

"No, actually, I was trying to spare the both of us. But now that you've brought it up, I think I should give the decision a second thought. Since I'm so selfish, as you say, maybe I should accept the position after all."

The surge of heat creeping up the sides of her neck had now made its way to her cheeks. "Don't be ridiculous. You're only doing this out of spite, not because you care about the cause."

"Oh, and you do, huh?" Travis shot back as he brushed past her to leave. "Just remember what I said."

"No, you remember what *I* said." She followed closely on his heels. "Tell your little girlfriend to stay out of my way, or the next encounter won't be so friendly."

"And that's *fiancée*, not girlfriend," Travis reminded her.

Fiancée. Leave. Her. Alone. For some reason, his words hit like a sharp shooter's arrow. Makayla stood stoically still. She wasn't one easily knocked off her kilter, but she didn't have a comeback for him this go-round. The best she could do was give him a look layered with contempt. He could barely exit before she slammed the door behind him, almost literally letting the doorknob hit him where the Good Lord split him.

She firmly pressed her back against the door and closed her eyes. "Asshole," she muttered to herself. *He's just being a jerk at this point, pretending to seriously be considering the position. He doesn't even care about the congregation. All he's interested in is membership growth and weekly tithes. Daddy is usually spot on with his leadership assignments but this ... this is a reach.* She felt depleted of the energy she'd had only moments earlier when she was dancing to the sounds of her favorite tunes.

"How are you, son?" Pastor Randolph greeted in an excited tone.

"I'm doing well. Thank you for making time to see me." Travis lowered his head as he took a seat at the small conference table in the corner of the pastor's office. Silence crept into the space the two men occupied.

"You know, I was just about to pour myself a cup of coffee. Would you like some?" Pastor Randolph offered, breaking the awkward silence.

"Sure." He nervously tapped his fingers on the chair's armrest. Although he hadn't discussed this decision with Regina, he was certain she'd be pleased for more reasons than one. But now that he was here, he was having second thoughts.

"I was hoping I'd hear from you." Pastor Randolph placed a cup of coffee in front of Travis before relaxing in his chair. "So, shoot. I'm all ears."

"Hmm ... now, how can I say this?"

"Just say it."

"Well, let me start by saying that I appreciate you thinking of me for this opportunity. I really do. But I just got engaged, and I don't want to bring unnecessary drama into my relationship. Regina is important to me, and I'm already seeing signs of strain, and I haven't even accepted the position yet."

"Makayla? Does this have anything to do with her?"

"Yeah, it does."

"How so?" the pastor asked.

"Well, the two of them had words recently, and I'm not all that sure Regina is comfortable with the idea of me working with my ex."

"I'll be honest with you, Travis; Makayla is my baby girl. And I understand that she can be a little difficult at times, but—"

"A little?" Travis interrupted.

"Well . . . let's just put it this way; she's a strong-willed woman, and she's always been that way, from a little girl. But that intense, focused personality isn't a weakness; it's a strength."

After meditating on Pastor Randolph's words, Travis said, "Can I ask you a question?"

"Sure, ask me anything."

"Why did you pick us to lead the singles ministry?" He stirred his coffee, anxiously awaiting an answer.

"I know you don't want to hear this, but you and Makayla complement one another. She's the sword, and you're the shield. Both serve a purpose. You're lucky if you have one but blessed if you have both." Pastor Randolph leaned forward, stroking his beard. "What does a sword do?"

"It strikes."

"Exactly. And the shield provides protection. Makayla is ambitious, full of these big ideas, but she doesn't always know how to tie it all together. Then there's you. You calculate the risk to determine the best way to execute a vision. You two balance each other."

Travis let out a disbelieving laugh.

"I get that there's baggage, but that isn't necessarily a bad thing," Pastor Randolph added, blowing into his coffee cup.

"I get it, I do. I just don't want our past to get in the way of our purpose." If he and Makayla could move beyond themselves, he was certain they could create something profound. He was willing to push their issues to the side. But he wasn't sure she could do the same.

"Does this mean that you're turning down my offer?"

Travis weighed the pros and cons. The pros: exposure to new facets of the church, a pay raise, access to new opportunities. The cons: Makayla Desirae Randolph. He briefly recalled the confrontation this past weekend. She'd basically called his bluff, and being a man, he couldn't see himself caving in, not even one last time. So, he replied, "No, I have concerns, but I'm in. I'm accepting the offer."

Pastor Randolph let out a boisterous laugh. "I knew you'd say yes. It will be good for Makayla having you by her side, steering the ship."

And once again, Makayla had gut-punched him. Not once did she mention she'd already accepted the position. "So, she said yes?" His teeth bore down on the inside of his cheek.

"Yes, the very next day. My daughter can never walk away from a challenge. Now, I want you to know that I am entrusting this to you two. You both have my full confidence. Jason and Raeann took the singles ministry as far as they could. The time is ripe for an infusion of new energy. You and Makayla are going to take this thing to the next level. This is going to be great. I'm excited. Are you excited?" Pastor Randolph asked as he stood.

"Yes?" The tone of his voice didn't convey his excitement.

"Good." The pastor patted Travis on the back. "I want this transition to happen fairly quickly, so you and Makayla should meet with the McPhersons."

"Got it. Thanks again."

"Of course. Tami will provide you with the HR packet. There are some forms you'll need to complete. The packet also lays out the job description, benefits, and salary."

"OK, thanks." Travis offered a sliver of a smile. On one end, he was relieved the decision was no longer hanging over his head, but on the other, he was embarrassed that Makayla had played him once again.

Travis spent the next twenty minutes in the reception area. Tami had nearly talked his ear off about the singles ministry and all the things he needed to do to improve it. When he finally made it to the lobby, he opened the job offer packet and flipped through the documents, looking for the only paper that mattered: total compensation. His eyes scanned the document feverishly as he tried to locate the relevant information. As the money guy, he knew the starting salary for a ministry leader, and his compensation package was five percent above starting. Opening the calculator app on his phone, he crunched the numbers. By now, his head was spinning with excitement. He blew out his cheeks as he opened and read an incoming text from Regina.

> Regina: Let's go out to dinner later. I still have that gift card I won at my job.
>
> Travis: I have a better idea. Let me take you out to dinner ... STK.
>
> Regina: Too expensive. That's the kind of place you go to on special occasions.
>
> Travis: 😏
>
> Regina: ???
>
> Travis: Just be ready when I get there in an hour.

A grin sprang across his face. He would tell Regina the news over dinner.

Chapter 7

Midweek church services were held on Wednesday evenings. It was when comprehensive church announcements were made, which included details on what was happening with the various groups and auxiliaries at Life Church. It wasn't Makayla's favorite service to attend by far, but as a ministry group leader, attendance was mandatory. And it was especially important she attend the midweek services now because she was going to be leading one of the largest ministries in the church.

She scurried over to the far-left side of the sanctuary and sat down next to Porsha.

"You love being late, don't you?" Porsha teased as she lifted her purse off the seat she was saving for Makayla.

"Girl, I had to run to the gym after work. You know I joined the gym again?"

"Who is it this time? 'Cause it's gotta be a man," Porsha whispered, chuckling under her breath.

"I'm thirty now. I have to keep it tight and keep it right."

"Mm hm. It's a man," Porsha mouthed.

"Shhh" was all Makayla said. Because she had gone through a dating hiatus for nearly a year, she was excited to be back in the game. And the cherry on top was the fact that Hosea was crazy about her. In fact, he was coming into town in a few days. Coincidentally, he was speaking at a conference at the Christian Fellowship Center, a nondenominational church in Alpharetta, Georgia, which was not too far from her townhouse in nearby Roswell.

Makayla glanced over at Porsha, who was clutching Colin's hand. A pang of jealously reared its ugly head. Why couldn't she find her special someone? Makayla already knew the answer to that question: she was single by choice, not due to a lack of options. Besides, Makayla had vowed not to concentrate on comparing her life to Porsha's. Yes, her sister was married, but Makayla got the sense that love wasn't a big part of their union. To her, Porsha was more in love with the status and privilege Colin's money afforded her than Colin himself.

Porsha never talked about how much she adored Colin like most newlyweds. She never called him sweet names. And now that Makayla was thinking about it, Porsha hadn't even told her how good or bad the sex was. Makayla was genuinely interested in what sex with a white man was like, having never experienced it for herself. But the few times she'd asked, Porsha gave her one-word answers like "Great" or chastise her for being nosy.

Trying to erase the none-of-her-business thoughts from her mind, she closed her eyes and hummed along with the choir as they wrapped up their solo selection.

When the choir had finished their song, Pastor Randolph crossed the stage and stood in front of the glass podium. "Let's give the choir a round of applause. They are a group of anointed voices. Brother Kemp has done an amazing job."

A chorus of amens and hallelujahs could be heard from the congregants.

"Before I minister the Word tonight, I have a few announcements," he continued. "At Life Church, we are constantly looking for ways to improve the services we provide and leadership's capacity to service this congregation. That said, we are making some big leadership changes." Pastor Randolph paused for dramatic effect, always putting on a show. "The married ministry will now be led by Jason and Raeann McPherson." Pastor Randolph pointed toward the congregation. "Jason, Raeann, why don't you stand." Applause and celebratory chatter broke out throughout the congregation.

Makayla turned to look at Jason and Raeann as they stood and offered acceptance waves. She didn't know her father was going to announce the leadership changes this Wednesday night. He hadn't mentioned anything.

"Jason and Raeann's move leaves leadership vacant in the singles ministry," Pastor Randolph said with a bright smile.

Makayla tipped forward in her seat. Her mouth hung suspended as she tried to anticipate her father's next few words.

"I'm excited to announce that Travis Holmes and Makayla Randolph will take over leadership of the singles ministry."

A surge of heat swept over Makayla, a knot forming in her belly. Fanning her face with her hand, she felt weak and queasy. Not noticing any of this, Porsha clapped wildly. "There you go, baby sis. Go get your man back!" she whispered in Makayla's ear.

"I hate him," a visibly upset Makayla mumbled under the vivacious cheers from the congregants. Yes, Travis threatened to take the job when he barged into her home on Saturday, but she assumed it was just his bravado talking, and once he cooled down, he'd return to his senses.

"Did you hear me?" Porsha nudged Makayla in the side.

But she didn't flinch; she hadn't heard what Porsha said to her. To be honest, in this moment, she couldn't care less. She stared straight ahead, ignoring the smiling faces around her. "You have to stand up," Porsha repeated, this time, tapping Makayla on the shoulder, prompting her to stand.

The cheers from the congregants seemed muffled, and the smiling faces seemed to fade away, all except those of Regina and Travis. There they stood, side by side, soaking up all the praise and glory seemingly bestowed upon them. No doubt, many church members were Team Travis and Regina. To them, Travis and Makayla were a faint memory. Whether she admitted it or not, she was bothered by the fact that Travis had moved on.

Suddenly, Makayla could now hear the faint sounds of the congregants, who were cheering her on as well. She managed to display a smile, one her grandmother, Lady Grace, would have called a "Barbie doll" smile. In other words, it was fake and painted on, just like the plastic dolls. And if she had the power of Sissy Spacek in the movie *Carrie*, everything near her would have blown up in smoke and ashes. After a few more seconds of standing, giving the congregation a chance to gawk at her, she took her seat again.

Makayla felt played, not only by Travis, but by her mother and especially her father. She couldn't focus on the words her father was now uttering, and truth be told, they didn't matter. Her only goals in life were making it through this service without losing her shit and getting out of the church as fast as she could after benediction.

"Something tells me this announcement took you by surprise," Porsha leaned over and whispered into Makayla's ear.

"Surprise ain't the word," she said through clenched teeth.

To say that she was in a trance for the remainder of the service would have been an understatement. She was more like in another world, thinking about how she was going to express to her father her disappointment about his surprise announcement; thinking about how uncomfortable she was going to be in a few weeks, having to work alongside Travis; thinking about how she was going to get him back for misleading her and taking the position anyway. *What if I resign the day I start?* Makayla thought. She was a pro at playing to win. All sorts of schemes ran through her mind as she sat in service.

After the final prayer, she jumped up and began to rummage through her purse in a desperate attempt to locate her car keys.

"Makayla, can we talk for a minute?" Travis's voice rang out behind her.

Exhaling, she hissed out a breath, turning around slowly. Just how he had managed to make his way over to her before she could dash outside was beyond her. She didn't respond verbally but glared at him as if she could see straight through him like an X-ray machine.

"I was just hoping we could talk." Travis shuffled his feet.

Makayla ignored him as she continued to search for her car keys in her cluttered tote bag.

He leaned in. "Did you hear me?"

"Yes, Travis, I heard you," she finally responded, her lips spreading into a bitter line.

"Can we talk?" he repeated, his jaw tightening.

"We're talking now." She tossed her notebook into her tote bag.

"That's not what I mean, M-Kay."

"It's Makayla," she snapped. He didn't have the right to call her by her nickname, and she wanted him to know it.

"OK . . . Makayla." He paused, waiting for her to give him the nonverbal cue to proceed.

"What do you suppose we need to talk about other than the singles ministry?" If she had just been honest with herself, she wouldn't be in the predicament she now found herself in—working with the man who broke her heart years earlier. But she had a point to prove, albeit to no one but herself.

"Please, can we go to Bean There, Done That, grab a coffee and talk?"

"It's late. I need to get home." The last thing she wanted to do right now was go anywhere with him. The plan was to go home and scream into her pillow until she could think straight.

"OK, how about tomorrow? We could meet at the Bean There, Done That down the street at nine."

"Two." She didn't have plans tomorrow at nine, but she wasn't going to make this easy for him.

"OK . . . great. See you tomorrow at two." Travis offered a smile.

Makayla dashed out of her row, heading straight for the church parking lot so she could get into her Mercedes and zoom off. She was almost successful in doing so, that is until Mrs. Chandler, also known as "Auntie Di" stopped her as she was exiting the worship center.

"Congratulations, sweetheart," she said, reaching both arms out to hug Makayla.

"Oh, hey, Auntie Di," she said as cheerfully as she could muster.

There was no way she could allow her disappointment to show. Auntie Di was her mother's oldest and closest friend, so Makayla needed to be on her best behavior or suffer a verbal lashing from First Lady Randolph.

"Now, Eugene done made the right decision putting you and Travis in charge of that ministry. Travis is such a nice young man. It's a shame you two didn't work out. You guys were such a beautiful couple." She flashed Makayla a sympathetic smile.

This was not the first time she had to listen to people comment on how great she and Travis used to be together. How happy they both seemed. How surprised they were when they heard they'd split. Most of these comments were followed by the same look Auntie Di was giving her now.

Makayla offered a muted smile. "Hey, Auntie Di, I gotta get out of here. I'm trying to make it to the pharmacy before they close," she lied.

"OK, baby. You go on. Maybe we can all celebrate soon. It'll be me and Uncle Charles's treat."

"Yeah, that'll be nice." Makayla pressed the exit button on the lobby wall, but she was no luckier than she was just moments ago trying to get to her vehicle. She was stopped again, this time by her mother.

"That's my baby girl!"

Makayla showed no reaction.

"What's wrong, honey?"

"Your husband is what's wrong," she said matter-of-factly.

"Did I miss a memo or something? Your father just upgraded your leadership status, and you have an attitude about it?"

"Come on," Makayla said, ushering her mother out the door. The two women scurried over to Makayla's vehicle, stopping only twice to wave and say thank you to church members expressing their congratulatory wishes to Makayla. "Get in, Momma," she said, unlocking the doors to her sedan.

First Lady Patricia Randolph opened the passenger door of

Makayla's Mercedes and plopped down on the seat, closing the door afterward. Makayla sat in the driver's seat, releasing a tight breath. She was glad to have finally made it to her vehicle.

"Now, what in the world is the matter with you, Makayla?" her mother asked as she fumbled with buttons and knobs, trying to turn on the interior light.

"Daddy never mentioned to me that Travis had accepted the position."

"Well, was he supposed to?" her mother asked with obvious confusion.

"Of course, Momma. He was supposed to let me know. Give me a heads up."

"This is a business, Makayla," her mother corrected. "Your boss doesn't need to give you a heads up when he hires a new team member."

"But I'm—"

"His daughter. And because you're his daughter, you think he owes you special treatment. Look, your dad has a lot on his plate, more than you girls will ever know. Maybe it slipped his mind, or maybe he was just trying to be neutral. Give him some credit. Your dad's not perfect, but he is fair. That I do know."

Makayla's shoulders sank into a rounded heap. Maybe she was being irrational. "I guess," Makayla said, acquiescing.

"I'll tell you what; why don't you come by on Saturday? We'll throw you a little celebration get-together. Let us make it up to you. I'm sure your dad wouldn't have deliberately tried to throw you off guard. Lady Grace will be there too."

Makayla's pouted lips now formed a warm smile. Lady Grace was her paternal grandmother, and at ninety-one years old, she was no longer a Georgia peach; she was a Georgia apricot. She had seen everything and watched it come back again. In other words, she was outspoken, rarely holding her tongue. Her motto was that growing older allowed you to say exactly what you felt, and if feelings got hurt in the truth-telling process, then it was a small price to pay.

"Deal?" First Lady Randolph said, leaning closer to look into Makayla's eyes.

"Deal."

Chapter 8

"Travis! Black coffee with three sugars for Travis," the barista called out. Jumping up, he grabbed his drink before returning to the corner table in the coffeehouse. He was waiting for Makayla, but she was running late as usual. Travis spent the time responding to emails and text messages congratulating him on his new position. His phone had not stopped blowing up since the announcement at the previous night's service.

He was already jotting down notes about his plans for the singles ministry. This job could provide the experience he needed to ultimately secure the director of operations role he desired. Pastor Randolph was sixty-five years old, and he'd mentioned his interest in scaling back his day-to-day participation at the church. How Travis performed in this new role could make or break his career aspirations. Although he was unsure of how Makayla would receive it, his intention was for the two of them to meet and lay down some ground rules.

Makayla came sauntering into Bean There, Done That as though she wasn't fifteen minutes late. Time waits for no man, but Makayla Randolph had missed that memo.

"Sorry I'm late." She flashed a strained smile as she approached the table where Travis was seated.

He gave a clipped nod. Time management had never been her strong suit.

Removing her coat, she draped it over the back of the chair. "I'm gonna grab a drink. Do you want anything?" she asked, turning away before he could reply.

His eyes followed her as she walked away and stood in line to place her order. Her hair was slicked back into a long, braided ponytail. Before he knew it, his eyes had traveled from her hair straight down, captivated by the burgundy wide-legged corduroy jeans she wore, which hugged her curves. Trying to tame his thoughts, Travis averted his attention to a picture on the wall of a couple who appeared to be laughing over a cup of coffee.

"You got a cinnamon roll?" he said as she set the pastry and a small coffee on the table. The cinnamon roll brought back distant memories. Like Makayla, Travis had a sweet tooth. On more than one occasion, they found themselves at the neighborhood bakery at five a.m., ordering two black forest donuts hot out of the oven.

"It was just sitting there calling my name. Why, do you want some?" She worked a stiff frown onto her face. Sharing dessert was a non-starter and he knew that.

"Ah, you know, I'm good." Travis waved her offer off but still eyed her sticky bun. "But . . . are you offering? 'Cause I don't wanna be rude." He'd missed lunch, and his stomach was rumbling louder than the voices of the customers that buzzed in and out of the coffee shop.

Makayla raised her eyebrow as she cut the gooey, icing-covered pastry into two, giving Travis the bigger half.

"Thank you," he said, flashing an easy, wide smile.

"Consider it a peace offering."

"I definitely want peace. That's why I suggested we meet. I thought we should hash out our differences, so going forward we can start with a clean slate." He slid his hand through the space between them as if he was pushing something away.

"I don't have any issues with you. I'm ready to move forward, full steam ahead." Makayla warped her lips into a smile, using a fork and knife to cut into her cinnamon roll.

Travis's shoulders shivered from a deep laugh. "So as far as you're concerned, it's all good?" he said with a hint of inquisitiveness. He knew what she'd uttered was a lie. *If everything is good, why did she avoid saying more than three words to me last night? If everything is good, why did she say those things to Regina?* "I don't share your optimistic view, so if you'd indulge me, I think we need to lay out some rules."

"Whatever floats your boat."

"Rule one, Regina is off limits." Training his gaze on her face, he hoped to drive his point home. For Travis, this was non-negotiable.

Makayla's eyes flickered. "I totally agree. Our significant others should be off limits," she said, licking her sticky fork.

His left eye twitched slightly; he was not going to take the bait. *Our? She isn't seeing anyone. She doesn't have a partner, significant or otherwise.* Makayla liked throwing hand grenades and watching them explode in his face. He decided not to acknowledge her attempt to initiate an armed conflict.

"OK." Travis puffed air through his nostrils. "Next, I plan to be totally professional and respectful, and I expect the same in return." This seemed like a no-brainer. Respect was the cornerstone of any co-worker relationship. Sure, they would disagree about the direction of the ministry, but the last thing he wanted was for those disagreements to turn into verbal slug matches.

"Respect, check," Makayla agreed, giving him a thumbs up.

"Finally, it's important that we set the tone. I don't want our personal shit to create unnecessary stress at work." Leaning back, he drank the last of his lukewarm coffee. "If you have anything you want to add, now's the time."

Makayla gave Travis a round of applause. "That was a great speech. Did you practice it in the mirror last night? You always say the right things . . . at church or with my father, such a nice young man." She repeated the phrase people often used when describing him. "I'm not interested in keeping the peace. I'm interested in keeping it real. You shouldn't have taken this job." Makayla's face rumpled with disdain. "But now we're here, and I'm not going to pretend like everything is okie dokie artichokie to make you feel comfortable. You don't get to make the rules, and you don't get to dictate how I should act or feel."

Keeping his voice measured, Travis inched forward. "All right, you wanna keep it one hundred, then let's keep it one hundred. No one hates this situation more than me. I know I'm gonna have to watch my back because the minute you get a chance, you'll stab me or throw me in front of a bus."

"Nope." Makayla's ponytail swung like a pendulum as she vigorously shook her head. "I'm just gonna sit back and watch you drown because you're in way over your head."

"One thing you should know about me is that I don't lose."

"You lost me. And that was a huge loss, a devastating one." She smirked.

"Or maybe I just dodged a bullet." From the twitch in Makayla's right eye, he could tell his arrow had hit its mark.

The crocodile smile faded from her face. "Rule number whatever: the past is the past. I'm not looking to exhume old feuds." Her chair squeaked as she pushed it back from the table and stood. Grabbing her purse and coat, Makayla planted her feet, staring directly into Travis's steely eyes that almost appeared gray in this light. "Do your job and stay out of my way." She turned to exit, practically leaving a smoke plume in her wake.

Holding his breath, he counted to five before releasing it and taking in fresh air. Makayla, always had to have the last word. Travis chuckled to keep himself from punching something. She had just made it perfectly clear that she wasn't interested in a harmonious working environment. For Makayla Randolph, there was no I in team, but there was a ME.

Chapter 9

Spritzing Flowerbomb perfume on the inside of her wrist, Makayla admired herself in the full-length mirror. Hosea would be there any minute, having finished his speaking engagement at the conference. It was important that she look her best, giving Hosea a reason to keep coming back for more. With her nails freshly manicured and her hair tumbling over her shoulders in thick spirals, she twisted her body in every direction before giving herself an approving thumbs up. Pleased with her appearance, she proceeded to head downstairs to wait for Hosea. She was midway down the stairs when she heard the sounds of a car pull into her driveway.

Makayla picked up her pace, sweeping the living room one last time, making certain nothing was out of place. Straightening her body-hugging hunter green ribbed dress, she used her fingers to comb through her bouncy curls. As the doorbell rang, she checked her breath to ensure it was kissable before heading toward the door.

"Hi," Makayla greeted him with a big smile.

A cheery-eyed Hosea was standing on the opposite side of the door. He looked dapper in a navy blue suit.

"Well, hello," he said, taking her all in. "These are for you." He handed her a bright bouquet of purple hydrangeas, pink roses, and orange lilies.

"Wow! They're beautiful. Thank you," a shocked Makayla said. "Come on in," she invited. "Welcome to my modest home . . . well, townhome. You can have a seat in the living room, right here," Makayla said, pointing. "I'm just gonna put these beautiful flowers in some water and come in there to join you."

Hosea made himself at home, perusing a shelf with photographs of her and her sisters. His eyes came to rest on a picture of Makayla in a bright yellow swimsuit, her arms raised triumphantly over her head. "Damn," he whispered under his breath.

"What's that?" Makayla called.

"Uh … nothing." He cleared his throat.

"How was the conference?" Makayla asked as she unwrapped the black-and-white-striped tissue.

"It was good. I think my speech went well." Hosea stopped in his tracks, taking notice of the colorful painting on the mantle. "Is that from paint night?"

"Yeah. Guess what it is," she said, covering her mouth with her hand to stifle a laugh.

"OK, don't tell me. Uh, OK . . . is it abstract?" Hosea asked, scratching his head.

"No, it's realistic. A spot-on representation of the subject." Makayla turned her face to conceal a smile.

Hosea balled his fist under his chin. "I'm gonna need a hint."

"Sure, I'll give you a hint; it's an animal," Makayla offered.

He moved closer, studying the canvas. "OK, I'm gonna need several hints."

"It's an owl," Makayla yelled out playfully. "Couldn't you tell?"

He shook his head. "You want the truth?" His mouth formed a cheeky smile.

"Of course, I do." Makayla freed the cluster of flowers from the wrapping.

"You're smart and funny and beautiful. But this painting is God-awful." He laughed deep and loud.

"So, you don't like it?" Makayla asked, placing the floral arrangement on the counter and putting her hands on her hips.

"You know what I like? I like you."

She let the insult of her unique artistic abilities slide. "So, where would you like to eat?"

"I'm not picky. No place in particular. But if I'm being honest, we could just order in. I'm tired from the flight and the conference. You don't have to entertain me by showing me the sites in ATL. We can do that another time. Plus, my flight leaves at eight. And with me having to turn the rental car in, that only gives me a little over four hours before I have to head back. So, if you don't mind, I'd really like to spend as much time with you as I can, so can we just dine in?"

Although she hadn't planned on entertaining him at home, what Hosea was saying made perfect sense. "Do you like Caribbean food?"

"Love it," Hosea said, walking toward her.

"How does jerk chicken, rice and peas, and cabbage sound?"

"Just add some platanos, and I'll be in heaven." He rubbed his hand over his stomach in a circular motion.

"Great. There's a Jamaican restaurant close by that delivers."

"Sounds like a plan." Hosea wrapped his arms around Makayla's waist from behind as she filled a glass vase with warm water.

The scent of his cologne penetrated her nostrils, and she closed her eyes. His presence was undeniable as he pressed his hips into her backside. Then, she remembered that it was too soon, too soon to be wrapped in the arms of a man she didn't really know and too soon to let her guard down, not just for Hosea but for any man. Breaking away from his embrace, she headed into the living room to retrieve her cellphone. "Let me call and order the food."

Hosea followed her back to the living room, watching intently as she placed the food order. "Did I overstep?" he asked as she ended the call.

"Excuse me?" She tried to act as though she didn't know what he was referencing.

"Hugging you back there. Did I offend you or make you uncomfortable?"

"Um, not really. It's just been a while since a guy made a move so—"

"I find that hard to believe," he said, taking a step forward, causing a ribbon of excitement to twirl inside her.

"I guess I should say it's been a minute since a guy I actually liked made a move." Her love life was on life support and had been read its last rites. But the second date wasn't the time to get into her complicated and pathetic dating history. His attempt at physical affection had caught her off guard, but she was more than open to the idea of getting to know him in the biblical sense.

"I apologize. The last thing I want to do is make you do something you're not ready for. I'm sorry. I should know better. I'm totally cool with just getting to know you. Consider me hands off from here on out." He slid his hands into his pockets.

"Oh God, I hope not. Maybe we can find a happy medium." Her pulse quickened its throb.

"I love a good compromise."

Hosea was a breath of fresh air. Confident but not cocky, assertive but not aggressive. Truthfully, she was ready to jump his bones, but he was a pastor and she wasn't completely prepared to abandon her dating rules. It was time to give love another shot, and not just because Travis was on the fast track to wedded bliss, although that was one hell of a motivator. She wanted to be with someone who could sense how she felt, someone who was going to protect her and not compete with her, someone who wouldn't lie to her or mislead her. Yes, that's what she wanted, and she realized it was way too early to know if Hosea was that person. But she was willing to stick around to see.

Makayla was late for the family dinner, but she didn't care. She took her time as she reminisced about her lunch date with Hosea the entire forty-minute drive to her parents' house. His cologne clung to her dress, filling the cabin of her car with his scent, and she could still feel his lips pressed against hers.

"Get it together, Makayla," she uttered out loud, trying to remind herself not to let her guard down too soon as she pulled in front of her parents' house.

She didn't even have a chance to put her key in the front door before it flung open to reveal Summer, Makayla's oldest sister who, in Makayla's opinion, often acted as if she were her mother. Standing at almost six-feet-two, Summer was a lot taller than both Makayla and Porsha. She was also much lighter in complexion than them, and she didn't quite resemble her parents or siblings. Her soft, reddish-brown hair also made her stand out from the pack of Randolph descendants. But when she opened her mouth, there was no doubt she was a Randolph through and through.

"You know you're late to your own party, right?" Summer said in between bites of the red velvet cupcake she was devouring.

"It's just six o'clock. And besides, this was really just a dinner for Lady Grace, and Momma just threw my celebration in at the last minute," Makayla said, stepping into the foyer of the house.

"Two things. You're wrong; it's 6:18. And I would hardly be over here just for a dinner for Lady Grace." Summer closed the door behind Makayla.

Both women bubbled with laughter. The last time they all got together, Lady Grace called Summer a fast-assed heifer, so there was no telling what she would say tonight.

"What did Momma cook?" Makayla asked as the two women walked through the entryway.

Summer lifted her head and sniffed the air. "Is that cologne I smell on you?"

"Huh?" Makayla answered, trying to act oblivious.

"Don't 'huh' me. If you can huh, you can hear." Summer leaned in to get a better whiff of the scent.

"Girl, get away from me," Makayla jokingly said, trying to speed up her pace.

"Yep, that's cologne, all right. So that's why you're late . . . out there gallivanting with a man. Who is he?"

"Nobody . . . I mean, just a guy I met. But don't say anything,"

Makayla whispered, simultaneously holding her index finger up to her mouth as the two women entered the dining room where everyone was seated.

"Look who decided to grace us with her presence," Porsha teased as she stuffed a hefty forkful of macaroni and cheese in her mouth.

"Ew, who invited you?" Makayla joked back.

"Mom and Dad said they wanted their favorite daughter in attendance, so here I am." Porsha winked at her.

Makayla made her way around the table, giving hugs and kisses to Lady Grace; her father's sister, Aunt Jennie; her husband, Uncle Brett; and her parents. She tapped Porsha on the head and sat in the empty seat next to her, waving at Miles, Summer's husband, and her nephew, Cordell.

"Hey, M-Kay. Your dad told me about your new job," Aunt Jennie said as she took a sip of water from her glass.

"Yes . . . yes, I accepted the position as leader of the singles ministry," Makayla announced. This time, butterflies didn't dance in her belly. She felt different making the announcement, as if she now owned the position.

Still full from the meal she had with Hosea, she surveyed the dishes in the center of the large dining table. After settling on the collard greens, she helped herself to a small serving. It was her maternal grandmother's original recipe, which her mother had perfected to a tee.

"Is that all you're gonna eat?" her mother asked, inspecting Makayla's plate from a distance.

"I'm not that hungry."

"Why don't you tell us why you're not hungry," Summer blurted out.

Makayla shot a glance at Summer from the corner of her eye.

"Oh, she wasn't fooling nobody. Come in here smelling like a gentlemen's lounge," Lady Grace said, letting the cat out of the bag.

Pebbles formed on Makayla's forehead, and she indiscreetly

wiped them as she pretended to move her hair from her forehead. All eyes were now on her for details.

"So, who is he?" Porsha said, whipping her head in her sister's direction.

"Nobody," Makayla said, now taking a gulp of ice-cold water from her glass.

"Oh, we're waiting," Summer instigated as she tapped her wine glass with a spoon.

"Y'all, leave my baby girl alone. When she's ready to talk about her new little friend, she will," her father said, coming to Makayla's defense.

Embarrassed by his remarks, she cringed. "Please don't call him 'my little friend.'"

"Well, then who is he?" he asked.

"I went on a simple date, that's all."

"With who? What's his name?" Porsha leaned back in the chair.

All eyes were on her, so she felt obligated to respond. "His name is Hosea Wright. He's a thirty-four-year-old pastor." She tried to keep it nonchalant.

"You're dating a pastor?" her mother squealed. Makayla could hear the delight in her voice.

"No. I went on two dates. That's it," Makayla corrected.

"Following in your mother's footsteps, I see," Lady Grace said.

"Yeah, she is. She has great taste in men. If that's what you wanna call following in her mother's footsteps, then you got that darn right," her mother said.

Makayla did not want to talk about Hosea at the family dinner. She was the last single Randolph daughter, and her mother had moved beyond hinting and had begun to strongly suggest that she would love to see Makayla settle down with a nice man.

"Go ahead, honey. Tell me more," her mother said, focusing her attention back on Makayla.

She breathed out deeply from her mouth with the realization

that her nosy family was not going to let this go. "He leads a church in Houston, Texas."

"Houston?" Porsha questioned.

"Yes, Houston."

"What's the name of the church?" Summer said, shaking a generous amount of hot sauce on every item on her plate.

"Brook Willow Church," Makayla replied, a prideful smile ruffling her lips.

"How'd you meet him?" her mom asked.

"While I was on business," Makayla answered without providing additional details. This was all the information she planned on divulging. She knew all too well that was all her mother needed to know to start a full-fledged investigation. By the next morning, her mother would know where Hosea went to college, where his family came from, and have copies of his college transcripts and financial records.

"Well, all I'm gonna say right now is that Mr. Houston, Texas better be prepared to move to Atlanta, Georgia, or it's a non-starter," her father said, grabbing his glass of Cabernet.

"When do we get to meet him?" her mother asked.

"You don't. Not right now, because we've just gone out a couple of times."

"Well, can't I be a little excited? I can't remember the last time you mentioned the words *man* or *date*," her mother said, passing the bread basket to her husband. "Makayla, you are such a beautiful woman; you could have your pick of the litter."

Gentle laughter tickled Makayla's throat. *Pick of the litter*, she thought. The comparison to men as dogs was not lost on her.

"I'm pretty sure this family has more exciting things to talk about other than my love life," Makayla said, trying to change the subject.

"Actually, we don't." Summer smirked.

"Yes, we do," Aunt Jennie chimed in.

Makayla gave her aunt Jennie an appreciative smile. She

purposely limited discussions about her romantic life. Her family was worse than Annalise Keating from *How to Get Away with Murder* with all the questions. The entire Randolph clan was opinionated and had issues with boundaries. Anytime she mentioned a guy's name, her mother and sisters would swoop in to tell her exactly what she needed to do. Makayla wasn't looking for any unsolicited advice. She wasn't looking to just land a guy. If she was going to date someone again, she wanted things to work out better than they had with her last serious relationship . . . with Travis.

Chapter 10

Makayla sat in the McPherson's Cape Cod-styled home, listening to Raeann talk in excited tones about the changes in leadership. The two women saw this new and exhilarating opportunity, Raeann's words not hers, very differently. A ball of worry and foreboding twisted in her stomach. Maybe she had been too rash at her coffeehouse meeting with Travis. She had every intention of listening to him in search of common ground. But that was before he started talking to her like she was a child and insinuating that she was the one who needed to change.

"There he is," Raeann said, standing to greet Travis.

"Good to see you." Leaning into her hug, he glanced in Makayla's direction. "Hey," he said, acknowledging her presence.

"Hey," Makayla replied. She relished the surprised look on his face when he realized she'd gotten there early and before him.

Surveying the room for a place to sit, Travis took a seat at the opposite end of the sofa where Makayla was already comfortably seated.

Jason carried a pitcher of sweet tea and glasses into the family room, setting the tray on the coffee table. "I'm glad we're finally getting a chance to get together. Raeann and I were in Seattle for a few days. My brother just had a baby." Jason poured everyone generous amounts of tea in their glasses.

"Ah, congratulations. Boy or girl?" Makayla asked, picking up a glass and a napkin.

"A big old boy, almost eleven pounds," Raeann said, pulling up a picture on her phone and handing it to Travis.

A smile pulled at the corners of his mouth as he observed the tiny rolls and chubby face. "Whoa, now, that's a healthy baby. Brings back memories. Babies are always a blessing." Travis passed the phone to Makayla.

Her heart tanked into the pit of her belly, where all of those other uncomfortable feelings dwelled. Sweat beaded her upper lip as she glanced at the picture and nodded, acknowledging the traits Raeann had pointed out.

"Cute." She hoped the expression on her face wasn't complementary to what she was experiencing inside.

Jason settled in on the love seat opposite Travis and Makayla, and Raeann joined him.

"So, are you guys excited?" Raeann said, eyeing Makayla for the answer.

"Well, technically, we don't start until next Monday, but we've been . . . at least, I know *I've* been prepping already." She finally looked over at Travis for a span of longer than five seconds.

"Me too." He gave Makayla a slight nod, a smile shadowing his mouth.

Jason grabbed a notepad from the side table and began flipping its pages. "That's good because you'll stay plenty busy in your new roles. And that's the reason Raeann and I wanted to schedule this transition meeting. So, for starters, I guess we can discuss the most important event, which is the singles retreat. I know it's not until the beginning of next year, but for an event like that, the planning starts early."

"In Savannah, right?" Travis asked, opening the notes feature on his phone.

"Yes," Raeann said. "We actually have a site visit for the hotel scheduled in June. Just to confirm the quality of the location. But it's pretty much a go."

"I'll email you guys the info for the visit so you can change over the reservations." Jason scribbled a note on his yellow legal pad. "It's an overnight trip. You'll want to tour the local sights to get a feel for what attractions the city offers. We like to recommend local activities so the attendees have fun things to do in their downtime."

A concerned looked shadowed Travis's face as his shoulders deflated.

"Uh oh, what's that look for, Travis?" Raeann asked.

Travis's mouth worked into a dubious pucker. "Did I give a look? It's all good over here. Just taking notes."

"What else needs to be done for the retreat?" Makayla lifted her glass of tea, taking a sip. Her eyes glossed over as she pretended to listen intently while Jason laid out the long list of things they would need to accomplish before the three-day singles retreat. Her mind began to wander. Taking over for Jason and Raeann was no small feat. The McPhersons were amazing leaders, despite what Auntie Di thought. They made leadership look effortless. If she was leading this ministry with anyone else, she wouldn't be worried.

She fidgeted in her seat, the weight of all she and Travis would need to accomplish, the retreat, engagement events, and creating and presenting singles workshops, finally sinking in. Maybe she shouldn't have been so closed off at their coffeehouse meeting. If he failed, she failed with him because now her success was dependent on him. Accepting the job meant being willing to set the drama aside. Luckily for Makayla, failure wasn't part of Travis's vocabulary. He would get the job done, even if he had to carry the singles ministry on his back and limp all the way to the finish line. *If he's genuinely willing to try, I can meet him halfway.*

"That's really the meat and potatoes of it all," Jason said, wrapping up the details of the meeting. "But like I said, I'll follow up with an email that summarizes everything we discussed today," he continued, setting his notepad aside.

"Any questions?" Raeann said, still bubbly and excited.

"Nope, no questions. This has been informative. I'm sure once my head stops spinning, a few questions might pop up," Travis said before resting his eyes on Makayla, who was seemingly in another world. Her eyes were focused on the wall behind the McPhersons. Travis leaned over and tapped Makayla on her thigh, causing her to flinch.

"Do you have any questions?" Travis asked.

"We didn't bore you, did we?" Raeann teased.

"No . . . no. I'm sorry. Just thinking about all we have to do. This was very helpful, thank you," Makayla said before flashing a concerned glance in Travis's direction.

His face relaxed into a smile as his gaze latched onto hers. Could he see the rising alarm swimming in her eyes? His focused eyes and casual smile acted as an anchor helping to steady the jitters that were growing inside. Tossing her spiral notebook with the saying "Today Is a New Beginning" written in gold lettering across the front into her oversized purse, Makayla was anxious to leave.

"Oh, one last thing," Jason said.

"What's that?" Makayla scooted to the edge of the sofa, checking the time on her phone.

"The space," Jason said.

Raeann chuckled, nodding her head. "Yes, the office space."

"What about it?" Travis's eyes shifted between the two of them.

"It's tight . . . real tight. It can be a challenge being on top of one another all the time," Jason said.

"It was a good thing we were married because I don't know how we would have made it some days," Raeann added.

"Honey, why don't you tell them about our agreement?" Jason patted his wife on the knee.

"Oh, yeah. Well . . . truth be told, we had to lay some ground rules. We couldn't bring personal problems to work. We agreed not to discuss anything that wasn't related to the singles ministry while at work. And trust me, it was hard to do some days. But you have to be committed to the task at hand."

Travis smirked. "Well, I . . . I mean, we did have a meeting like that. Well, sort of. It didn't end too well." His eyes swung Makayla's way.

"Well, I know you guys have some ... history, so my advice to you both is to set those ground rules. Tackle any issues that might interfere with your work," Raeann said, looking directly at Makayla.

Leaning back on the sofa, Makayla knotted her arms over her chest. She had a sneaking suspicion that Travis had talked to the McPhersons in advance of their meeting. Three pairs of eyes were all focused on her, and she didn't like being teamed up on. *I'm not the problem*, she thought.

"Know what I mean?" Raeann emphasized.

Makayla's eyes moved furtively from one face to the other. "Oh, trust me, I get it. Teamwork makes the dream work." She tilted her head in Travis's direction.

Travis cleared his throat. "I look forward to this opportunity. And working with Makayla is just the ... sour cherry on top of it all. Makayla is sharp as a tack. She ... is ... determined. She finds a way when it seems like there is no way." Travis folded his mouth shut.

She eyed Travis suspiciously. The nice-young-man routine was an act, and she could see right through it like a robe that had been washed one too many times. Her jaw trembling with anger, she did her best to reapply a smile.

Raising his hand to his chin, Jason considered the pair. Even though they were both smiling, the tension in the room was palpable. "I'm going to leave you two with this. God stretches us through our circumstances. Growing pains can be uncomfortable, but if you push through it, the reward is worth it," Jason said, slapping his hands against his knees.

Makayla shook her head, pretending to take Jason's words to heart. She couldn't deny working with Travis was going to stretch her. Hopefully, she wouldn't end up being ripped to shreds.

As he headed toward his car after the meeting, Travis could hear Makayla's brown suede boots clicking behind him like a horse trot.

"What was that back there?" Makayla yelled, pushing him in his back.

Caught off guard, Travis spun around instinctively. "What are you talking about?" He was a bit shocked because he thought the meeting had gone reasonably well ... until they neared the end.

"You guys were all piling on me like I'm the problem." Balling her hands into fists, her frustration was written all over her face. "Who do you think you are? I'm not exactly jumping for joy to work with you, but I'm not going to be an obstructionist."

"Look, Makayla, this is what I was trying to avoid. It's the reason I wanted us to meet before we started working together. To set some ground rules, just like the McPhersons said."

"Yeah, you called the meeting, all right, trying to dictate rules as if you're my boss. Let's get one thing straight right here and right now: we are *co-workers*. You don't get to tell me what to do," Makayla shouted with a flip of her hair as she walked with determined steps toward her S-Class.

"That wasn't my intention." He grabbed her arm.

Makayla reeled toward him, ready for a fight as she glared at his hand, which was still clutching her arm. He shrunk back, removing his hold. Was it too late for him to back out? His pleading eyes searched her face silently, begging her to listen to him.

"That wasn't my intention," he repeated, flipping his palms up. "I just want this to work."

"I do too," she muttered, her shoulders curving.

Travis saw this as his chance. Maybe she was tired of this adversarial Ping-Pong match. The McPherson's had just unloaded a shitton of work on their laps. Makayla was worried, and he understood because his chest was heavy from the overwhelming weight of all their new responsibilities.

"I know we can accomplish amazing things together. We always made a great duo."

Makayla winced. "Great duo? Great duo? You don't get it, do you? You just don't get it!" Makayla shouted as she disarmed her car alarm, climbed in, started the engine, and drove away as though she was Dale Earnhardt Jr. racing in the Daytona 500.

Travis rested on his heels, stoically still. *Don't get what?* There was a time when he knew exactly what she was feeling at any given moment, no need for words. Talking to her now was like talking to a stranger. All their shared memories, inside jokes, bedside confessions, gone. *What am I missing?* He pondered for a little while longer until he remembered he had bigger fish to fry, like how he was going to break the news to Regina that he had an overnight business trip with Makayla coming up in the next few months.

Chapter 11

Walking into his new office, Travis set a large box on the floor next to his desk. The office was small, just like the McPhersons had warned. There was just enough room for the two desks. He didn't want to focus on the fact that he and Makayla would be in close quarters for eight hours a day, Monday through Friday. Sizing up the area, he envisioned what could be done to make the space more inviting, but first it needed to be cleaned.

For Travis, an organized and spotless workspace was a must. His motto was "Every item in its place, and a place for every item." Cleaning would also help keep the nervous energy that was coursing through his body at bay. He had enough first-day jitters that he could act as a one-man cleaning crew, sweeping through the fifty-thousand-square-foot building until every corner sparkled and shined. Pulling out his Clorox wipes from an adjacent box, he decided to tackle the biggest item in the room, the desk.

"Knock, knock," Phor said, entering the already cramped space. After signing on to the role, Travis enlisted Phor as his number two. Phor was now part of the small singles ministry staff he and Makayla had recruited to help with the day-to-day operations of running a ministry with over four thousand members. Travis needed someone he could count on, and as his best friend, Phor, would always have his back. The hope was that Phor would act as a buffer, forcing Makayla to be on her best behavior. And for Makayla, her best was still pretty bad, including insults and eye rolls that were so protracted he wondered how her brown eyes remained in the sockets.

"Hey, good morning." Travis gave Phor dap, gently tapping him on the back.

"This office . . ." Phor looked around, tugging on his beard.

"Yeah, I know. Great, right?" Travis warped his lips into a smile. It was an inside joke. They were thinking the same thing: close quarters for two people who were like oil and water.

"How are you and Makayla going to function in this space?" Phor asked, lounging against the empty desk.

"Jason and Raeann seemed to manage just fine." He wiped down the desk phone, picking up the receiver, paying close attention to the mouth and earpiece.

"Jason and Raeann actually enjoyed one another's company." Phor released a snort as he walked over to the small rectangle window that showcased a beautiful view of a nearby smaller building.

"Listen, I have an office, and you are not going to dampen this moment. Look . . ." Travis walked over to the office door, shutting it. "I can close this door and have complete silence."

"Yeah, the lion's den was probably peaceful too, but that doesn't mean I want to be locked in it."

"Daniel made it out alive, and so will I," Travis replied. Phor was not going to ruin this day for him. New job, new office, and new opportunities. He was happy to be out of his cube, even if the office space wasn't much bigger. Travis believed in the power of positive thinking, and he was going to actualize the hell out of this job.

Taking a seat behind Makayla's vacant desk, Phor stretched his arms over his head. "OK, boss, what are we doing first?"

"I think we need to plan an event. Kind of like a grand reopening. Under new management type deal. Everyone knows us, but they don't know us as the leaders of the ministry." Travis's eyes doubled in size as if he had an aha moment.

"So . . . like a meet and greet?" Phor said, swinging his feet on top of Makayla's desk.

"Yeah, I need to talk it through with Makayla first. But once we confirm, we can work on the logistics." Moving from the phone, he was now wiping down the armrest of his chair.

"You might wanna chill with the wipes. I'm getting a little lightheaded."

Tossing the wipe aside, Travis dropped down onto his chair.

"How's the wedding planning going? Have you guys picked a date yet?"

"Um, we've talked about maybe the early part of next year. But we just got engaged, so there's no rush."

"Does Regina feel the same way?"

"Not exactly." He squirmed in his seat. Right now, jumping the broom wasn't his priority. This new position would require long hours as he tried his best to get up to speed. Regina would have to understand that reviewing files and new-member outreach was going to consume his time for the foreseeable future, so things like photographers and finding the perfect shade of dusty rose would have to take a back seat.

Before Phor could respond, the door swung open and Makayla walked in. Crashing to a halt, she traded glances with Travis and Phor, who had made themselves at home in her office. She placed the bags in her hands on the floor next to her desk, which Phor was occupying.

"Are you comfortable?" Makayla asked, sweetly batting her long lashes as she thrust her gaze over to him.

"Very comfortable, thank you." He placed his hands behind his head.

Her plump lips flattened into a thin line as she waited for him to get the hint.

"Do you want me to move?"

"Yes." She waved her hand for him to get out of the way.

Phor jerked to his feet.

"Thanks."

"So, imma go," Phor said, pointing his finger at Travis.

"You don't have to go," both Travis and Makayla said in unison.

Phor ignored them. "Happy move-in day, you guys. Hey, Travis, we'll talk later." Phor paused at the door. "Open or closed?"

"Open," Makayla said.

Travis resumed cleaning. The small space smelled like a hospital ward. The air was stale, and a strong scent of disinfectant lingered over top, singeing his nostrils.

"Do you wanna wipe down your desk? All kinds of stuff could be lingering on it," Travis said, placing the wipes in front of her.

"Like what?"

"I don't know. Jason and Raeann were married so . . ."

Makayla stepped back from the desk. "You're saying Jason and Raeann had sex on this desk?" she whispered.

"No, that is not what I'm saying. But ..." Travis was thinking of dirty diapers and toddler germs from the McPherson's kids, but she made a good point. His gaze latched onto hers, their eyes entangled long enough to throw Travis's heart out of cadence.

Shrinking away from his eyes, she said, "Yeah, give me a wipe."

For the next few hours, the two worked in complete silence, wiping down every surface and decorating their modest office. Makayla kicked off her shoes, grabbed a framed inspirational poster, and climbed precariously onto her swivel chair to hang the frame from the nail in the wall. As she attempted to descend, the chair wobbled, forcing her to throw her arms in the air in an effort to maintain her balance. But she could already feel herself losing this fight with gravity as she braced her body for impact. Luckily, Travis crossed the distance just in time to catch her in his arms. Makayla pressed her body against his firm chest and freely allowed her arms to wrap themselves around his neck.

"Thanks." She gulped down a steadying breath, her gaze soft as silk.

"People who trip over their own feet shouldn't be climbing things," Travis teased, lowering her to the floor, his arms still maintaining a secure grip. Reaching, he tucked a wayward lock of hair behind her ear, accidentally brushing against her cheek. Goose bumps sprang on her arms as her skin sparked from his touch. Makayla narrowed her brow, searching his serious hazel eyes, although she was unsure of what she was hoping to find. But one thing she knew for sure was that he needed to let go of her waist. Coughing, she backed away.

"You good?" He adjusted his view to examine the poster she'd almost broken a limb for.

"Yep," Makayla replied, unable to meet his eyes. Stepping back into the middle of the office, she admired their work. *We actually worked together toward a common goal without going at each other's throats. Sure, it was cleaning a space the size of a closet, but if we could come together on this simple task, maybe there's hope,* she thought.

Closing her eyes, she took in a deep, cleansing, lemon-scented breath. This was a bit surreal, seeing Travis seated at the desk right in front of hers. Her phone vibrated from her pocket. Retrieving it, she eyed an incoming text message from Hosea: Hope your first day is going well, it read with a smiley face next to the text. Hosea was a welcomed distraction. She didn't have time to think about anything other than looking forward to his texts throughout the day and his phone calls in the evenings. For a busy pastor, she didn't take the attention she was receiving from him for granted.

Removing her laptop from her tote bag, she plugged it into the nearest outlet. "I think we should craft an email. Something simple to introduce ourselves and our plans for the ministry."

"I like that. I was just telling Phor we should plan an event to kind of kick off the change in leadership."

"You talked to Phor?" Her stomach pitted into tight coils, angsty about the response from her new work partner.

"He's my number two."

"Don't you think you should come to me first with things since we're running this show together?"

"So, I can't talk to anyone about anything related to the ministry until I confer with you first?"

Her head bobbed to the side. "Yes. If *we're* leading the ministry, Phor shouldn't know things before I do." *This is common sense, and if the roles were reversed, he would be having a fit right now.*

"He doesn't know anything. You're being ridiculous." Travis waved his hand, brushing away her concerns.

"Don't be dismissive."

"Don't be paranoid."

His tone was harsh, causing a burning rage to boil her blood. Makayla stood, her swivel chair spinning into the wall. "I am not being paranoid." She pinched her fingers together for emphasis. "We are supposed to be a team. So, you should act like it."

"If we're a team, then you need to trust me."

"Trust? I trust what I see, and what I see is you undermining me."

Rubbing his forehead, he fixed his attention back to his laptop, signaling he was done with this conversation.

Makayla dropped to her seat, stealing a glance from the corner of her eye. She watched as he took out his frustration on the keyboard. She opened her mouth to speak but stopped short, not wanting to say the wrong thing. Makayla perused her calendar to keep her eyes from traveling in his direction. The sound of his leg bouncing up and down made her painfully aware of his presence. This morning had gone so smoothly, but now, she felt foolish for thinking, even for a brief second, that this could work.

After the meeting with the McPhersons, she decided the best course of action was to find common ground. Bickering back and forth would ensure nothing got accomplished. Her father was expecting results, and if they were unsuccessful, Travis wouldn't hesitate to blame it all on her. Makayla drove her teeth into her lip, anger retreating from her eyes as she looked over at Travis, who was scowling at his laptop screen.

Leaning back in her chair, she said, "So, what were you thinking?"

"What?" Travis asked, inching his eyes toward her.

"I'm all ears." She closed her laptop, hoping he could tell she was trying. The old Makayla would have ignored him for the remainder of the day, but the new kumbaya Makayla was trying to turn the page and forge a path forward. This wasn't the private sector; there was no place for backbiting in the house of the Lord.

He slid his chair out so he could get a better view of her face. With a raised eyebrow, he laid out his idea. "I was thinking we should put together some type of event." Travis paused, expecting her to object. When the objection never came, he continued. "Our first event as ministry leaders. It should establish the vibe for what we want the group to be going forward."

"So, what kind of event did you have in mind?"

"Maybe a karaoke night or a movie watch party." His face relaxed into a tentative smile. "What do you think?"

"Thinking outside the box has never really been your forte. Don't get me wrong, you're on the path; you just need to be pointed in the right direction."

Clasping his hands, he said, "OK, hit me with your dazzling suggestions."

"Well, we need something interactive, something that gives people the opportunity to mix and mingle." Her words were slow and deliberate like she was teaching her ninety-one-year-old grandmother how to send a text message. "You haven't been single for quite some time, so you wouldn't know this, but people want a collective experience, like a game night."

"I'm single, and I know what people want, thanks." He clicked his tongue.

"You have an entire fiancée," Makayla corrected him.

"Yup, I do, but I'm not married yet, so technically, I'm still single."

"Oh, is that how that works?" A twisted smile pulled at her lips. "You sure do like your technicalities."

"You know what, Makayla—" Travis stopped mid-sentence.

Makayla watched as he closed his eyes, exhaling sharply. He was probably praying for patience or a sharp object to poke her with. Clearing his throat, he finally said, "I think you're right. Game night sounds like it could be fun."

Chapter 12

Travis's sneakers squeaked as he jetted for the ball. As he made contact with his racquet, the ball whacked the wall and returned in their direction, forcing his friend Calvin to extend his arm in an attempt to make contact. The ball flew past Calvin, just inches from his racquet.

"Fifteen to nine. Good game," Travis said, lifting his shirt to wipe his face.

Calvin Mitchell and Travis were roommates at Clark Atlanta University and had remained friends ever since. Calvin wasn't a member of Life Church. He wasn't a member of any church, causing the two to clash from time to time because of their different ideologies.

"Shit, my game is trash today." Calvin swung his racquet, trying to get his groove back.

"Your game is trash every single time we play," Travis joked.

"Don't play me, T. You just gonna forget about last month when I whooped your ass?" Calvin waved his arms.

"I was sick and had a fever." His smile switched to a frown.

"I still beat you, though." Calvin squirted water into his mouth. "I'm gonna need a ten-minute break before the last set."

Travis leaned against the wall and slid down, sitting on the polished hardwood floor.

"How's the new gig?" Calvin asked, sitting next to him.

"It's been two weeks, and I'm still alive, so I guess that's a win," he said, lightly bouncing the ball against the floor.

"You need to chill. M-Kay ain't even that bad." Calvin rummaged through Travis's backpack, looking for a snack.

"To you. She isn't that bad *to you*." Calvin knew Makayla from college, back when they were all friends. Those first two years of college, she was just one of the boys. "That's what's so messed up about her. With me, it's all stinger, but then she turns around and offers others honey."

"Is that some kinda sex analogy?"

He pulled off his goggles. "No. Everything isn't about sex, Cal. Dang."

"To you. Everything ain't about sex . . . *to you*." Calvin worked up a cocky grin, opening a granola bar. "Honestly, can you blame her?"

His rosy face washed of color. "I don't think she's ever forgiven me."

"You fucked up, Travis. Expecting her to forgive *that*." He clicked his tongue, rumpling his face. "That was a hard pill to swallow."

Calvin was right. Travis couldn't disagree. Expecting forgiveness was probably asking for too much. Grabbing his bag, he retrieved his phone from one of the small compartments. He skimmed the barrage of text messages he'd received, with almost half of them coming from Regina. He read them one by one.

> Regina: Hey, I know you're playing racquetball, but call me as soon as you get this message.
>
> Regina: Hey, did you get my message?
>
> Regina: Travis?
>
> Regina: Tiffany from the Trolley Barn called. Someone canceled their appointment, so she can

put us in their place. I need you to confirm that you
can make it.

Regina: Travis?!!!

Regina: I went ahead and confirmed with Tiffany
for two o'clock. Can't wait!! If you can't make it, I'll
just go by myself.

"Dang," Travis said.

"What?" Calvin took a bite of his bar.

"Regina confirmed a two o'clock for us."

"Wedding stuff?"

"What else?" He huffed with a slight scowl.

"You don't sound too excited. What's up?" His eyes swung in
Travis's direction.

"It's not that. It's just . . ." Travis stopped mid-sentence, unable
to string together words that would accurately capture what he'd
been feeling.

"You know who you sound like, don't you?"

"Who?" Travis asked, dumbfounded.

"My brother, Jaylin."

"Go ahead. I ain't nothing like Jay."

"Yes, you are. Jay knew he wasn't in love with Mia, but he married her anyway. Dude's been miserable ever since. I don't know what
it is about you church people who stay in your misery because you
claim God doesn't like divorce. Hell, I don't like misery, and I'll be
damned if I stay in it."

Travis chewed at the corner of his mouth. "I never said I didn't
love Regina. I love her . . . a lot."

Sucking his teeth, Calvin asked, "You sure about that?"

"What is this, one-on-one premarital counseling?"

"Nah, I'm the last one to try to offer you marital counseling, but
I *do* know you." He pointed his long index finger at Travis.

Here we go again. Calvin wasn't a fan of Regina, but Travis had hoped the two would grow on one another. His best friend was convinced that he should try to fix things with Makayla. It had been five years, and it seemed like he was the only one who'd moved on. "Cal, what are you trying to say?"

"You love her, but are you *in love* with her?"

Travis paused.

Tilting his head, Calvin asked the question again. "Are you?"

"Yes . . . yes, of course, I love her . . . am in love with . . . her. Just because we're not one of those obnoxious couples who can't keep their hands off of each other doesn't mean I don't love her." Regina was the first woman that made him feel like happily ever after was still possible after his split from Makayla.

"You mean how you and M-Kay used to be?"

"Yep, and look how that turned out. All fluff, no substance."

"Looks like I hit a nerve," Calvin teased.

"No, you didn't hit a nerve. I'm good, real good. But enough about me. What's up with you?" Comparing the two women wasn't fair. Makayla was his first real serious relationship. That type of love hit different. That type of love also cut deeper, leaving behind lasting scars.

"How do you church folk say it? Blessed and highly favored. Work's busy as hell. I just got assigned to a new project. But things are great, couldn't be better."

"Happy to hear everything is falling into place." Travis clambered to his feet with a big stretch. "Look, Cal, let me get outta here. We'll have to finish up next weekend. I need to go home and get myself together so I can view that venue with Regina." His lips pinched upward.

"How about we get together for happy hour this Monday?" Calvin gathered his things from the floor.

"Sounds like a plan."

As Travis headed to his car, he knew Calvin wasn't going to let go of the marriage debate. He'd had variations of this conversation with Calvin before. *Are you sure she's the one? Marriage is forever. You hardly know her.* No matter what Travis said, Calvin remained unconvinced. At the end of the day, he knew Calvin would be standing next to him on his wedding day, but his friend would continue to voice his concerns right up until Travis and Regina jumped the broom.

Regina stood under her apartment carport, waiting for Travis. She was frantically looking down at her phone when he drove up. He didn't even have a chance to get out and open her car door for her; she opened it herself.

"Finally," she said in a sarcastic tone.

He lobbed her a look. "What do you mean 'finally'?"

"I thought you'd be here before now. You know I hate rushing."

"Babe, we have forty minutes to get there. The place is only twenty miles away. We'll make it."

She screwed up her nose. "Yeah, but I just like being early. Anything can happen, traffic or whatever."

Exiting the apartment complex, he pulled onto the main road, heading for the expressway.

"If you weren't hanging with Calvin, we could have grabbed the one o'clock slot. I sure hope you don't plan on spreading yourself this thin after we get married. It's bad enough I have to deal with you working with your deranged ex every day," she said as she fumbled through her purse.

"Regina ..." Travis paused. "You can't be serious. This job requires a level of sacrifice. I'm no longer pushing papers across my desk. I'm actually interacting with people. I thought you understood that. Between Bible studies and baptisms, counseling sessions and planning meetings, this is my life now."

Her eyes slammed into him. She didn't need to say anything; her eyes spoke for her.

"*Our* life," Travis corrected himself. "Right now, work is going to demand a lot of my attention, especially with the transition. So yeah,

I don't think it's too much to ask if I wanna go work out or occasionally grab a drink with the guys."

"I'm making sacrifices too. When do I get to go out and hang with my friends?"

"What friends?" As an Atlanta transplant, the only friends Regina had were the ones he'd introduced her to.

"I have friends," Regina said with a sharp click of the tongue. "I just keep my circle small."

"If by small you mean nonexistent, then yeah, you do." He changed lanes.

Her back snapped straight. "Maybe I should make friends with Makayla. I'm sure we'd have so much to talk about."

Turning on his hazard lights, Travis pulled over to the side of the road. "What is this about, hm? Are you looking to get into an argument on the way to the wedding venue?"

"I don't know. Since you started this job, I hardly see you. And when I'm with you, I have to share you with the church, with Daisy, with Calvin, and now I have to share with your ex-girlfriend."

"*Ex* being the operative word. She's my ex, and that's it. You and I discussed the job before I accepted the promotion. Heck, you even told me to accept it. So, what I don't want to hear is you throwing it back in my face." This moment right here was exactly what he was trying to avoid and why he initially wanted to turn the job down. Even after all these years, Makayla was like gum on the bottom of his shoe. No matter how hard he tried to rub the sole on the pavement, the gum refused to come off.

A worried expression marred her face. "Baby, I'm sorry. I just . . . I just don't know. It's just that Makay—"

"Don't say her name. Please don't say her name. You're getting yourself all worked up over nothing." He caressed her face, meeting the questioning look in her eyes. "I know I'm wrapped up in work right now, but it won't always be like this. I just need to get my bearings. It's still you and me. Don't ever doubt that." Leaning in, he planted a quick kiss on her lips before pulling back onto the main road.

Travis's knuckles tightened against the steering wheel as he drove in silence. The knot in his jaw spasmed, a reminder to unlock his teeth, which had been clenched since picking up Regina. Usually, she was fine with following his lead. But lately, she'd been making it clear she didn't appreciate the direction he was steering them in. As he headed for their freeway exit, he could hear the foundation of his perfectly crafted life cracking.

As they approached what looked like a big green barn, Travis and Regina were greeted by a middle-aged woman standing outside with a clipboard and an inviting smile.

"Hello. You two must be Travis and Regina. I'm Tiffany Davis," she said, extending her hand.

"We are so excited to tour the property today," Regina gushed, her head on a swivel, not knowing what to take in first.

"Well, first, on behalf of our CEO and general manager, we want to thank you for considering the Trolley Barn for your special day. You're going to love this place," she said, leading them to the right of the building. "First, we'll tour the suites where you'll be getting dressed. And for the ladies, the bridal suite even has an area for makeup and hair."

Regina and Tiffany walked ahead, chatting about the property while Travis lagged behind, taking in the rustic scenery, for which he wasn't a great fan. He and Regina had different upbringings and different tastes. While Travis was raised in "the 'hood" as they say, Regina grew up in the country, Vermont to be exact. She was used to fields, farms, bed-and-breakfast spots, and lots of natural scenery. Travis, on the other hand, was a city boy, growing up in Oakland. He was used to concrete, congested street traffic, and the occasional gunfire.

Large trees enclosed the space, making it intimate and cozy. A walking path was off to the left, leading to a thicket of trees. Regina glanced back at Travis and smiled.

"What?" he asked, sure he'd missed what she'd said.

"Did you hear that? The barn has been here since 1889."

"Wow." One of his eyebrows crept upward, semi-impressed.

They stopped in front of a cottage. "This is the bridal suite. It's six hundred square feet, which is perfect for you and your wedding party to get beautified. The groom's suite is similar, and it's on the other side of the property." Tiffany moved aside to allow them to view the space.

"This is so cute. I love it." Regina grabbed Travis's hand, giving it a squeeze. "Don't you love it?"

Travis looked around the well-outfitted suite. "It's kinda small. Are you going to be able to fit all your bridesmaids and the makeup and hair people?" Regina didn't have any real friends to speak of in Atlanta, but she had lifelong friends in Vermont and a gang of sorority sisters from her college alma mater.

"So, you don't like it?" Regina whispered, letting go of his hand.

"I didn't say that. I just think we need to keep our options open. It's not like we don't have options."

"But I really like this place. It's cozy and intimate."

Travis inhaled patience, deciding to bite his tongue, fearing one more comment would end in a squabble like the one they got into on the way to the venue.

"Let's check out the first potential ceremony site," Tiffany said, leading the way to the other side of the property. "Have you picked a date yet?"

"No, but we were thinking early next year," Regina said.

"Or spring, summer, fall of next year," Travis added, sliding his hands into the pockets of his jeans. They didn't have a date. Wedding event planners were worse than car salesmen, always trying to get them to set a date and lock in the venue. They'd already looked at several places, and the playbook was always the same: pressure to sign contracts and leave a deposit because available dates were going fast. As far as he was concerned, there wasn't a rush.

"Tiffany, ignore him. It's going to be early next year. We just need to pick an exact date." Regina threw him an icy glare.

Tiffany smiled. "No worries. You have a general idea, and that's good. The first ceremony site is straight ahead."

"Hey, Tiffany, can we meet you there? I just wanna confer with my hubby-to-be," Regina said in a sing-song tone, hooking her arm around Travis's.

"Sure. It's straight ahead. You can't miss it," Tiffany said, disappearing from view.

"What was that about?" Regina shifted her weight to one side, dropping his arm.

"What are you talking about *now*?"

"The wedding date, Travis. The wedding date. You know, the day we're supposed to say 'I do' to each other."

"We've never settled on a day. Never. I'm getting the sense that . . . never mind." He didn't understand why they had to rush. Was she going to turn into a green, warted ogre if they didn't get married soon? Why weren't they allowed to enjoy this new phase of their relationship? There were no rules that said that once you get engaged you have to immediately start planning the wedding.

"And I'm getting the sense that you don't really want to get married."

"Oh, my God. I can't believe you're going there again."

"Yeah, Travis, I'm going there again. I want to be your wife, and the sooner the better."

Travis paused. Regina was getting upset, causing dread to contract his stomach. He was fearful that tears would follow. When someone cried, Travis turned into a sweaty mess, unable to form coherent sentences. More accurately, this happened when he was the cause of the tears. His gaze flitted about the forest, spotting two other couples who were receiving a tour of the property. And like him, the men were lagging behind while the brides-to-be were leading the charge during the tour. If Travis were an animated character, a lightbulb would have brightened above his head. Regina wasn't overreacting. She was no different than these other women. Maybe he had dragged his feet long enough.

"OK, Regina. Let's set a date. And if you like this place, we'll book it."

The sadness in her eyes was converted to that of joy and excitement. "Really?! Are you serious?" She nearly jumped into his arms.

Travis gave her a lopsided smile. He leaned in, placing a soft kiss on her thick lips.

Lying in his bed that night, Travis recalled the events of the day: his conversation with Calvin; his arguments with Regina; his apprehension on setting a date; signing the wedding contract for the venue, which felt like signing away the rights to his firstborn child; and last but not least, being on permanent lockdown. His temples throbbed and the base of his skull hummed. All this wedding planning was giving him a headache.

Chapter 13

"Hey, good morning." Travis placed his backpack in his desk chair.

"Morning. I was just about to text you." Makayla looked away from the laptop screen to greet him.

"Did you need something?"

"After you finished your meeting with Pastor—"

Travis let go of a single chuckle.

"What's funny?" She was puzzled by his smirk.

"Why do you say 'Pastor'? Why don't you just say, 'Dad'?"

Her eyebrow rose in a slow arch. "Because . . . I guess in this role, it just sounds kinda funny for me to be walking around here calling him 'Daddy' when everyone else calls him 'Pastor.' Know what I mean?"

"I guess." He lifted a blasé shoulder. "Did you need something?" he repeated.

"I was gonna ask you to stop by the café and pick me up a—"

"Tall double chocolate chip Frappuccino with whipped cream, melted fudge, and crushed cherries on top," he recited, finishing Makayla's sentence, still remembering her favorite drink.

A streak of heat moved along her skin. She was impressed by his memory.

"We can grab one on the way to our meeting at Coin-Op. You're still planning on going, aren't you?" Opening his backpack, he retrieved his laptop.

"Yes. It's on my calendar. Meeting with Chaz Baker at one."

"Cool." He powered up his laptop. "We riding together?"

"We can." Her heart stuttered before regaining its normal beat pattern.

Before he could respond, Phor came bursting into their office uninvited.

"Congratulations, my dude!" Phor said, rushing over to Travis, catching him by surprise.

Makayla looked in their direction. *Congratulations?*

"Ah . . ." Travis uttered. A panicked expression flittered across his handsome features.

"Heard you guys finally set a date," Phor said as the two shook hands.

Travis's face washed of color and sweat sprung from his pores. "Yeah, yeah. Got my arm twisted this past weekend by Regina and the lady at the venue. You know how they are; the two of them were like mobsters."

Makayla jerked her head back to her screen, certain Travis and Phor could hear the pounding sound of her heart beating. Focusing her attention on her inbox, she stared at the boxes and the blurry words in them. Perspiration dotted the roots of her hair, causing her smoothed edges to curl. She desperately wanted to be anywhere but in this cramped room. The last thing she wanted was to come off as the bitter, jealous ex-girlfriend Travis claimed she was. Since an invisibility cloak wasn't readily available, she decided to speak.

Clearing her throat, she offered a genuine-sounding congratulatory wish. "Hey, no secrets around here, Travis. I didn't know you guys had set a date. Well, anyway, congratulations to you . . . and Regina."

With nervous strokes, he straightened his shirt. "Thank you." Shooting his best friend an irritated look, he said, "Hey, Phor, I came in late today, and I have to make some headway before our afternoon meeting."

"No problem. Congrats again. See you later," Phor said.

"Not if I see you first, buddy." Travis scowled as Phor exited.

As hard as she was trying, Makayla was losing the battle with containing her tears; a few had escaped their ducts and began to slide down her cheeks. Eyeing the door, she knew she needed to get out of there before it became blatantly obvious that she felt some type of way about hearing the news.

She swallowed in an attempt to clear the knot that had formed in her throat. "Hey, I'll be right back. Gotta run to the ladies' room. Might be TMI, but I think it's that time of the month," she lied as she stood up from her desk, grabbing her makeup case from her purse. Doing her best to shield her face from view, she crossed in front of his desk to exit the office.

"OK," he said without looking up, too busy trying to discreetly mop away the sweat that slicked his brow.

Makayla dashed through the reception area and lobby to the east side of the church, which is where the private lounge for the first lady was located. With the keys her mother had provided, in case she ever had a need, she let herself in and hurriedly locked the door behind her. She slid against the door onto the floor. The levee broke, and a warm, salty flow of tears began to cascade down her cheeks.

Get it together, Makayla. You and Travis are over. You've been over. You left him, remember? What did you expect to happen? People who get engaged tend to eventually get married. You need to let this go. You're gonna end up alone, and you don't even like cats, so you'll have no one to keep you company. You need to focus on Hosea; he's crazy about you. In a year or so, you may end up with a ring of your own. Travis has moved on; it's time you do the same.

No matter how true the conversation she had with herself was, it didn't take away from the fact that, for some reason, hearing that Travis and Regina had set a date stung. It probably stung worse than hearing they were engaged. Makayla didn't know why; she just knew it did. Why couldn't the tables have been turned? Why wasn't she the one getting married instead of Travis? This thought made her mad all over again, mad that she had pushed away every suitor, never really giving anyone a fair shot, mad at herself for taking this new position at the church. After all, she knew working with him was going to be challenging, based on the mere fact they could never see eye to eye. If she said the sky was blue, Travis would chime in, saying that, actually, the sky was an amalgamation of colors.

Makayla realized she could rehearse as many scenarios as she wanted, but she couldn't talk herself out of feeling the way she felt. Rationally, she knew she had no right to be as upset as she was, but her feelings for Travis had never been rational. Her love for him was the same way Icarus loved the sun, too close, entirely too close. And when that love faltered, she settled on hating him just so she could still feel some part of him inside of her. Pushing through her thoughts, she acknowledged the need to get back to her office; otherwise, it would be obvious to Travis that she was bothered by the news and had probably gone off somewhere to cry. Although it was true, she wasn't going to allow him the satisfaction.

Glancing down at her watch, she realized she had been gone for twenty-three minutes. She rose to her feet and went to the sink to touch up her face. When she was pleased with her look, she squirted two drops of Visine in her eyes and exited the lounge, making sure to lock the door. Infused with a hefty dose of pride, Makayla strutted through the lobby to the reception area, where she was stopped by Tami.

"I just dropped off a package for you," she said, her smile wide and gleaming.

"Package? For me?"

"Well, it's not really a package, per se, but it's a delivery for you," Tami said, spinning an ink pen between her fingers like a baton.

Makayla wasn't expecting anything, but it wouldn't have been out of the ordinary to have an order come in her name since she was using the corporate AMEX card for purchases and other supplies.

"OK. Thanks." She walked through the reception area, picking up her pace with each step.

Her eyes took up her whole face when she noticed the large floral arrangement of pink and white roses in a glass vase with a gold ribbon tied around the middle. Without looking at Travis, she walked straight to her desk, slowly bending over to smell the roses. *Yes, Makayla, smell the roses,* she reminded herself.

Curious to know who the suitor might have been, Tami followed Makayla into her office.

"Somebody's got a secret admirer," Tami joked, walking over and taking a sniff of the flowers as well. "Who you over here entertaining?"

"I don't know yet." Makayla retrieved the note card from the envelope.

"Read the card," an anxious Tami suggested.

"No."

"Why?" Tami placed her hand on her hip.

"Because it's private," Makayla said. And for the first time since she'd made it back to the office, she turned to look at Travis, whose gaze awaited hers. His eyes had been fixated on the gorgeous floral arrangement that took up nearly half of Makayla's desk.

"Beautiful flowers," he said before turning his attention back toward his laptop.

Before Makayla could read the card, Tami snatched it from her hand and began to read it out loud.

> *"Makayla,*
>
> *I miss your laugh. I miss your smile.*
>
> *I miss your eyes. I miss your style.*
>
> *Can't wait to see you once again. In my book, you are a ten.*
>
> *H.W."*

"Oh, my goodness! Who is Mr. H. W.?"

Heat tickled the back of Makayla's neck as she snatched the note card back from Tami. She was the last person Makayla wanted in her business. Tami was the office gossip, and Makayla knew in a matter of thirty minutes, the entire church staff would know Makayla had received flowers from a mysterious suitor.

"Who is he?" Tami repeated.

"He's none of your business." Makayla tucked the note card back in the envelope and placed it in her top desk drawer.

"Uh oh," Tami instigated as she whirled around, facing Travis. "I don't know about you, but it must be real awkward to have some dude send flowers to your ex-fiancée."

"We were never engaged," Travis corrected her.

"Damn near, the way you two were always holding hands and laughing at your inside jokes. It was like a Hallmark movie. *Passion and the Pulpit.*" Her eyebrows mashed together into a frown. "OK, that's a horrible name, but you know what I mean."

Ignoring Tami, his eyes traveled from the flowers to Makayla one last time before settling back on his work.

"Well, those are some beautiful flowers. Do you want me to add some water? It's looking a little low."

"If you could, that would be nice. We're heading out to a meeting, and I won't have time to do it."

"My pleasure," Tami said, scooping up the floral arrangement.

Makayla grabbed her purse and placed her makeup case back in it. It was almost noon, and if she and Travis were going to grab that Frappuccino before heading downtown, they needed to leave now.

"Are you ready?" She packed up her laptop.

Without looking at her, he answered, "Yeah . . . We better get going. I'll meet you in the back lobby." He closed his computer without powering it off, shoved it into his backpack, and jetted for the door.

Makayla opened her top drawer, pulling out the note from Hosea. Reading his card, a smile brushed her lips. The good Pastor Wright was applying some serious pressure. Flowers, calls, text messages with smiley faces and heart eyes. Last week, he had a two-hour lay-over in Atlanta, and she'd met him at the airport for an early dinner. A shiver overtook her spine when she recalled how he kissed her before he went through TSA. Tucking the note in her purse, she grabbed her belongings and followed Travis. And although neither one of them would say it, she knew it was going to be one uncomfort-able afternoon.

Chapter 14

After touring Coin-Op, an arcade and gaming room, Travis and Makayla agreed they had found the location for the game night event. Travis used his company card to reserve the space, happy to be able to cross this task off his growing list.

"Ready to head back?" he asked.

"Yep."

Travis's phone vibrated with an incoming call. Holding his hand up, he signaled to Makayla he was going to need a minute before walking to the opposite side of the room.

"Hey," Travis answered.

"What up? We still on for happy hour, or does your girlfriend have you on curfew?" Calvin said on the other end.

"Yeah, we're still good. I just have to run Makayla back to the church."

"Wait, M-Kay's with you?"

"Yeah. We're downtown, just reserved a space for our first singles event."

"She should come too."

Travis's laughter ended with a snort. "Get the hell outta here."

"It'll be fun. Plus, I haven't seen Makayla in a minute. And you're already downtown, so you can save some gas."

"Your definition of fun and my definition of fun are two totally different things." His eyes swung in Makayla's direction as she aggressively smashed the buttons of a Mortal Kombat machine.

Calvin was silent on the other end before offering a compromise. "Well, at least put her on the phone so I can say hi."

With a low hiss, Travis acquiesced. If this would get Calvin to shut up, it was worth it. Walking over to Makayla, who was smiling at the arcade screen after successfully defeating Scorpion, he shook his phone. "Calvin would like to talk to you."

"What?" she said.

Calvin's voice chimed in over the speaker. "Damn, how quickly they forget."

"I could never forget you, Cal." Makayla took the phone, beaming at the screen. After some good-natured ribbing, Calvin went over Travis's head, asking Makayla to happy hour himself.

"Yo, M-Kay, Travis and I are going to happy hour; you should come through."

Travis reached in, trying to grab the phone. "OK, give me the phone back."

"Stop being a cock blocker!" Calvin yelled.

Travis wrestled the phone from her hands. "Cal, I'm sure Makayla is busy," he said, looking at her, hoping she'd agree.

"I don't want to impose on your guys' night. Maybe next time," Makayla said, slinging her purse over her shoulder.

"M-Kay, you're one of the guys; you can't impose. Just stop by for one drink," Calvin suggested, his voice almost pleading.

Travis rubbed the back of his neck, pressing his lips together tightly. His eyes pinged toward Makayla, trying to gauge her temperature.

"OK, one drink sounds like fun. As long as it's OK with Travis." She flashed him a weak smile as she waited for his response.

"Yeah, no, it's totally fine," Travis said, working his jaw in a tight circle.

Calvin roared with laughter, dipping his maki sushi roll in spicy sauce. "Remember when Travis walked around in Birkenstocks?" he asked.

"For months. I tried to get him to stop wearing them, but every day without fail, I'd look down at his feet and there they were." Makayla burst into a laugh, pointing her chopsticks in Travis's direction.

"They were comfortable," Travis said, squeezing lemon into his ice water.

The plan for one drink had morphed into several drinks and sushi rolls.

"They were Birkenstocks, and you're a black man," Calvin said, a quick no jerking his head.

"Black men wear Birkenstocks," Travis said.

Trading a glance, Makayla and Calvin erupted into a fit of uncontrollable laughter.

"I found them at the Goodwill for three dollars. They were in mint condition," Travis said over their cackling.

"That doesn't make it better." Calvin wiped tears from his eyes.

"That was three dollars too many," Makayla said, covering her mouth with her hands in an attempt to muffle her laughs.

"Haters, both of you. Plain and simple," Travis said, popping a lotus root in his mouth. Makayla and Calvin wasted no time catching up. Without missing a beat, they fell into their normal routine of making Travis the butt of their jokes. Travis would have preferred it if Makayla had not tagged along, but he had to admit, with Calvin around, she appeared to let her guard down. The last time he'd heard her laugh like this ... Honestly, he couldn't remember the last time they'd shared a genuine laugh. Recalling their most recent conversations, her laughter was always laced with irritation or discontent. Calvin's presence seemed to act as a shock absorber, dulling the sting of her animosity.

"So tell me what else is going on in your world," Makayla said, nudging Calvin on the arm.

"I bought a house," Calvin said with a sly smile.

"What? Cal, that is huge," Makayla said with a bright smile.

"Yeah, Travis was there when I signed the papers. He took a gang of pictures like he was my mom and I was five years old, graduating from kindergarten."

"Did he stand up and scream, 'That's my baby'," Makayla teased, shaking hot sauce on her California roll.

"It was a momentous occasion, and it needed to be memorialized," Travis said.

"Awe, you're so grown, Cali," Makayla said in a baby voice. "Seems like everyone is making big moves. You bought a house, Travis set a wedding date."

Calvin's eyes bulged as he leaned back. "You set a date?"

"Yep." Travis scratched at the back of his neck.

"Why am I just hearing about this now?"

Travis's glare settled on Makayla as his jaw worked back and forth.

"I'm sorry, I thought he knew." A shrug rolled over her shoulders.

"It happened this weekend. I was gonna tell you."

"That shit's crazy." Calvin snorted out a laugh. "I always thought I'd end up living in y'alls guest house after you two got married. Life's funny." The smile faded from his face. "We were always together, and then we weren't. I guess my question is how do you go from everything to nothing? I'm not saying you two are still in love, but there has to be something there in one way or another."

Travis cast a challenging glare in his friend's direction. "Cal ..." This wasn't the time or the place for them to have this conversation.

"Best friends, deepest darkest secrets ... to nothing. How does one do that exactly?"

A pinched frustration filled Travis's face. "It's growth. People move on. It happens every day."

"Oh, so you just outgrew Makayla? I got it." Gulping his sake shot, he poured another.

Makayla flashed Travis a look of concern. She hadn't spoken to

Calvin in a while, so his outburst most likely caught her off guard. This was exactly why Travis didn't want to get the band back together. Revisiting these ancient feelings helped no one. Most relationships failed. He and Makayla weren't soulmates; they were statistics. When Makayla left him, her friendship with Calvin was just collateral damage. Travis didn't understand why Calvin was taking this so personally.

Makayla reached for Calvin's arm. "You seem upset."

"Damn right I'm upset. I haven't seen you in over two years." Calvin thrust his hand in Travis's direction. "And Travis seems perfectly fine with acting like you never fucking existed."

"Because it's been five years. Get over it," Travis said with an impatient sneer.

"Oh, like you're over it?"

"Cal," Travis's voice warned. His friend had indulged in the half-priced drinks, and was now shit-faced drunk, violating all types of regulations and bylaws of the Bro Code.

"You're not over it. You pretend like you are, but you're not." Calvin scrubbed his face with his hand.

Travis had moved on, but according to Calvin, moving on from a situation was very different from being over that situation. He knew his friend meant well, but getting sloppy drunk and airing his dirty laundry was messed up. Heat burned his neck as sweat coasted down his spine. Travis could feel Makayla's eyes on him, sizing him up, trying to determine if Cal's words rang true. For once, Travis wasn't interested in meeting her gaze. Always worried about what her eyes would reveal, he never stopped to consider what could be found in his own. Travis closed his eyes, and when he reopened them, the mask that Calvin had shifted with his words was firmly back in place. "So I see we have progressed to the part of the evening where Cal gets drunk and starts saying crazy shit."

Luckily, Makayla followed his lead. "You really can set your clock to it. If he's not cussing someone out—"

"He's crying and telling you how much he loves you," Travis said, tossing his napkin on his plate.

"I just want you to know that I ride hard for you. You're my best friend, man," Makayla said, imitating Calvin's voice, pretending to cry. Now it was her and Travis's turn to share a laugh.

"You know what ... fuck you guys," Calvin said.

"I wish I hadn't passed on dessert at the restaurant," Makayla said, her bottom lip poking out.

Travis grunted in response as he pulled next to her car in the empty parking lot at Life Church.

Stepping out of his car, Makayla looked over at the building. "Thanks for the ride. I'm gonna run in. I have to pee. Have a good night."

"I'll wait."

"You don't have to wait; I can handle myself."

"I know if anyone jumped out of the bushes and tried to attack you, you would probably roundhouse kick them—"

"Ten years of taekwondo, baby." Makayla positioned her body into a ready stance.

"Still going in with you. Let's pull our cars to the side entrance." Buckhead was a fairly safe neighborhood, but it was late, and he had no intentions of leaving her alone.

Jumping into their separate cars, they both headed for the entrance on the west corner of the building. Travis used his keys to unlock the door, stepping aside so Makayla could enter first.

"Thanks. I'll just be a minute." She headed to the restrooms near the back of the lobby.

Calvin had really messed up Travis's plans for a chill night, first by inviting Makayla to tag along and then by dumping his emotional baggage over sake and sushi. You would think Calvin was the one who got dumped and not him. And what was that shit about how he wasn't over Makayla? No one wanted to talk about that. But Calvin was drunk, and when Travis loaded him into his Uber, he had apologized profusely, saying, "My bad, bro. I think I said too much."

Makayla returned with a bright smile. "Tank is officially on E."

"Are you still jonesing for dessert?" Travis blurted out, even though he promised Regina he was headed to her place.

"What, are you gonna pull a cupcake out of your pocket?"

"No, but close. Follow me." Travis led the way to the café. "How does a milkshake sound?"

"Sounds great, but the café is closed."

Travis searched his key ring, each key labeled. Selecting the café key, he inserted it, and a loud click signified it was safe to roll back the metal gates.

"Wait, you have keys to the café?"

"I have all the keys." He shook his key ring.

"So my father just gave you keys to the entire building?" Her eyebrows inched upward. "I don't even have keys to the entire building, and I'm his daughter."

"How often have you lost your keys in the past ... oh, I don't know ... year?"

Makayla's features softened. "Good point."

Inside the café, Travis dropped his keys on the counter and got to work, pulling ice cream, milk, and chocolate chips from one of the refrigerators. After mixing the ingredients in the blender, he poured them each a cup.

"Thank you." Her shoulders hopped as she used a spoon to dig in.

"Sure." Sitting at the table with her, he took a sip.

"It was good to see Cal again, despite his outburst."

"Yeah, he's great when he's not shit-faced drunk."

"I didn't realize he had such strong feelings about our breakup."

"Well, he cared about you too. And it hurt that you didn't return any of his calls." He tossed her a side eye.

Makayla released a tight breath. "Because he was your friend first, and I was trying to make the split as easy as possible. I got the television, and you got Calvin."

"If I knew I had an option, I would have fought harder for the TV," he joked.

Even in his drunken stupor, Calvin had made some valid points. Travis had held out hope for a long time that they could be friends again. Like a twelve-year-old who still believed in Santa, despite all the evidence to the contrary. But with every evil eye or snide remark, Makayla made it very clear that wasn't possible.

Her face lit up with recognition. "I forgot to mention, your mom sent me the nicest card congratulating me on the new job."

"Not surprising. When I told her we were gonna be working together, she was pretty excited." Excited was an understatement. His mom was thrilled and subtly hinted at a potential reconciliation, just totally ignoring the fact that he was engaged.

"So she's doing well?" She poked at the thick chocolate shake with her spoon.

"Yeah, she asks about you a lot and tells me how I was an idiot for messing it all up."

"Your mother is a wise woman. I've always said that."

The corner of his mouth ticked upward into a grin. "She's always had a soft spot for you."

"I'm sure she treats Regina the same."

"Nah, I mean they get along, but it's not the same. In her mind, she already had a daughter-in-law. I don't know why, but for some reason, she loved you. And she has compared every other woman I've ever dated to you, the standard." An amused look coasted over his eyes.

"I've always done well with the parents, the actual guy, not so much." Makayla winked playfully.

"See now, I don't believe that for a minute. You could have any guy you want."

"Don't let the pretty face fool you. Apparently, I'm an acquired taste. That's what Porsha said." Makayla flashed him a questioning look, biting down on her lip.

"That just means you're special. It means you're rare."

"Or I could be a dying breed."

"Rare people are valuable. I can say unequivocally that I have never met a woman like you. I'd rather be an acquired taste than everybody's cup of tea."

"Porsha thinks I should change." She fiddled with her diamond hoop earring.

"What do you think? I love your sister, but she doesn't know what she's talking about. I hope whoever sent you those flowers knows how amazing you are. Because you deserve to be happy, M-Kay."

Makayla's eyes landed on him, soft and vulnerable, causing his heart to glitch before resuming a normal beat pattern. "Thank you," she said.

Calvin's words echoed in his head: *"How do you go from best friends to nothing?"* Makayla was the kind of friend you would call when something funny happened so you could laugh together; the kind of best friend who would text you in the middle of the day to tell you some useless, random fact; the type of best friend who, when you had a bad day, would do her best to cheer you up, and if that didn't work, she'd just sit next to you in silence so you didn't have to be alone. This woman knew everything about him, and because the love part of their relationship didn't work, he'd lost his confidant. If he was being honest, that's what made him the angriest, losing his best friend.

Chapter 15

Makayla laid her yoga mat on the hardwood floor next to Porsha's, then scooped crumbs out of her purple mesh sports bra. She'd gobbled down a banana nut muffin on her way to the yoga studio, and some of the crumbs had missed her mouth. Stretching out on her mat, she waited for the class to begin.

"You're just gonna act like you didn't get flowers the other day, huh?" Porsha said, raising her hands above her head and giving them a stretch. "I heard all about it. Heard they were gorgeous."

It appears Tami's gossip train is still running on time. "They were just flowers, not a ring, Porsha. Calm down."

"You act like you're not excited."

"Porsha, they were just flowers ... roses."

"From that pastor guy?" Porsha retied her shoelaces.

"His name is Hosea."

"OK, OK, Hosea. So, that's a good sign."

"I guess."

At the light sound of a chime, Alicia, the super-toned yoga instructor, addressed the class. "Grand rising. Welcome to hatha yoga. For the next hour, we will focus on the balance of our physical and mental energy, which is all grounded by our spiritual energy. Let's start with some simple breathing exercises. Inhale a deep, cleansing breath and hold it for five seconds."

"OK. Back up, back up ... Hosea sent flowers to your job ... to the office you share with Travis?" Makayla could hear the gears turning in Porsha's head and smiled, trying to imitate the instructor's perfect posture. "All right, I want all the details. All of them." Porsha reached for her toes.

"There's not really much to tell."

"Did his jaw drop?"

"I didn't notice." Makayla wasn't looking to gloat, although it did feel a little good to catch Travis off guard.

Porsha tossed her a side eye. "Well, it sounds like this is getting serious with Mr. Houston, Texas."

"After a few dates?" Makayla breathed a laugh through her nose. "I don't even know his middle name. This isn't serious." She stood, preparing for full-body yoga poses.

"Whatever. Obviously, he likes you." Porsha pulled at a wedgie as she stood.

"They all like me until they get to know me." Makayla bent at the waist and turned her torso. She knew how this would go. Hosea would ask her on a few more dates, then he would start to feel uncomfortable by her self-reliant lifestyle. He'd question if she even needed a man because it would appear as though she had it all together. The visits would stop, and the calls would become less frequent, until one day she received a text message telling her it wasn't her, it was him. Or worse, a text that told her it *was* her, and he didn't see a future because she was too independent, or distant, or closed off.

"OK, M-Kay. I'm just gonna be real with you." Porsha planted her feet while everyone else was in dolphin pose.

"Not the time or the place. Try to focus." Makayla rolled her eyes, attempting to shut down the conversation. Porsha loved to tell her what she was doing wrong. It had been six months since her wedding, and now she thought she was an expert on love and relationships. Porsha's famous saying was "Now, what you need to do . . ." In Makayla's opinion, what Porsha needed to do was mind her business. Sure, her sister meant well, which is why she tolerated her sticking her nose in her affairs or lack thereof, but collecting Porsha's two cents was getting old. Makayla didn't want someone second-guessing her life; she did that enough already.

"All right, you guys, great class," Alicia said, her long legs now crossed on her mat. "Repeat after me. I change my thoughts."

"I change my thoughts," the group said in unison.

"I change my world."

"I change my world," the group repeated.

Porsha wasted no time jumping back into their conversation. "I see a pattern with you."

"What do you mean 'pattern'?" Makayla's eyes darted toward the exit.

"You sabotage your relationships."

"No, I do not." She crossed her arms over her chest.

"What happened to the last few guys you dated?" Porsha asked, clasping her hands. "I've watched you find an issue with every guy you go out with. What happened to that lawyer guy you dated a couple years back?"

"Lamonte?" Makayla grimaced. "His name was Lamonte. I tried to look past it, but you know how I am with names. I don't want to introduce people to my boyfriend, Lamonte. That's such a cheesy name." She shook her head, muttering.

"So?" Porsha's head flinched back slightly, waiting for a reasonable explanation.

"It didn't work, Porsha. It just didn't work."

"What about Gerald?"

Porsha was making it seem as though she was the problem in her relationships. Makayla decided it was time to set the record straight.

"Do you want to know what happened with Gerald . . . with Travis, and with whomever else from my past?"

Porsha didn't answer.

"Well, let's start with Gerald. He dumped me because he said I wasn't making him a priority. Peter, he pursued me hard, and when I finally gave in, he said we were moving too fast. And then there's Travis. Everyone thinks Travis is the all-American boy, huh?" She snorted a laugh. "Well, let me tell you about Travis. He was a story-teller. He sold me a dream, and I fell for it, hook, line, and sinker. I gave him everything I had, and he made me regret it. All that per-formative bullshit, only for him to turn around and get..." Makayla stopped short, falling silent. Her arms were tired from digging up the past.

Concern grew on Porsha's face. "All I'm saying is give Houston, Texas a chance."

"I am. I have. It's too early for predictions. He seems like a great guy, but only time will tell. We're talking about a couple dates. I don't understand why everyone is pushing me down the aisle." Makayla rolled up her mat. She hadn't given up on love, even though it seemed like love was done with her. Despite all the heartbreak, deep down, she still believed everyone had their person, their soulmate. She needed to remain positive and trust in God's timing. *Change your thoughts, change your world, right?*

Chapter 16

Parked outside of Atlanta International Airport, Makayla waited for Hosea. After wrapping up final preparations for the game night at Coin-Op, she managed to run to the nail salon and squeeze in her bi-weekly manicure and pedicure before heading to the airport.

Pushing the large, twisted curls from her braid out over her shoulder, she glanced at the clock on her dash: 7:33 p.m. Fiddling with the radio dials, she searched for something other than a commercial. Although the two had FaceTimed almost every day, it had been a few weeks since she'd last seen Hosea in person. After serious consideration, which included a coin flip and a pros and cons list, she decided to invite him to game night. And Hosea, being the man that he was, moved around his schedule so he could support her this weekend.

Makayla normally liked to keep her romantic endeavors private, preferring to fly under the radar at church, a lesson she learned after her very public breakup with Travis. That privacy, however, didn't necessarily keep her name out of people's mouths. When you don't give people something to talk about, they'll often come up with their own theories. Makayla knew bringing Hosea tonight would get tongues wagging but she didn't care. She had a little something to prove, and not just to herself but to anyone who thought she was still stuck.

Adjusting the bangles on her wrist, she checked her phone.

It read 7:34 p.m., only one minute had passed, although to her it seemed like an hour. A loud knock on the passenger window made her jump. From the other side of the window, Hosea smiled with an enthusiastic wave.

"Pop the trunk," he yelled through the glass.

Makayla complied, watching him walk to the back of her Mercedes and put his luggage in. She gave herself one last look in the mirror before he hopped in on the passenger side. A shiver traveled up her spine. *This man is fine and could be all mine*, she thought.

"You made it." She bit her lip, allowing her eyes to scan his body.

"Hey." Hosea leaned in, lowering his lips to hers. His tongue was like a match and her body gasoline. The warmth of his kiss set her insides aflame. "You smell amazing," he muttered against her lips.

Makayla could not contain her smile as her heart became a mess of pitter patters. "We should go."

Pulling back, he secured his seatbelt. "I'm looking forward to game night. I hope you can handle a little friendly competition," he said, placing his hand on her thigh, giving it a gentle squeeze.

"Boy, I'm about to whoop your tail." A playful smile crossed her face.

Travis went back and forth between the upper and lower levels, ensuring everything was running smoothly. Casting an eye toward his watch, he scanned the boisterous crowd of singles in search of Makayla. The event had started thirty minutes ago, and she was nowhere to be found.

Phor approached Travis with a pat on the back. "Hey Travis, quick question about the bar . . ."

Ignoring Phor's words, Travis asked, "Have you seen Makayla?"

"No, not yet. Why, what's up?"

He tucked his pencil behind his ear. "Nothing. I guess she's just gonna be late to our first event."

A smile played at the corners of Phor's mouth. "That's about par for the course with her." Everyone at Life Church knew Makayla Randolph couldn't be on time to save her own life. "Look, the bartender was asking about . . ."

As Phor rambled on about an issue with the non-alcoholic drinks, Travis caught sight of Makayla walking in with a tall, dark mystery man right behind her. He sloped his head to the right to get a better view around Phor's massive frame. His eyes grew wide as he intently watched Makayla introduce the mystery man to ministry members. *Is this the guy who sent her the flowers?* The color drained from his face. This event had taken a month to put together, and in one fell swoop, she was ruining it. Who brings a date to a work event? Even though Regina was also in attendance, he considered that apples to Makayla's oranges.

Travis interrupted Phor, who was still delivering a dissertation about the issue with the drinks. "Hey, do you know that guy with Makayla?" he asked, pointing his chin in her direction. As Phor turned his head, surveying the man who stood next to Makayla, rubbing her back, Travis winced. He had hoped Phor would be low key.

"He doesn't look familiar." Phor bobbed his shoulders.

Travis shut his eyes tight, unable to hear himself think over the ringing and buzzing of the arcade machines.

"What do you want me to do about the drinks?" Phor asked, following up with his previous conversation.

"Handle it. I trust you." He lifted his lids and shooed Phor away. The list of things he had to check on were as long as his arm, but it was as if his feet were glued in place; he couldn't turn away from watching Makayla and the man who was standing way too close. After making her rounds like she was Miss America accepting her crown, she headed in his direction. He whipped around, dropping his gaze toward his clipboard, hoping to appear in full event-coordinator mode.

"Hey." Makayla tapped him on the back. "Sorry I'm late. I had to pick up my friend from the airport." She gestured toward Hosea, who was in what seemed to be an animated conversation with some men from the church.

Travis lifted his head but did not focus his eyes in the man's direction. "No worries," he said.

Moving closer, she leaned in. "Can you believe this turnout? It's not even nine." She observed the growing crowd, excitement dancing behind her eyes.

"Yeah, you called it. Looks like game night was the right choice." His tongue burned with the urge to know more about her friend, curiosity gnawing at him until the words tumbled from his mouth. "So, you brought a guest?" Flashing a perfect set of teeth, he tried his best to sound disinterested.

"I did." A smug smile slid over her face.

Tucking the clipboard under his right arm, he didn't respond. Hoping she would offer more information, he just stood there, chewing on his bottom lip, the rowdy voices in his head fighting to be heard. *Who the hell is that guy? She's just trying to make you jealous. Is she dating this dude?*

Their eyes battled one another, hoping the other would crack and silently reveal some deeply held secret. Though they hadn't dated for years, she knew him well enough to know that he wasn't going to ask any additional questions. "I'm gonna mingle, make sure things are on point and everyone is having a good time," she said, walking away.

Travis's eyes followed her across the room, and as if in a trance, he finally uttered the word, "Bye," but Makayla was already back in the arms of the mystery man.

Hosea bent over and whispered, "Don't mess this up," a devilish grin plastered across his face.

Makayla, with her game face on, squatted. She was in deep concentration, trying to remove the large wooden Jenga piece. Whether it be Taboo, Charades, or Spades, the spirit of competition coursed through her veins. She liked Hosea all right, but she wasn't going to hold back. *I'm a winner, and he might as well get used to second place now*, she thought.

"Could you stop? I'm trying to concentrate," she said, blowing on her hands to ensure optimal grip.

"I'm just trying to motivate you. This is important, and I don't want you to freeze." He examined the Jenga tower for her potential options.

She pushed on her piece, carefully moving around the two-foot tower, hoping to pull it out from the other side. The tower swayed to the right, and she held her breath, raising her hands. When the movement ceased, she made a second attempt, slowly tugging at her piece. The tower wobbled, crashing to the concrete patio floor with a loud bang. A collective groan erupted from onlookers in the crowd. Makayla threw her hands on her head, bending at the waist in defeat.

"Ugh, that sure is a shame," Hosea said, not even trying to hide his smile.

"You do realize I'm your ride to the hotel. If you keep gloating, you may have to call an Uber," Makayla teased, adjusting her rose gold nameplate necklace.

Leaning in, he whispered in her ear, "No, I don't want that." He planted a soft kiss on her cheek. A half-moon smile spread across Makayla's face. Public displays of affection usually made her uneasy, but she needed to prove some points, to both Hosea and Travis.

From the moment she'd walked into Coin-Op with Hosea, Travis's eyes zoned in, following her around the room like he was Inky, Blinky, Pinky, and Clyde and she was Ms. Pac-Man. From the corner of her eye, she could see him watching them as Hosea tossed his arm over her shoulder. She rested against his strong, firm body, laughing loudly at a mildly amusing joke he whispered in her ear. All this flirting was bound to come back to haunt her; by tomorrow, she would receive a call from her mother asking questions about the tall, dark, and handsy brother she was seen with the night before.

cℬ

Having made it to level fifteen of Galaga, Travis hunched over the arcade buttons in his quest to shoot as many invading aliens as he could. He was startled by a scream from across the room.

"I won!" Makayla shouted. "I won!"

The commotion drew his eyes from the screen for what he thought was a split second, but when he turned back to the game, a sound chimed, indicating that his space jet had been shot down from the sky by an aggressive alien army.

"Hey, gamer boy," Regina said.

Turning his eyes toward his fiancée, he forced a smile.

"Thought you might like this." She handed him a pomegranate mojito mocktail.

"Thanks," he said, taking a long swig of the minty, sweet concoction.

"Game night was such a genius idea. Everyone's having so much fun. Good job, baby." Planting a kiss on his lips, she stroked his cheek.

"Thanks. I wish I could take full credit, but I can't. It was a team effort. Makayla and I did it. And Phor and all the rest of the crew helped as well."

"Mm hm." She looked out into the crowded gaming hall. "Makayla's not getting any attaboys from me. While you're busy keeping the event running smoothly, she seems more interested in showing off her arm candy. Honestly, who brings a date to a work event?"

Travis tipped his head to the side with a raised eyebrow.

"We're different." Folds bracketed her mouth. "This isn't even a date; you've been so busy tonight, it's been more like a girls' night out."

"I guess." He brushed off her comments with a dismissive wave of his hand.

"I heard he's from Texas. Seems like he's really into her. He's hardly left her side all night."

Travis took a gulp of his drink. While Regina gave him a rundown of the goings on at the event, he scanned the room. It took a minute to find them amongst the crowd, but his eyes locked in just in time to witness Hosea's hand wrap around Makayla's waist, resting lightly on her buttocks.

After watching his ex-girlfriend like a chicken hawk all night, Travis saw an opening. Makayla walked away, leaving her rooster unattended, and he was ready to pounce. Hosea was standing next to a WrestleMania pinball machine, counting out coins.

"Hey, how are you?" Travis tapped on the glass of the pinball machine. "Having a good time?"

"Yeah, I am. It's been a fun night."

"Travis Holmes." Extending his hand, he flashed his brilliant smile.

Hosea clenched his teeth from the pressure of Travis's firm handshake. "Hosea Wright, Brook Willow Church in Houston, Texas."

The minute Hosea said his name, Travis knew exactly who he was. He'd visited his church a few years back. He remembered Hosea gave a great sermon.

"So, what brings you to Atlanta?" He was done playing with his food; he was ready to go for the jugular.

"Just visiting." Hosea pointed to Makayla, who was near the bar, talking to a group of women.

"Oh, you know Makayla?" His eyes stretched wide, trying to act surprised.

Hosea repaid Travis's grin with an amused one of his own. "Yeah, I do."

"How?" Travis shoved his hands in his pockets. Any trace of his once-vibrant smile was gone.

"Ah . . . we met in Houston." Hosea raised a challenging eyebrow.

"And you decided to come all the way to Atlanta for game night?" He crinkled his face.

Hosea leaned in, whispering, "Actually, I came for her. Can

you blame me? Other than the obvious reasons, she's pretty exceptional." He tapped Travis on the arm, causing his eyebrows to mash together into a frown, the contact to his arm felt more adversarial than friendly, leaving behind a bit of a sting.

"Yeah, she's definitely something." He tried to hide his reddening cheeks with his hand. "So, are you guys . . . dating?" Travis hoped he sounded dispassionate, just a normal conversation.

"Yes." Hosea beamed.

Travis's heart didn't drop to his stomach; it dropped to his toes as Hosea's words sunk in. "A couple?" His voice cracked and sounded a few octaves higher than normal. "You two are a couple?"

"Not exactly. Not yet anyway. I'm working on it," Hosea said with a wink.

A wave of relief washed over him. He couldn't explain why knowing Hosea wasn't her boyfriend comforted him. *Makayla's free to date whoever she wants. And I'm engaged, happily.* Travis shook the conflicting thoughts from his head. "That's great. That is so great." He clenched and unclenched his fist.

Makayla returned, carrying two electric blue drinks, handing one to Hosea. "I see you met Travis."

"I was just making the rounds. Saying hello to any new faces," Travis said, jingling the change in his pocket. The last thing he wanted was for Makayla to think he was nosing around in her personal affairs.

"Well, get used to this face 'cause you're gonna be seeing a lot of it," Hosea said, draping his arm around Makayla's shoulder.

Travis noticed the wide grin spreading across her face. He had no doubt that her body was releasing mini endorphins at the thought of one-upping him. Makayla owed him nothing. One lesson his mother had taught him early on was that actions always have consequences. His careless actions ended up producing long-term consequences, the latest of which was this random dude with his hand securely around his ex.

Chapter 17

Following a day of go-carting and picnicking in the park, Makayla and Hosea headed back to her place. Scrolling through Pinterest, she pulled up the simplest chicken recipe she could find, trying to figure out her next step, with Hosea watching her every move. Last night, on the way to the Hyatt Regency Hotel, he mentioned he wanted to ask her a question. Makayla could only imagine he wanted to make things official. The thought made her nervous. She wasn't good at long-distance relationships. Truth be told, she wasn't good at relationships that were in the same zip code, so how would she manage one that was several states away?

"Do you need any help?" he asked, nicking a piece of cheese from the charcuterie board.

"No, I've got this. You just relax and let Chef Makayla do her thing." Makayla's culinary skills began at cheesy scrambled eggs and ended at spicy ramen noodles. Growing up, she had watched her mother, grandmothers, and aunties work their magic in the kitchen. Despite all those hours spent as a kid eavesdropping on grown-folk business, she never really learned the cooking part. Now, the tasting part she was great at. Referring back to the recipe, she seasoned the chicken with every spice in her spice rack.

"I had a good time at game night." He popped a marinated olive in his mouth. "It was nice meeting some of your friends."

"Yeah, you were definitely a topic of conversation." Makayla cut into an onion.

"Travis seems like a nice guy." He brought a twist to his lips, his gaze awaiting hers.

"Uh huh." She shoved the over-seasoned chicken and potatoes in the oven.

"So, you and Travis used to date?"

Washing her hands, she wiped them dry on her ruffled apron. "Why would you say that?"

"Because he was staring at us, staring at *you*, the entire night."

Moving across the kitchen, she put the unused items back in the fridge and pantry. "Really? I didn't notice." Of course she'd noticed. Last night was all about giving Travis a taste of his own medicine. For months, she'd sat back and watched him parade his girlfriend around the church. Watched when Regina announced their engagement at a singles event a few months ago. He didn't even have the decency to give her a heads-up. So now, it was his turn to watch as Hosea swept her off her feet and changed her relationship status from single to taken.

"Well, you were too focused on winning," he said. "I didn't realize you were so competitive."

Makayla removed her apron. "Why lose when winning feels so much better?" A playful smile sprung to her face.

His eyes followed her movements as she cleaned the mess she'd made. "What's the story with you two?" he asked, grabbing the chicken stock and placing it back in the refrigerator.

Makayla rolled her eyes. There comes a point in any relationship when you have to have the dreaded conversation about past partners. In Makayla's opinion, she and Hosea had not reached that point. Releasing a protracted sigh, she said, "There isn't one. We used to date, and now we don't."

Hosea didn't respond, but his eyes tightened at the corners as he sized her up.

Exiting the kitchen, she headed for the dining area to finish setting the table. Her dating history was a sore subject, and it would require several glasses of wine before she was willing to tell that sob story.

Hosea followed her but stopped short of entering the dining room area and took a seat on the sofa. "How long did you guys date?" he followed up.

Clicking her tongue, she pushed a curl from her face. "Why?" she said, not turning to look at him.

"Just curious."

"Curiosity killed the cat," she said firmly, clanging plates and silverware down with a thud.

"I get it. I have exes too. I don't think any of them are still in love with me, though." He leaned back into the sofa cushions.

She tipped her head back with a hoot of laughter. "Travis is not in love with me. We barely get along. Actually, he's engaged, just set a wedding date."

"Yeah, well, sometimes love and hate present similarly. You know, the whole thin line thing."

Hosea studied her face like he was taking inventory of every twitch, nostril flare, and rumination of her jaw. She didn't have to explain herself to him. If Hosea was disappointed that she had a past, he could jump in his rented Acura and leave right now.

"You mentioned you wanted to ask me something. What was it?" Ignoring his last comment, she sat on the ottoman in front of him.

"Oh, so you're just going to go there. Spoil the surprise." He reached for her hand.

Pulling her hand away, she said, "I don't like surprises." If this wasn't going to work, she'd rather know now.

"What about the go-carts? That was a surprise."

"Yeah, and I didn't like it." Hunching her shoulder upward, an inflexible bend formed in her jaw. She knew she was being a brat, but she didn't feel like being nice. Hosea's fixation on Travis had rubbed her the wrong way. If she listened closely, she could hear gates locking, bridges being drawn, and the alligators snapping in the moat she'd built around her heart.

The corners of Hosea's mouth twitched. "Are we fighting right now?"

"No." She shook her head with a false smile. Stubborn was Makayla's middle name, and once she stumbled down a path, it was hard for her to correct her course.

"Are you sure? Because it kinda feels like you're mad at me." He squeezed her knee.

"Honestly, I'd just like to talk about something else." She smiled, trying to thaw some of the ice that was building between them.

"OK, let's talk about something else," he said with a reassuring smile. "I wanted to invite you to Houston."

Makayla's jaw dropped. This wasn't exactly a confession of his undying love for her, but in her mind, it was a start.

"I wanna show you my city and introduce you to my friends."

"Your friends?" This time, the smile on her face was genuine.

"Yeah. They are going to love you."

"Mmm, most people do find me delightful," she teased with a twirl of her hair.

"Of course, I'll pay for everything. Plane ticket, hotel." He rubbed the side of her thigh.

"OK, yes. Sounds like fun." Normally she would make a million excuses for why she couldn't go, but she was trying to actively receive what God was putting before her, whether it be professional, personal, or romantic growth.

"Excellent, I'll have my people call your people." He grabbed Makayla's waist, pulling her on top so she straddled him. "How long till dinner?"

"About forty minutes." Sliding her hands over his biceps, she inched closer.

"Whatever will we do to pass the time?" A naughty smirk crossed Hosea's mouth.

Leaning in, Makayla kissed his lips softly, causing Hosea to return the gesture with an intense longing as if he'd been wanting to kiss her all day.

"Hosea?" Makayla breathlessly whispered.

"Hmm," he mumbled, kissing her shoulder.

"What's your middle name?"

"Actually, Hosea is my middle name." He placed a trail of kisses from her cheek to her chin.

Backing away, Makayla grabbed his face in her hand. "Then, what's your first name?"

"Rufus." He tried to release his face from her grip so he could kiss her lips.

She leaned further back. "Wait, your name is Rufus Wright?"

"Yep, after my father Rufus Wright Senior," he said, massaging her thighs. It appeared he didn't want to talk. During several late-night conversations, Hosea had told her exactly what he wanted to do to her, and now he seemed ready to back up every last word.

"Huh, it has a nice ring to it," Makayla lied. Rufus Wright Junior pulled her toward him, nuzzling her neck. *Rufus? Why has every man I've met been named after a '70s Motown artist?* she wondered.

"Can I take this off?" Hosea tugged at her shirt.

Makayla froze. Were they at the take-your-clothes-off stage of this relationship? She did some simple math in her head, trying to calculate if this was too soon. After all, she was the daughter of a prominent pastor and that meant walking this imaginary line. Bumping uglies with Pastor Wright wasn't an approved stop on that impossibly straight line.

"What?" The heat of a blush made its way across her cheeks.

"I just wanna feel your skin against mine."

The thought of his skin on hers gave her heart palpitations. Why not? She raised her arms, giving him the green light. Tossing her shirt aside, Hosea ran his hands across her back and arms. The contact fired off the neurons underneath her skin, sending her brain into free fall. Burying his face in her breasts, he sucked her nipples over her bra.

"Wow … It must be so difficult being a pastor. Like I get it; as a pastor's kid, I would hear it all the time. I still do." Words were tumbling from her mouth. She wanted achingly for these words to stop. Hosea did not care about her difficulties growing up as the child of a pastor. When she was nervous, her brain had a mind of its own, and Hosea's touch was making her very nervous. "They think church kids are the worst ones, always drinking, and doing drugs, and having sex. And I was doing all that, but still. It's a lot of pressure to be perfect, and no one can live up to those ridiculous standards. I'm mean—"

"Makayla, are you gonna talk the entire time?"

"No, of course not." A shriek of laughter escaped her throat.

Hosea repositioned so she was lying underneath him on the couch before removing his own shirt.

"Oh my God, you're taking off your shirt." Her eyes grew wide, trying to register all his muscles.

He paused, looking down at her, eyes wild, chest heaving. "Are you always this weird before you have sex?"

"Am I being weird?" Her body tensed. She bit down on her lip, fearful she was messing this up.

"It's OK, I actually happen to like weird," he backtracked. "You can talk about the migratory habits of the ruby throated humming-bird as long as you continue to swivel your hips against me."

"I haven't had sex in over two years," she blurted out. "Like with a person." Why did she add that part? In fact, it had actually been fifteen months, but the last guy didn't count. She wasn't going to add subpar sex to her overall score. If there's no big O, it's a no go.

"Would you like me to help you with that?"

A low and pleasant hum warmed her blood. "Yes … that would be so kind of you. And I need so much help."

Hosea descended on her, his mouth brushing against hers, causing heat to spark in her chest. She loved the fact that his hands didn't neglect the rest of her body as they traveled up the length of her form, cupping her neck and gently caressing her back before finding their way back to her waist and thighs.

As he ran his lips along her collarbone, she couldn't contain herself. "This is great. You're really good at that. I'm sorry ... I won't talk any more, I promise."

"No, it's fine. I want you to tell me exactly what you need."

Makayla's eyes lit up. There was one thing she desperately wanted. "If you could just put your lips ..." She pointed down. "That would just be swell."

Following her directive, he grabbed her leg, planting a kiss on the inside of her knee before slowly advancing upward. She smiled to herself thinking, *My drought is about to be over.* This must've been what the earth felt like after months without rain, the first drop bringing relief and the promise to soften the soil, making it new again. As Hosea's mouth hit her inner thigh, she braced herself for a monsoon.

A loud, shrill sound pierced the silence. Makayla's eyes fluttered open. "Shit, the kitchen's smoking."

Pushing him off, she ran to the kitchen, tugging at her skirt, with a shirtless Hosea on her heels. Fanning the air, she coughed, not sure what to do. She only used her oven to warm up day-old pizza, but she knew it wasn't supposed to do all that.

"What did you have the oven set to?"

"I don't know, high?" She grabbed a hand towel, fanning the air.

Hosea jumped in, turning off the oven, opening windows, and silencing the alarm. Makayla moved her arms back and forth, trying to push the smoke-filled air out of the room. The world's longest drought was in Chile; it lasted for 172 months. At the rate her love life was progressing, it was very possible that her sex life would beat that impressive record.

Makayla assessed the damage. The chicken was burnt, the mood had been ruined, and she was standing in her kitchen partially undressed, frustrated, embarrassed, and unsatisfied. "Put your shirt back on, and I'll take you out to eat. My treat."

Chapter 18

It was the end of a long day, and Makayla was intent on making it to the gym before heading home. Mondays were always jam packed with meetings, many of which she believed could easily have been emails. Going from a budget meeting to a fundraising meeting to an outreach meeting wasn't a constructive use of her talents or time. As she approached her car, she stopped in her tracks. The back tire on her S-Class was flat. Crouching down, she assessed the damage and determined almost instantly that she wasn't going anywhere on it.

"Ugh, will this day ever end?" Makayla shouted. Throwing her stuff on the passenger seat, she popped the trunk. With the hair tie from around her wrist, she pulled her hair into a low ponytail and made her way to the trunk. The gym bag she removed from her trunk landed on the ground with a soft thud. She lifted the trunk cover, revealing a full-size spare tire, jack, and lug wrench. With jack and wrench in hand, she headed back to the airless tire.

"Need help?" a deep, familiar voice called out from behind her.

"Nope, I got it." Makayla groaned as she used her full weight to release the first lug nut.

Travis dropped his backpack next to her gym bag. Rolling up his sleeves, he knelt next to her. "Let me do it."

Lowering the wrench, her eyes swung his way. "I am more than capable of changing a tire."

"I know you're capable, but you're also in high heels and a pretty dress. Just let me help." He reached for the wrench.

She fixed her mouth to object, but she was reminded of Porsha's words: *"Just because you can do it doesn't mean you have to."* It was the end of May, and Atlanta was in the middle of a heat wave. She could already feel her edges curling up. Makayla loosened her grip on the wrench.

"Knock yourself out," she said, rubbing her hands together, trying to remove the soot. Leaning against a car next to her own, she watched as Travis removed the remaining lug nuts with ease. She couldn't help but take note of his strong back and firm backside. He typically wore jeans, but today, he was in a button-down shirt and slacks. His slacks gripped his thighs and butt just right. Tilting her head to the side, she languished in the comfort of a familiar heat emanating inside. Makayla twirled a loose strand of hair as she enjoyed the view. Before she realized it, he was standing right in front of her, moving his mouth, but she didn't hear a word.

"What?" she asked, coming back from her naughty wonderland with visions of full-body massages and deep moans that danced in her head.

"Hold these." He dropped the lug nuts into the palm of her hand.

"Do you need me to get the spare?" she asked, feeling a little useless.

"Woman, would you just let me take care of it?"

Makayla never liked to ask for help, raised to believe the only thing she could count on was herself and God. Man could disappoint you, but God never did, her mother would say.

Reaching into the trunk, he pulled out the spare.

"I appreciate this," she offered.

"Of course. What would I look like leaving you out here to fend for yourself?" He rolled the spare tire on the ground.

"Well, you're better than me. If your tire was flat, I would not help you," she half teased.

"You wouldn't even offer to call Triple A?"

"Nope." Her lips danced around a smile.

Jacking up the car, he said, "That's what makes us different. I'm always gonna look out for you. I don't hold grudges."

Her smile melted into a scowl as she shuffled the lug nuts in her hand. "And I do?"

"Yeah." He thrust his chin upward.

Makayla had a difficult time letting things go. She still held animosity toward the girl who was named prom queen in high school. "I was robbed," she would claim.

Her face bore a quizzical expression. "Don't I have a right to?"

"Honestly, with me, yes." His shoulders twitched as he pulled off the deflated tire.

Furrowing her brow, she said, "Just so you know, I'm not holding grudges. I'm just not interested in forgiving people who do me wrong."

Travis stood and turned to look at her, rubbing his face with the back of his hand. "Even when those people were genuinely sorry and were willing to put in the work to make it right?"

"Fool me once, shame on you. Fool me twice, shame on me." As their eyes linked, she could tell that was not the answer he was hoping for.

Air escaped his flared nostrils, turning his attention back to the tire.

She wanted to let the past go. Maybe she and Travis could forge a congenial friendship. It could never be what it once was, but it didn't have to be cantankerous all the time. She was trying, but then he'd say something insensitive about forgiveness like it was all just that simple. Forgiveness wasn't guaranteed, and forgetting was easier said than done. Forgetting was like erasing the past, and she didn't want that, even if clinging to the good parts also meant holding on to the pain that tagged along with it. These past few months hadn't made anything any clearer, being in close proximity to Travis had unearthed some skeletons. Feelings she claimed had long died were now shimmying, shaking, and lurching side to side like the zombies in the "Thriller" video.

Tightening the last lug nut, he threw the flat tire and tools back in her trunk along with her gym bag. With a wet wipe from his backpack, he cleaned his hands.

"You're all set."

"Thank you." *Porsha's right. It does feel good to let go and let someone help. Maybe I need to cut Travis some slack.*

Scanning his face, she stepped forward. With a lick of her thumb, she reached up, wiping a speck of dirt from his cheek. The touch of his warm skin caused a fluttering in her chest as his eyes latched on to hers, holding her in place. Traces of his aroma wafted in her face, a mixture of cedarwood and basil from the cologne she'd introduced him to years earlier. Travis's intense hazel eyes traveled back and forth from her eyes to her mouth. With her hand still resting on his cheek, Makayla absentmindedly stroked his face. Goose bumps rose on the back of her neck as he placed his hand on her waist, gently guiding her closer. Their eyes were entangled in an intense standoff as he slowly leaned in, their lips so close they were exchanging the same air.

"Y'all have a good night," Tami yelled, eyeing the two standing inches from each other.

Pushing him away, Makayla scrambled, trying to explain. She yelled back, "I had a flat tire. Travis just fixed it."

"Mm hm," Tami said, not once breaking her stride.

Makayla turned to Travis, her mouth spread in a grim line. The last thing she needed was for the office gossip to misconstrue what was going on and have rumors floating around the entire congregation.

Travis purposely avoided her gaze, wiping his brow that was now dripping buckets. "I gotta go." He scooped up his backpack and headed toward his car.

"Tha-thank you. Thanks again," Makayla called out in a stammer. Climbing in her car, she berated herself. *Stupid, stupid, stupid.*

Chapter 19

Swimming from the six-foot depth of the pool to the shallow end, Makayla walked up the iridescent glass-tiled steps. She wrung the water from her hair and dried her body with an extra-large sea green pool towel stitched with a letter D monogram. The backyard was massive, with a pool, spa, and cabana that rivaled the Ritz Carlton or Four Seasons. When Porsha married Colin, his parents gifted them with a substantial down payment on a house. They purchased a starter mansion in a gated community. Needless to say, Porsha had been busy over the past few months working with an interior designer to pick wall colors and accent pieces.

"So, spill the beans. How are things going with the good Pastor Wright?" Porsha asked, slathering sunscreen across her sepia skin.

Makayla plopped down on the pool chair next to Porsha. "Great. Well, sort of."

"Sort of?" Porsha asked inquisitively.

"I almost burned down the house trying to cook for him. But other than that, great."

Porsha let out a sigh. "Makayla, you really need to learn to cook. This is ridiculous."

"Why? I've survived this long without knowing how to broil, roast, or sauté."

"Last time I checked, it was still Makayla party of one." Porsha adjusted her floppy straw sun hat. "No guy is going to wife a woman who can't cook. You barely clean. I hope your hips are putting in work."

"I do not have to conform to the patriarchal standards of womanhood. Why can't the man cook?"

"Girl, now you know you don't give a damn about the patriarchy. You're just lazy."

"Travis cooked when we were together."

"Travis was a unicorn. How you let him get away is beyond me," Porsha said absentmindedly, taking a sip of lemonade.

Makayla sat up. "What is that supposed to mean?"

Porsha sputtered, "Travis was . . . he is a catch. Smart, handsome, funny." She counted out his positive attributes on her fingers. "He cooked, loved to clean, and worshipped the ground you walked on."

"OK, so what? It's just eff me, and go Team Travis all the way?" Makayla grunted through her nostrils. She didn't let him get away. He cheated. In her mind, he made a choice, and she made hers.

Porsha swung her legs to the ground so she could face her sister. "I'm not saying that. I remember how hurt you were, and you had every right to be. But he tried for months to make it right, and you wouldn't even hear his side."

"Team Travis. I got it." Makayla crossed her arms, leaning back in her chair.

"I'm only Team Travis because . . . I don't think you're over him." Porsha sat on the edge of Makayla's lounge chair.

Makayla sliced her head left to right. This wasn't the first time her sister had broached this topic. Porsha was convinced that Travis was Makayla's soulmate and that all her relationships faltered because she was still secretly pining for him. Yes, working with Travis had stirred up some feelings she thought had long dissipated, but none of this mattered now. They were on different paths, and it would take a water-to-wine type of miracle to repair the ocean of hurt between the two of them.

"OK, I'll bite. Even if I did have . . . feelings, which I do not," she pointed at Porsha, "what exactly would you have me do?"

"Tell him!" Porsha exclaimed matter-of-factly.

"He's engaged. They set a date."

"I know you don't wanna look stupid. But for love, you're gonna need to drop that pride."

Makayla was trying to move on, and everyone around her—her mother, sisters, and father—were stuck in the past. "Why are you doing this?"

"Because I want you to be happy."

"I *am* happy," Makayla shouted, heat radiating off her chest.

"No, you're not, M-Kay. You're pigheaded, though." Porsha's cell phone pinged, and she looked down at it. "I have to get the door," Porsha said as she stood.

The tendons in Makayla's neck twitched, and even though the weather was a pleasant eighty-five degrees, she could feel beads of sweat forming on her forehead and upper lip. Porsha was wrong. She didn't still love Travis. Maybe she felt slightly nostalgic for what they had, but love? No. Of course, she missed certain aspects of their relationship, like bedtime snuggles with her face tucked into the crook of his neck; drinking in his soapy fresh scent; or the way his eyes would light up when he talked about things he was passionate about, his hands flying and his speech at double the speed as the corners of his mouth curled up into a smile.

Then there was his touch. The way he would take his time savoring every part of her body like it was the first time. The way he looked at her like a kid on Christmas morning when she undressed. The fact that she never had to ask; he just always knew exactly what her body was craving and delivered every single time ... she missed all of it. But missing something and wanting that something back were not mutually exclusive.

Her phone chimed and vibrated on the side table next to her; it was a text message from Hosea. Maybe Hosea could be the one to make her happy. He definitely had the potential to make her legs quiver, so that was a start. She'd enjoyed the last few months getting to know him. Since breaking up with Travis, she'd been stuck in quicksand, but perhaps now, she was finally ready to work her way out.

"Wings are here." Porsha held up a bag with a greedy smile on her face.

"Thank God! I'm starving." The aroma from the lemon pepper and Louisiana-rubbed wings was making her mouth water. Porsha handed her a container packed with wings and fries. She popped one of the crispy crinkle-cut fries in her mouth.

"Hosea invited me to Houston," Makayla said, hoping to move on to a different topic, one that wasn't going to put her on the spot.

"Shut the front door!" Porsha exclaimed. "He wants you to meet his momma?"

"He didn't mention his mother, but he did say he wanted to introduce me to his friends and show me his city." Makayla opened a packet of hot sauce and drizzled it over her wings.

"So, when are you making the trip?"

"Not for a few more weeks." Her lip curled out dejectedly. "My schedule is packed with all the singles events on the weekends. And his calendar is fuller than mine with speaking engagements and church business." The distance had been a difficult obstacle to overcome. Makayla was certain if Hosea was based in Atlanta, they would already be a couple. She had to hand it to him; even with the miles between them, he made the effort, calling and texting her every day and video chatting at night with conversations that got her pulse racing.

"Sounds promising, but if you don't work through the Travis stuff, it's never gonna last." Porsha raised a hand to the heavens.

Makayla's eyes tightened at the corners. "There is no 'Travis stuff.'"

"OK, whatever you say." Porsha crunched down on a celery stick.

"Porsha?" She did not appreciate the tone in her sister's voice.

"You can't fake the funk with me, M-Kay." She wagged a blue-cheese-covered wing in her direction, accidentally dripping some of the dressing on the ground. "You and Travis need to have an honest conversation. Let him say the things you refused to hear all those years ago."

"What purpose would that serve?"

"Closure . . . or maybe a fresh start. Girl, don't act like you haven't thought about all this."

"I haven't." She was lying; she had definitely entertained thoughts of an alternate universe in which she and Travis were still together. Makayla was a planner, and before the split, she had their entire lives plotted out. Engaged at twenty-six, Travis would have asked for her hand in epic fashion, which included her closest friends and family. Married at twenty-eight, their wedding would have been a classic black-tie affair, with lush flowers and romantic lighting. By now, at thirty, Makayla would probably be sporting maternity chic in anticipation of a new addition to their family.

"Um hm," Porsha said, throwing a clean chicken bone onto a napkin. "Well, hopefully Houston goes well."

Makayla jostled her shoulders. She could sense her sisters lack of enthusiasm. If Porsha had her way, Makayla would go back groveling on her knees, begging Travis for a second chance. It would be a cold day in hell before she did that.

Regina's gaze stalked Travis as he walked back and forth from his dresser and closet, packing his clothes in the duffel bag that was sprawled out on his bed. She nervously crossed and uncrossed her legs as she sat at the foot of the bed.

"You should take a jacket. It could get chilly at night in Savannah." Regina repositioned a pair of slacks in his bag.

"Good point." Travis winked as he folded a pair of jeans.

"So, what's the plan for tomorrow?"

"The plan hasn't changed since the last time you asked," he said, placing a pair of dress shoes in a plastic bag.

She chewed at the corner of her mouth as she helped him fold his T-shirts. "What time are you picking up Makayla?"

"Six a.m." He headed toward the bathroom.

"And you're going to call me when you get to the hotel, right?"

"Yes, when I get to the hotel, I will call you like we talked about," he shouted back, grabbing his leather toiletry bag from the bathroom cabinet. Drawing a thoughtful breath, he lingered in the bathroom, tossing aftershave, cologne, and a fresh razor in his bag. Regina was giving off heavy game-show-host vibes with all her questions. Travis had repeatedly promised to check in regularly while he was gone. She was acting like he was going to All-Star Weekend in Miami and not on a business trip.

"Are you two going to eat together?"

"I don't know. We have to eat." Travis returned to the bedroom, adding the folded T-shirts to his bag.

"Yes, but it doesn't have to be together," she instructed, raising a challenging brow.

"Well, we have to be mindful of expenses. So, we'll have to play it by ear." He moved the duffel bag aside, lying back on the bed. For every question he'd answer, she'd come up with another obscure one.

"I can't wait until this trip is over." Climbing on top of him, Regina kissed his lips.

"Me too." Closing his eyes, he allowed himself to enjoy the kisses Regina planted on his face and neck. Paying close attention to his ears, she kissed, nibbled, and sucked them, fully aware that she was driving him crazy. Her soft hands slipped under his shirt as she gently ran her fingernails down his chest and stomach before pulling at the waistband on his shorts. In one fluid motion, Travis pulled her under him so he was now in control. Gently wrapping his hand around her neck, he parted her mouth with his tongue. The ringing of his phone interrupted the sound of Regina's mouth moaning over his.

"No, don't answer it," she whispered breathlessly as Travis reached for his phone next to him on the bed.

Peering at the screen, he said, "It's Makayla."

"Send her to voicemail," she said, the airy quality in her voice now gone.

"It could be an emergency." Untangling himself from Regina's grasp, he rose from the bed.

"Then she needs to call someone else," Regina said, tugging at his shirt.

"Hello?" he answered.

"Hey, it's me ... Makayla."

"Yeah, I know. I have caller ID."

"I just wanted to confirm that you'll be here at six in the morning."

"Yep." Travis stopped pacing long enough to look at Regina and roll his eyes.

Regina leaned forward on the bed. "What does she want?"

"Does it really have to be that early?" Makayla asked. He could hear the distinct sound of a tea kettle whistling on the other end.

"If we want to get there by noon, yes, we have to leave early." Travis dared to sneak a glance at Regina, who was shaking her head and frowning.

"Are you packing something nice to wear for dinner or just going casual?"

Regina snapped her fingers in his direction. "What the hell, Travis?" she yelled.

"Is that Regina? Tell her I said hello."

"Yeah, no ... I'm not gonna do that." He could hear Makayla's smirk over the phone.

"I'll just pack a few options. Better to be prepared," Makayla said.

"OK." He threw his hand in the air with a shrug. Did she call him to just shoot the shit or was there something more she wanted?

"See you bright and early in the morning at the crack of dawn."

"Yep."

"Good night."

"Sweet dreams." Ending the call, he tossed his phone back on the bed.

"Sweet dreams?" Regina shot him a furious glance.

Travis held up his hands, palms forward. "I was being polite."

"You were being familiar, too familiar. Makayla Randolph shouldn't be calling you at ten o'clock at night. Tell her your business hours are from eight to five."

Regina was upset. What else was new. When he worked late, she got upset. When she asked about his day and he mentioned Makayla's name, she got upset. When his co-worker called to iron out details related to work, she got upset. It was late, and he wasn't interested in another fight. He wanted to finish packing and head to bed.

"I love it when you get all riled up like this. It's sexy." He winked, hoping to release some of the tension that was hanging between them.

"Don't make fun."

He ran his thumb over her pouting lips. "Never."

"No more after-hours conversations with Makayla." Grabbing his face, she looked him square in the eyes. "Tell me you understand."

"Got it."

Chapter 20

The warm summer rain pelted the hood of Travis's hybrid Honda Accord as he waited outside of Makayla's townhouse. They were headed to Savannah to check out the hotel they hoped to reserve for the singles retreat. Glancing at his watch, he hissed out a breath; he'd been waiting for ten minutes, but as always, she was running late. Makayla came trudging toward the silver Accord with an umbrella protecting her head from the increasing downpour. Reaching for the door handle, she gave it a tug, but the door didn't open.

"It's open," he yelled.

Makayla jiggled the handle. "It isn't open," she yelled back.

"Move your hand. Stop pulling." He hit the lock button. "OK, try it now." He let her struggle with the door for a while, pretending to unlock it, watching her pull the handle to no avail. Finally, when he unlocked the door, she tossed her overstuffed weekender bag in the back and climbed in the passenger seat, shooting him an aspirated look.

"Sorry about that. I might need to get that checked out." A look of false concern crossed his face. "Ready to go?"

"Yep." Makayla wiped drops of rain from her face.

Pulling out of the driveway, he turned left at the stop sign and headed to the highway.

"Fun fact," Makayla said, pointing at him. "If you press your foot down on the acceleration pad, the car—wait for it—accelerates."

She swiveled her neck, watching as cars zoomed past them on the interstate.

"Do you wanna drive? 'Cause I can pull over and let you drive." Signaling, he moved to the right lane.

"No, I don't. It was just a suggestion." Makayla adjusted her seat, getting settled in for the almost four-hour drive to Savannah.

"I don't need driving instructions from the woman with the lead foot. The only reason you think I'm going slow is because I'm actually driving the speed limit." He adjusted the wiper speed.

"No one drives the speed limit."

"I do, and everyone should, especially in inclement weather like this." He ignored the smirk on her face as he scanned the radio stations.

"Can I pick the music?" She reached for the control panel.

"My car, my radio, my choice," Travis said, playfully swatting her hand away. John Legend's "All of Me" began to play.

"Aw, that was Porsha and Colin's song." She swayed side to side.

"What?" He changed the station. There would be no sappy love songs on this particular drive.

"Porsha and Colin danced to that song at their wedding. It's their song that represents their relationship. Every couple has a song. We had a song, remember?"

He pulled out a bag of trail mix from the center compartment. "Of course, I do."

"What is it? I mean ... what *was* it?" She raised a disbelieving eyebrow.

"You don't think I remember our song?" After throwing a handful of banana chips, peanuts, M&M's, and cranberries in his mouth, he handed the bag to Makayla.

"No, I don't." Sorting through the bag, she picked out all the banana chips.

He glanced over at her expectant face. "'I Only Have Eyes for You' by The Flamingos."

Makayla let a chuckle escape her lips. "I think you were the only nineteen-year-old boy on campus blasting fifties oldies but goodies from his dorm room."

"It was 1959 to be exact." Travis had always had an affinity for old soul music. Curtis, Dionne, the Isley Brothers; he inherited his taste in music from his mother.

"I'm not gonna lie, you put me on to some amazing music."

"I learned early on that women loved songs with begging-ass men. And they just don't make music like that anymore."

"So, you play that shit for the women?"

"No, I play it 'cause I enjoy it. If women like it too, that's just a plus. It worked on you."

"I was naive and gullible." Makayla tossed the bag of trail mix at his lap.

"Those are two words that have never been used to describe you."

"Honestly, I'm surprised you remembered."

A wrinkle cut across his forehead. "Of course, I remember. That was our song. Whenever I hear it, I immediately think of you."

Their eyes locked briefly. Travis's mind was like a highlight reel, firing off memories from their time together. Their first kiss in the hidden stacks at the university library. The perfect Saturday afternoons spent together both in and out of the bedroom. How she would squeal and her nose would wrinkle when his mouth grazed over a sensitive part of her body. The way her voice would lift whenever she said his name like it was taking flight. A knowing smile began to emerge across both of their faces.

Clearing his throat, he felt a bit discombobulated. "So naturally, I avoid it like the plague," he added.

Makayla leaned forward in her seat. "What's you and Regina's song?"

He stared straight ahead at the dampened road. "We don't have one. I already have enough songs on my CLT list."

"CLT list?"

"Yeah, cannot listen to. Because it's tied to some memory

associated with you. I'm not interested in adding any more songs I love to that list."

Makayla was silent. He swiped a quick glance in her direction and a question mark hung over her gaze. Turning his attention back to the rain-soaked road ahead, he decided to drop the subject.

Travis's phone rang. He was tempted to let it go to voicemail, but he knew Regina would just hang up and call right back.

Hitting the speakerphone button on his steering wheel, he immediately made an announcement. "You're on speakerphone, just so you know." The last thing he wanted was Regina saying something to antagonize Makayla.

"Hey, babe. I just woke up and wanted to check in, make sure you're OK," Regina said.

"Everything's good. Don't worry about me," he said, his hands at ten and two with a death grip on the steering wheel.

"You're still going to call me when you get to the hotel, right?"

"Yes, first thing." They hadn't been on the road for thirty minutes, and he'd sent her a "Good morning," text while he was waiting in the car for Makayla. Was this what he had to look forward to for the next twenty-four hours?

"I woke up this morning with the biggest smile on my face thinking about what you did to me last night."

The car swerved as Travis scrambled to take the phone off speaker. "Really?" he said, pressing his iPhone to his ear.

Regina giggled on the other end.

It was clear she had decided to make this ride as unbearable as possible. What he did last night was absolutely nothing. Makayla's call dampened the mood, with Regina leaving shortly after and him going to bed alone.

"I gotta go." A twinge of anger laced his voice.

"OK, I love you. Don't be so serious."

Travis flung his gaze in Makayla's direction, who had focused her attention outside of the passenger side window. "Talk to you later. Bye," he said before disconnecting the call. They drove in silence for a few minutes, the only sounds from a used car advertisement on the radio and the tapping of Makayla's fingernails against the door.

"Makayla? She was joking. We didn't do anything last night."

"You do not have to explain anything to me. She's your girl-friend ... oh excuse me, fiancée."

"I'm not explaining. I'm just letting you know."

"Great." She threw her hands in the air.

"Great." Travis's eyebrow twitched.

Of course, she was right; he didn't need to explain, but for some reason, he wanted to. No one wants to think about their ex being intimate with someone else. The fact that she was almost certainly getting her back consistently blown out by the pastor from Houston made his stomach churn. He could recall Makayla seriously dating one other guy after they broke up, some guy named Gerald, and for a time, he thought they might actually go the distance. Gerald wasn't nearly as put together as Hosea Wright. On paper, Hosea was Makayla's perfect match. He was a prominent pastor, leading his own church with a large congregation in a major city. Professionally, Hosea was leaps and bounds ahead of him. A few weeks ago, Travis was flipping the channels and came across Hosea on *Good Morning America*. Travis hadn't even been featured on the local news. Hosea had everything Travis wanted: the church, the platform, and the girl.

If Regina's plan was to make things awkward between him and Makayla it had worked. Makayla, who was a nervous chatterbox in uncomfortable situations, was unusually quiet. He tried to think of something they could talk about that would keep them in neutral territory.

"Any interesting summer plans?" she blurted out.

"Not really. My summers are usually spent at Chuck E. Cheese and playgrounds."

Her face flashed a sign of recognition. Travis's summers were always booked.

Makayla popped the last banana chip in her mouth. "Did

you hear about the new park with the zip line and massive rock-climbing wall?"

He tilted his head. "Yep, it's on the list," he said, drawing an imaginary check mark in the air.

"Of course. Always prepared."

"What about you? No sisters' trip to some tropical destination?"

"I wish." She rolled her eyes. "This summer is just too unpredictable with this new job and other obligations."

"Well, there's always winter in Coeur d'Alene or Aspen." He inhaled a deep breath. The air inside the car was perfumed with Makayla's floral-infused clean, crisp scent. She always smelled so good ... He hated that about her. How dare she smell that good, with him unable to pull her close or bury his face in her thick, shiny hair.

From the corner of his eye, he spied Makayla glancing at him inconspicuously as she slowly reached for the radio button. A frown spread across his face as she shuffled through the stations. She settled on "Where the Party At" by Jagged Edge, swaying to the beat. And as if on cue, Makayla belted out a live off-key performance of the song with dance moves. He couldn't resist nodding his head in time with the beat.

When the chorus chimed in, he belted out, "Uh-oh." Makayla dissolved into laughter, letting Travis rap the Nelly part as she danced freely beside him. Singing along at top volume, the two finished the song with synchronized dance moves that almost felt rehearsed as they traveled down the interstate.

Chapter 21

The rain appeared to let up as they pulled into the hotel parking lot. Makayla jumped out and reached into the back seat, struggling to pull out her heavy bag. Leaning from the weight of her luggage, she lagged behind as they walked toward the hotel entrance. Travis made an about-face, watching her struggle.

Holding out his hand, he said, "Give it to me."

"No, I've got it." She continued to walk with a limp.

"You're going to topple over. Just give it to me," he insisted.

She didn't protest any further. The bag was cumbersome, and she didn't want to carry it another step. Travis grabbed her designer bag and almost dropped it from the heft.

"What do you have in here?"

"Nothing much, makeup and shoes. You know, essentials." She tucked her three-day-old silk-pressed hair behind her ear.

"For an overnight trip?" He shook his head. "I see some things haven't changed." Lifting the bag, he swung it over his shoulder.

The hotel lobby resembled a rustic log cabin, with distinctive architectural features like tapered logs, stone-faced fireplaces, and rustic chandeliers. There were large windows that provided views of the lofty, beautiful trees that surrounded the property. Even though it was June, Makayla was tempted to sit by the hotel's massive fireplace. All she needed was a good book, a warm cup of bourbon and burnt sugar black tea, and a cozy blanket.

At the reception desk, they were greeted by a plump, freckle-faced clerk.

"Good morning. Welcome to the River Inn. My name's Diane. How may I help you?"

"Checking in, last names Randolph and Holmes." Makayla pulled her wallet out of her purse. Standing next to her, Travis dropped her bag on top of his.

The clerk pulled up the reservation. "OK, I have one room with a king bed for Makayla Randolph and Travis Holmes. I'll just need your identification and a credit card for room service and incidentals."

Travis's eyes tightened at the corners. "Excuse me, you said one room? You meant one room each, right?" He leaned forward, pointing at her computer.

"Um, no. I have an overnight stay with one room," Diane said, clicking her pen.

"No, there's two of us. We booked two separate rooms." Makayla wagged her finger. "Can you please check again?"

Drumming her nails on the counter, she refused to return Travis's intense gaze. It was her responsibility to change the reservation, and she knew he was chomping at the bit to blame her for this—or anything, really.

Diane looked up from her computer with a faint smile. "OK, I checked, and you only have one room booked."

Makayla's eyes grew big. Stepping back slightly, she rubbed her forehead, trying to calculate her next step. Travis's eyes were slowly boring a hole into the side of her face.

"Diane, can you excuse us for a second." Travis grabbed Makayla by the arm and pulled her over to the fireplace. "I thought you said the rooms were taken care of."

"I did. Jason and Raeann booked the rooms. I just emailed the hotel with the name change for the reservation."

"Jason and Raeann booked one room because they're married." He pointed in her direction to ensure she got the point.

Makayla's head gave a single nod. "I realize that now." She let out a dry chuckle that ended in a sputter.

"Is this funny? Is this funny to you?"

"No, it's not funny. But it's fixable. It's fine; I'll just get a second room. No need to freak out. I'll handle it." Makayla walked back to the long line at reception. She gulped down a dry lump in her throat, tugging at her top lip. "Totally fixable," she whispered to herself.

Back at the front desk, Makayla smiled brightly. "Hi, Diane. I'm going to need to book an extra room for Travis Holmes."

"Unfortunately, we're all booked for tonight," Diane said with a professional smile.

"Could you check . . . 'cause you didn't even check." Makayla tapped the top of Diane's monitor screen.

Diane clicked her mouse and typed on her keyboard. Makayla looked up at three rustic wagon wheel chandeliers above the reception area.

"Ms. Randolph, like I previously stated, we are all booked today. There is a huge anime convention in town this week. You would most likely be hard-pressed to find any hotel that isn't completely booked," Diane informed her.

She looked back at Travis, who was focused on his phone. The last thing she wanted to do was go back over there and tell him she had failed. Makayla understood she missed a very important detail, but she was going to sort this out. *I have to fix this*, she thought.

"Diane, I need another room." Clasping her hands together. "I will take a storage closet, a bathroom stall, a shed. If you could find a way to help us out."

"Ma'am, I wish I could, but I can't pull rooms out of the sky." Diane motioned to the next guest in line.

"Just one more second," Makayla said to the frustrated man behind her. "OK, this is the part where I beg. We can't be in the same room. We're not together. He's my ex." She pointed back toward Travis. "I would be forever in your debt." Makayla shook her clasped hands with a crooked, painful smile.

Diane let out a long swoosh of air. "OK, girl, let me see what I can do." She started to click on her keyboard rapidly. "OK, I changed you to a room with two queen beds. Y'all still have to share a room, but at least you don't have to share a bed."

Makayla had already asked for too much, so she didn't want to look ungrateful. "Thank you very much. We'll take it." She pulled out the church's AMEX card.

Diane handed Makayla the room key cards. "Here you are. Now, you stay strong because that tall drink of iced tea is finer than a frog's hair split four ways." Diane gestured over to Travis, who was still seated by the fireplace. "Don't let him tempt you by offering to rub your feet. The last time I let a man rub my feet, I ended up pregnant . . . with twins. So be mindful."

"Good to know." Makayla tapped her temple. "Thanks again." She grabbed their bags, dragging them over to where Travis was seated.

"Are we all set?" Travis asked, jumping up from the leather arm chair.

"Actually, I have good news and bad news." She displayed a strained smile.

"Just give me my room key, and we can talk later." He held out his hand.

"Bad news: there is a convention in town. Anime? Whatever that is." Makayla flailed her arms, hoping to distract him.

"It's Japanese cartoons." His hand was still extended.

"Wow, we really do learn something new every day." She put her hands on her hips.

"Can I just have my key?" He examined her with narrowing eyes.

"I still have the good news. They changed our room."

"That's great. My key." She pulled one of the keys from the sleeve, handing it to him. "Excellent. Let's go." Grabbing their bags, Travis headed to the elevator banks. Makayla slogged into the elevator, standing off to the side.

"What floors?"

"Eighth floor." Makayla stared at her floral Converse sneakers.

"Both of us?"

"Uh huh." She bit her lip, mentally preparing herself; she knew Travis was going to be mad.

On the eighth floor, they exited the elevator and headed left. She stopped at room 832, and he dropped her bag in front of the door.

"What room am I in?" He scanned the hall.

Makayla looked down at the key card. "Have you been working out?" She grabbed his bicep. "Because you are ripped."

"Makayla!" he yelled, pulling his arm away.

"I tried to tell you downstairs." She shrank back. "They changed our room from a king to two queens, so you don't have to sleep on the floor. Good news." She waved her hands like she was a cheerleader.

"None of that is good news." Travis dropped his bag.

"What do you want me to do? There's a convention in town. The hotel is booked. All hotels are booked."

"I wanted you to do your job," he yelled.

Makayla looked up and down the hall. She didn't want to cause a scene. "Can we please take this inside the room before we get kicked out?" she whispered, opening the door. Travis brushed past her, stepping over her bag and leaving it outside the front door. Pushing open the door, she dragged her bag in. "I know this isn't ideal, but it's where we find ourselves."

"Nah, I'm about to find myself in another hotel." He pulled out his phone.

"All the hotels are booked."

"I don't believe that." Lifting his hand to silence her, he Googled the nearest hotels.

Working a stiff frown onto her face, Makayla escaped to the bathroom and locked the door behind her. She slid down onto the cold tile floor. He was acting like this was her fault. It was an honest mistake. Yes, she should have paid closer attention to the finer details, but to be fair, she had a lot on her plate right now. The new job, a budding relationship with Hosea, and the fact that every day she had to pretend to be perfectly fine working with the man who was set to marry someone who wasn't her.

Hopefully, he was successful in finding a hotel because she didn't want to spend another second with him. She was tired of looking at his perfect handsome face, his piercing hazel eyes, his smooth walnut-honey skin, his captivating smile. Then, there were his hands, which she was particularly drawn to during the car ride as they casually gripped the wheel. Those strong hands, which once upon a time, he used to explore every inch of her body. Jumping up, Makayla splashed cold water on her bare face. Fidgeting with the neckline of her Hillman College T-shirt, she focused on her reflection in the mirror.

Damn, Porsha ... All that "Travis is your soulmate, and I just don't want you to have regrets" talk had gone to her head. She found herself scrutinizing his face, searching his eyes for a hint of what he was thinking. Working this closely together was muddying the water. Travis was an asshole, that was a fact. But then he'd smile at her and she was no longer so certain. "It doesn't matter what I feel or what he may feel. He's engaged, and I need to let this go." She studied her face, hoping her words sank in.

Shaking her head, she pushed away nagging thoughts of his body pressed against hers. Looking around the bathroom, she pulled back the shower curtain to examine the bathtub. Even if Travis was interested, she couldn't see herself begging any man for a second chance. She was the prize, and if you lost her, then you never deserved her in the first place.

Plus, he was never going to leave Regina. It would be too big a hit to his precious reputation: Travis Holmes, upstanding church member, hard worker, nice young man. She seriously doubted he'd give that image up to be with her. They were similar in that way; for better or worse, the way people perceived them mattered. As the daughter of a pastor, Makayla learned at a young age that she was a reflection on her family, and she needed to comport herself in a manner that was befitting of the Randolph name. The last thing her parents wanted was a whiff of impropriety. Destroying her ex-boyfriend's engagement would have tongues wagging for months, maybe longer.

There was a knock on the bathroom door, which interrupted her thoughts.

"Any luck?" She swung the door open.

"No." He released a resigned breath. "Sorry I yelled at you."

"You know, it could be worse. We could have—"

"We could be stuck in an airport for eighteen hours, forced to sleep on the floor."

Makayla's eyes twinkled with recognition back to the time they went to Isla Mujeres in Mexico and were delayed at the airport.

"I think I still have residual back pain from that fiasco." She rubbed her back, exiting the bathroom.

"You were pissed," he reminded her.

"And you kept looking for the silver lining. I wanted to punch you in the face." The two shared a laugh.

Makayla plopped down on one of the queen beds. "Look, I'm sorry about all this."

Travis tugged on his ear. "Excuse me, can you please repeat that?"

"No, you heard me the first time."

"I must be tired from the drive because I thought I heard you apologize . . . to me."

"Chill out, Holmes, it's not that serious." She laced her arms over her chest.

Travis sat down next to her on the bed, brushing his knee against hers. "I accept your apology." He nudged her playfully with his shoulder.

"Stop being a brat," she teased.

He chuckled. "Just think of it as another story to tell our kids."

Makayla audibly pushed air through her nose, her lips pressing together. When they were together anytime something unusual or exciting happened, one of them would joke that it was a story to tell their kids one day, "their" being the keyword. She didn't want to think about telling stories to future kids that weren't with this man.

He scrubbed his hand over his face. "This is why you're always mad at me, right? 'Cause I say stupid shit like that."

"Yep."

"Well, can I say this? I'm really happy that we're in a better place than we were a few months ago."

"Even if that place is a hot, cramped office space with no privacy?"

"If it's with you … yes."

His words activated something deep within, a tingling surge that started in her fingers and toes and worked its way to her center, leaving her gasping for breath.

His phone vibrated in his hand. "What time are we meeting the hotel guy for the tour?" he asked, jumping to his feet.

"Noon."

Walking toward the door, he said, "I'll meet you in the lobby at noon."

Lifting herself from the bed, Makayla called out, "See you later." As the door closed behind him, she surveyed the room before falling backward onto the bed, a relieved breath passing her teeth.

Chapter 22

Outside, the air was warm, and any traces of rain were beginning to quickly dissipate. With his arms outstretched, Travis let the warmth wash over him. There was a sign noting a trail leading to the river. He opted to take a walk to reset his thoughts. Pulling out his phone, he scrolled to Regina's name in his favorites contact list. Her smiling face popped up, a photo he saved from the night they got engaged. He needed to check-in, but if he told her he was sharing a room with Makayla, she might jump in her car, head to Savannah, and pull him out of the hotel by his ear. After calling several hotels and a few motels, he realized there were no vacancies. He was stuck. There was no use delaying the inevitable. Pushing the screen, he waited for her to answer.

"Hey, baby, what took you so long to call?" Regina asked.

"Sorry about that. The whole check-in process was insane. There's a convention in town, so there was a long wait." Travis peered up at the immense trees. Their branches, scattered with leaves as big as his hand, provided a cool shade from the sun.

"How's your room?"

"It's rustic. Lots of wood." He wasn't going to lie to her; he was just going to withhold irrelevant information.

"Where are you now?"

"I went for a walk to stretch my legs." This was true; it had been a long drive. What he didn't add was he also went for a walk because he needed a break from Makayla. Being around her, especially when she was being charming and funny and smelt so good, made it hard for him to pretend he disliked her. It was much easier to profess you hated someone when you weren't reminded on a daily basis of the qualities that made you fall in love with them in the first place.

"How was the trip down? Did Makayla even talk to you?"

"We talked a little bit. We mostly listened to the radio." Stopping at a bridge over the river, he listened to the water bubble as it passed over rocks and branches. "Speaking of the drive. What was that stunt you pulled in the car?"

"It was a joke," Regina defended.

He shook his head. "It wasn't funny."

Regina kissed her teeth. "What, did her feelings get hurt?"

"It was just unnecessary and mean."

"Why are you defending her?" He could practically hear the rolling of her eyes.

"I'm not. It's just that Makayla is a fighter, and if she feels like she's being backed into a corner, she will come out swinging. Most people underestimate just how hard she can punch."

"Yeah, well I can take care of myself."

The muscles in his jaw bunched. "This is my job, Regina. Why you want to make it more difficult than it already is, is beyond me."

"That wasn't my intention." Her tone was more subdued.

"Well, that was the result."

"I'm sorry. I was just having some fun."

"It's fine. Let's just try not to do that again."

This overnight trip was turning out to be more trouble than it was worth. He was trying to keep everybody happy and, apparently, he was failing miserably. Regina was acting out. Makayla was being agreeable. The world was topsy turvy.

"What else do you have planned for the day?"

"We're meeting with the hotel representative for the tour at noon."

He could hear Regina hiss out a breath on the other end before saying, "OK. Sounds good."

An awkward moment of silence crept in. He didn't like lying to Regina, but Travis knew she wouldn't be OK with the truth. There was nothing for her to worry about, so he decided to make sure he gave her nothing to worry about. "I'll call you later."

"Look, Travis, I know you hate this just as much as I do. I'm sorry if I did too much. I love you."

"I love you too." His breath resumed its normal pattern as he tucked the phone in his pocket. He'd survived yet another round of Regina's subtle interrogation. Now he just needed to get through the next twenty-four hours with Makayla so he could return to his regular life.

Back in the busy lobby, Travis thumbed through a shelf of tourist pamphlets, grabbing a few before searching the crowd for Makayla. He moved past a group of men dressed like Naruto to find Makayla in a far corner, slowly strolling the lobby, examining the artwork and fixtures that cluttered the walls. She had used the time alone in the room to change out of her T-shirt and yoga pants into a sundress. Her hair draped her shoulders and fell freely down her back.

The cover of the crowd allowed him to openly scan Makayla's womanly frame. When they dated, she wasn't this curvy. *She has grown all the way up in the last five years*, Travis thought, biting his lip. The yellow-and-white floral dress, with its generous neckline, complemented her skin and gave him full access to ogle her long neck and décolletage. Travis was a thief, stealing glances of her over the past few months at every opportunity. Makayla was a pain in his ass, but she was soft on the eyes, the definition of eye candy. He'd lost track of the time spent just sneaking peeks at her while in their tiny office. Turning, Makayla caught him staring at her. But he didn't avert his gaze or pretend to scroll on his phone. His eyes bathed her in.

Approaching, he asked, "What's the plan?" handing her a stack of pamphlets to throw in her purse.

"The event coordinator, Barry, is on his way out. Did you go for a walk?"

"Yeah, I walked to the river. It was nice and quiet. You should check it out." He tilted his chin in her direction. "I see you changed."

"Yep, told you that heavy luggage would come in handy."

"I guess I stand corrected. You look nice ... you looked nice before too. Who are we kidding, you always look good." *Where the hell is Barry*, he thought, fearing his tongue would continue to betray him.

As if on cue, a short, balding man in a bowtie approached. "Jason and Raeann? I'm Barry, nice to meet you." The bespectacled gentleman extended his hand.

Travis shook Barry's hand. "Actually, Jason and Raeann couldn't make it, so you have Travis and Makayla."

"Ah, well, nice to meet you both," Barry said, shaking Makayla's hand. "Thank you for choosing River Inn. I'm excited to show you around the property and answer any questions you two may have."

"We're looking forward to the tour. What we have seen of the property so far is beautiful," Makayla offered.

As they walked the property, Barry talked nonstop, showing them the meeting rooms, guest lounge, and business center.

"Over here, you have our renowned restaurant, Buckhorn," Barry said, walking them through, pausing at a wall of windows that overlooked the river. "At night, this place is all lit up, and the ambience is just as breathtaking as the menu." Barry nudged Travis with his elbow. "Perfect for a romantic dinner with the missus."

"Oh, no—" Makayla wagged her finger.

"No, we're not ... she isn't—" Travis and Makayla stumbled over one another, trying to correct Barry.

"We're not married," she was finally able to spit out.

"Oh, my apologies. Well, maybe you can work on that tonight." Barry winked in Travis's direction.

With a raised eyebrow, Travis gave Barry a glassy stare, clearly expressing his desire for their tour guide to move on.

Rubbing the back of his neck, Barry continued. "Anyway, did you get your invitation?"

"Yes, we did. It was in the email you sent," Makayla said.

"Great. I hope you two will be our guest tonight for a complimentary meal. Just present the invitation to the hostess when you get here."

"You had me at complimentary," Travis said, a gentle laugh tickling his throat. There was nothing he liked better than free, even if it meant Makayla had to be his dinner guest. He'd already perused the menu and decided on the filet mignon.

After Buckhorn, they toured the pool, spa, and gym. Stepping on a treadmill, Barry started running in his dress shoes to demonstrate the state-of-the-art gym equipment. Travis locked eyes with Makayla, exchanging a knowing look as they both tried to suppress laughs.

They made their way back to the lobby, which was still filled with people and luggage. "And that concludes our tour. Can I answer any other questions?" Barry asked.

Travis glanced at Makayla before answering for both of them. "No, thanks for the thorough tour. We appreciate your time."

With the tour behind them, they headed to the car. Travis had a list of local attractions for them to check out. He thought it best to get it done now so they could rest a bit before dinner.

After visiting Savannah's Historic District, Forsyth Park, and the Cathedral Basilica of St. John the Baptist, the two hopped off a trolley near the Savannah River.

"Do you remember that?" Travis asked, crossing the street.

"Remember? I was scared for my life. Her hair literally caught on fire."

"Lit . . . erally." A goofy smile spread across his face.

Wincing, she said, "I see what you did there, and I'm gonna allow it because that was lightweight funny." She scooped up the chocolate chip bits at the bottom of her cup with her straw. "To this day, I don't mess around when there are candles on a cake."

"It happened so fast. One minute, we're all laughing, and the next minute, her hair is smoking." He gently pushed Makayla, switching places with her so he was walking on the outside of the sidewalk, closest to the street.

Her face lit up, remembering another detail. "Yeah, then you sprayed her and the cake with the fire extinguisher."

Travis jerked his shoulder into a shrug. "I had to. She was on fire and wouldn't stop, drop, and roll to save her life."

"That's really all Smokey the Bear talks about."

"Nah, he actually only told us we could prevent the fires. He never really provided any instruction on how to stop said fire."

"What kinda name was Smokey? Kinda makes him the prime suspect, if you ask me." Makayla tossed her empty Frappuccino cup in the trash. "If there's a fire in the forest, who are you going to first? Hoppy the Frog, Swimmy the Duck, or Smokey the Bear?"

"Oh, Smokey would definitely be a person of interest." Travis bobbed his head in agreement. "Like, if you stumble across a bunch of mats, xen music, and candles, you know who you need to take it up with."

"Yogi Bear." Makayla waved her finger as a smile crept across her face in spite of herself. "I forgot you were super corny. But so corny that it's funny, you know?"

Pulling his vibrating phone from his pocket, he said, "I'm hilarious. I don't know what you're talking about." He pointed to a record store. "I have to take this. I'll be right back."

"OK."

"Hey, baby girl. How was your day?" he answered, making his way down the street, out of earshot.

Makayla loved Savannah; life here seemed laid back, simple, and a bit magical—the architecture of grand Victorian homes, the trees draped with Spanish moss, the sound of horse hooves hitting the cobblestoned streets. Plus, her traveling companion had also been a pleasant surprise. She was concerned that a full day with Travis would be filled with awkward silence and misunderstandings, but she was happy they were able to put their differences aside and actually enjoy one another's company.

Glancing down the street, she watched from a distance as he finished his call. Makayla wasn't the only one inspecting the goods. A group of women enjoying lunch outside were also intently checking him out. Travis was the type of guy who caused most women to do a double take. He was attractive, and he absolutely knew it. It was the silent confidence he exuded, commanding a room when he walked in. His dazzling smile that simultaneously melted and broke Makayla's heart. The steely hazel eyes that always betrayed him as they darted from her lips to her legs to her backside and back again. It appeared he was unaware of this frequent habit: his eyes always all over her, drinking her in.

Makayla's face flushed as he moved past the tourists on the street, his long strides bringing him back to her. When it came to Travis, she didn't have to imagine what his body could do to hers; she had memories. Vivid memories of his hands cupping her breasts, the low guttural growl he would whisper in her ear, or the feel of his lips on her neck, her stomach, her thighs, her ... She tried to tame her thoughts, thoughts that, in the last few weeks, had taken a naughty turn. Softly muttering to herself, she said, "You need to get laid." With a deep breath, she pushed the thoughts from her mind as she exhaled.

"Sorry about that." He looked toward the store front. "I thought we could check out this record store." Holding the door, he let her walk inside. Makayla squinted her eyes, adjusting to the lack of light. It was like stepping back in time, with stacks of records and posters of recording artists from yesteryear and present day plastered on the red brick walls.

"I picked this place because it's retro, and there aren't many places like this anymore." He ran his fingers across a stack of records.

"This spot is right up your alley." Flipping through records, she stopped at Aretha Franklin's *I Never Loved a Man the Way I Love You.* "Do you still have your record collection?"

"Of course, I do. Still adding one new record each month."

"I remember we could just lounge for hours, listening to music," Makayla said, pushing a strand of hair from her face.

"Listening to music, talking ... and some other stuff." The corners of his mouth twitched.

A warm sensation crept up the back of her neck and spread across her face. "A good way to spend the day."

"I can't disagree with you there."

Wandering further into the stacks, Makayla thought about their conversation in the car and his CLT list. She thought she was the only one with songs she couldn't listen to, restaurants she couldn't frequent, and friends she no longer called after breaking up with him.

"Can I play you something?" Travis's face lit up as he flipped through the records, looking for a specific album. Once he found it, he walked to a listening booth a little bigger than a phone booth. Holding the door, he allowed Makayla to walk in first, closing the door behind them. Makayla squeezed against the back wall to allow space between them. "I am obsessed with this song right now." He placed the record on the player, lifting the needle. The piano notes began to play as he nodded his head. A rich, full voice filled the tiny space. Makayla closed her eyes, allowing the music to wash over her.

"Do you like it?" he whispered in her ear, his warm breath tickling her neck.

Tipping her head upward, she looked into his eyes. His hand grazed against hers, causing her lungs to fill with breath. She wanted to backup, but there was nowhere to escape in the cramped box. Pulling her hands up to her chest, she tried to create room and protect herself. As she searched for space, she bumped into the record player, causing the track to skip before it restarted at a previous verse. Travis leaned forward, resting his hands on her hips, pulling her away from the record player and closer to him. He was too close ...

entirely too close. Makayla stared straight ahead, watching his chest rise and fall, almost as if in rhythm with the music.

She could feel his eyes on her—they were always on her—but she dared not look up. Her heart sputtered like a car engine. Makayla opened her mouth, hoping that more oxygen would flow in to give her chest some relief. With nowhere to turn, she was forced to lean her forehead on his chest; the last thing she wanted was to hyperventilate because she wasn't used to physical contact. When the song ended, all that could be heard was the hum of the needle circling the record and the throbbing of Makayla's heart. Travis reached out, removing the needle, slightly brushing her breast with his arm. The silence was broken by a buzzing sound from his pants pocket. He turned sideways to reach his phone. Looking at the display, he declined the call.

"Our dinner reservation is at eight, so we should head back," he said.

Makayla exited the booth, fanning herself, her heart still racing.

Chapter 23

Tugging at his shirt cuffs, Travis fidgeted in his chair. He'd left Makayla in the room so she could finish getting ready. She could never be on time and would most definitely be late to her own funeral. It was Makayla's world; everyone else was just lucky she allowed them to live in it. Since she was operating on CP time, it gave Travis a chance to give Regina a quick call, but he ended up getting her voicemail. The lights from the restaurant's orbed fixtures danced against the window. Barry was right; this place had a totally different vibe at night. Unfortunately, the vibe was romantic, with low jazz music and assorted circular glass vases with lit candles inside as table centerpieces.

Time slowed as Travis caught sight of Makayla entering the restaurant, like in one of those neon-colored '80s movies he loved to watch. She looked stunning; her hair was sleek and shiny, swinging from side to side with the movement of her curvaceous body. Draped over that body was a champagne-colored silk wrap dress. That color against her rich skin made her look like a goddess. Aphrodite, Athena, and Freya had nothing on this woman.

"Oh, my God. This was a bad idea. Why does she look so good?" he whispered under his breath. His temperature rose as beads of sweat formed on his forehead. He stood as she approached the table.

"Hey." A dopey smile spread across his face.

"Hey," Makayla replied with a smile of her own. Pulling out her chair, he watched as she glided into the seat, looking up at him frozen in place at her side. "Are you gonna sit?"

"Me? Of course," he said, taking his seat across from her. The waitress, dressed in a crisp white shirt, black slacks, and a long black apron, walked up to the table.

"Good evening. Welcome to the Buckhorn. Would you like wine this evening?"

"Uh . . ." Travis looked over at Makayla, who shook her head. "No, I think we're good."

"Because you are V.I.P. guests, the wine is complimentary with your meal," the waitress added.

"It's complimentary? The wine?" Once again, Travis looked at Makayla for confirmation. "Why not, right?"

She lifted a blasé shoulder with a light giggle. "Sure, let's do it."

"We'll take two glasses of the house red, please." Travis smiled.

"Excellent," the waitress said, walking away.

"I like this place. Free meal, free wine." He took a sip of his water. "This place is fancy." He bit down on his tongue; his nerves were turning him into a chatterbox.

Scanning the restaurant, Makayla said, "This place is nice enough. But fancy restaurants don't typically come with food vouchers."

"You're probably right." Travis rarely splurged, so he couldn't rate whether or not this steakhouse was a five-Michelin-star establishment. Sneaking a peek at his dinner companion, he watched the light from the candles dancing across her face, causing rivulets of excitement in his belly. Travis lifted his menu to cover his face, suddenly painfully aware that this felt like a date. Maybe agreeing to have a candle-lit dinner with his ex-girlfriend was a bad choice.

When he was around her, his tongue had an irritating habit of having a mind of its own, spouting out words that his brain had not approved. "You look . . . nice." Nice was an understatement. But he thought confessing that her beauty was unmatched and crowning her the fairest in the land was probably overkill. One thing about

Makayla; she was a girly girl. She paid attention to every detail: the nails, the toes, the shiny stuff in the corner of her eyes, and whatever it was that she lathered over her mahogany skin to make it look like she was glowing.

"Oh . . . thank you. Um, you look . . . you do too." She pointed in his direction.

"Thanks." Travis was wearing a blue iris suit that he'd purchased from a department store on clearance, then had expertly tailored so it adorned his toned physique perfectly. "Do you remember the last time we went out to a fancy dinner together?"

Makayla's eyes rolled toward the ceiling as she remembered. "Yes. Come to think of it, I think you had a coupon then too."

"Don't knock the hustle," Travis playfully chided. "That night was fun." He grabbed a roll, handing the basket to Makayla.

"Yeah, it was fun until the waitress spilled that tray of drinks all over you."

"That's right; I forgot about that." A sly smile spread over his face. "I never told you this, but I tripped her."

Makayla's brown eyes bulged. "Why in the world would you do that?"

"Because the coupon had expired, and all I had was a hundred dollars in my wallet."

"Oh my God, you're crazy," Makayla said, her mouth hanging open.

"It worked. She apologized profusely, and we got our meal comped."

"You should have told me; I could have helped out."

"I wanted to show you a good time. I couldn't have you pay. I felt really bad about it, but in my defense, I left the hundred dollars as a tip."

"Yeah, and you smelt like a brewery the entire drive home."

"Because of that night, I always triple-check my coupons." He winked.

"So, you're still using coupons?"

"Yep. There is no shame in my game."

"Regina OK with that?" Makayla squinted, pulling her bread apart.

"Yeah, I mean, you were the only one who was bothered by my financial situation."

Makayla was about to object, but the waitress returned with the wine. Pouring red wine into each of their glasses, she asked, "Do you want me to leave the bottle?"

"Is the whole bottle complimentary?" Travis looked up at the waitress.

"Yes, it is."

"Yeah, then leave the wine." He reached for the bottle with a smirk. Travis was happy to have it; he needed something to soften the edges.

"How is it?" he asked, swirling his wine in the glass.

"It works," she said, considering his face. "You know, I never cared about the size of your wallet."

"You pretended not to care, and I pretended to believe it."

"Is that what you really believe? That I was just some bougie princess?"

"Listen, I don't blame you. You wanted a lifestyle I wasn't able to provide, so you went out and hustled and created that life for yourself."

"So, you think I chose a lifestyle over you? I wanted to build a life *with* you." She tapped her finger on the table to drive her point home.

"Yeah, until I wasn't building fast enough."

Makayla placed her hands in her lap, leaning back in her chair. "Wow, you remember things so differently than I do."

"Oh, yeah? How do you remember it?"

"Money wasn't the issue. Was I worried about our future? Yeah, I guess. But we were good. If I had money, we had money. Because it was us versus everybody."

"How do you think that made me feel? I didn't want to rely on you for money. Makayla, you wanted to go on vacations and eat at fancy restaurants. I couldn't afford that." He could feel bands tighten across his chest. He didn't want to rehash grievances from the past.

"That isn't what I wanted." Hoisting her glass to her lips, she drained half her wine.

"Are you two ready to order?" the waitress asked, seeming to appear from nowhere.

Travis lifted his menu. "Yes, I think we are."

"Great, we'll start with the lady."

Makayla ordered the salmon and Travis opted for the steak.

"Excellent choice," the waitress said, placing the menus under her arm and walking away.

Makayla grabbed the wine bottle, pouring herself another glass.

Drumming his fingers on the table, he thought about what she'd just said. She was never going to admit that money was a point of contention for her. He grew up poor, so he chose to save. Makayla, on the other hand, always had access to money, so being told no was foreign to her.

Deciding it best to change the subject, he said, "How's Hosea." He told himself he wasn't going to bring that man up, but his curiosity had once again gotten the better of him.

"What?" She released a laugh so full and free, he could feel it vibrating through his body.

"I'm just asking how Hosea is." He smacked his tongue, tasting the black current and fig from the wine. He didn't know where Makayla and Hosea stood, but he was praying every night that Hosea would be called to build a church in Peru or Bulgaria. All Travis was asking was for God to place the seed of charity in Hosea's heart so he would pack his bags and head to a distant location with spotty cell phone service and no Wi-Fi.

"No, we are not talking about that." She dismissed the topic with a wave of her hand.

Travis's eyes searched the restaurant for their waitress, hoping she would appear with the food and rescue him from this awkwardness that was growing between them.

"Does your vegetarian girlfriend know you're cheating on her?" Makayla asked.

He swallowed with a cough as the wine tumbled down his throat. "Wha-what?" He fidgeted in his chair.

"You ordered a steak. I doubt she'd approve."

"I'm free to eat what I want," Travis said. However, he had no plans of telling Regina about this steak dinner, partly because of the meal but mostly because of the company.

"Does she realize that you are a hardcore carnivore, and you are never going to embrace that veggie life? I bet that would just steam her carrot tops." Makayla reached for her glass of water as the corners of her mouth trembled in an attempt to suppress a fit of laughter.

"It's really not all that bad. After a while, you don't even miss the meat."

With an incredulous sigh, she said, "Bullshit. Let me ask you this ..." Makayla shifted her body weight in her chair, leaning forward. "Have you had carrot bacon?"

The sides of his jaw tightened as he clenched his teeth. "Yes, but—" He raised a hand to object.

"Looks like I may have lost you. You're eating for the vegetarian team now." Makayla shook her head solemnly.

"Aw, yes, this from the woman who thinks that meat with a side of meat and meat drippings is a meal."

"What can I say, I'm from the South. I like the taste of meat in my mouth." She pursed her lips once the words escaped.

Travis rocked with a silent laughter, resisting the urge to make a joke like a twelve-year-old boy.

"Shut up, Holmes." She threw her napkin at him.

Catching it, Travis raised his hands. "What? I didn't even say anything."

The waitress returned with their meals, and after a prayer led by Travis to bless the food, they ate in relative silence.

Eyeing his dish, Makayla interrupted the sound of their forks and knives moving over their plates. "I think I have plate envy."

"My food is pretty tasty, I ain't gonna lie. I read reviews on Yelp, and people raved about this dish." Proud of his Googling skills, he gave a broad smile.

"Always prepared."

"It hasn't failed me yet." Travis wiped the corners of his mouth with his linen napkin. "Do you want a bite?" He pointed to his plate.

Makayla shook her head, but her words betrayed her. "If you're offering, yes."

Slicing into his tender medium steak, he added mashed potatoes, mushroom sauce, and a piece of the asparagus stem for a perfect bite. He turned his fork, guiding it toward her, his eyes trained on her plump lips the entire time. Makayla opened her mouth, allowing him to feed her.

"Delicious," she swooned, licking her lips.

He instinctively placed the fork in his mouth before setting it on his plate. Feeling a slight flutter at the top of his stomach, he wrapped his hand around his wine glass, taking another sip.

On her third glass of wine and her filter gone, Makayla leaned back in her seat.

"That's funny. You're funny. I don't remember you being funny."

"What are you talking about? I've always been funny," Travis said, pouring the last of the wine into his glass.

"No, not like this."

"Remember . . . 'member when I did that open mic night at the comedy spot, You Got Jokes?"

"Yes, I do." Makayla vigorously shook her head.

He threw his arms up. "I killed it, like the crowd was loving it."

"No, no, no." She wagged her finger. "You wanted to kill yourself after because you tanked and got booed off the stage."

Scrunching his face, he said, "That's not how I remember it."

"You love rewriting history."

"It's not a rewrite; it's just an optimistic spin."

"Uh huh ... OK, sure."

His eyes twinkled with mischief. "So, Hosea . . . he's . . . weird. Right?"

"What? No. He's not weird. You think he's weird?" Makayla asked, tucking her hair behind her ear.

Travis jerked his head back and forth. "Yes. He does this bizarro thing with his eyes."

"Hm, I never noticed." She searched her mental images for confirmation. In her defense, she was having difficulty focusing, the warm tingling effects of the libations clouding her thoughts.

"I'm surprised you haven't. It would creep me out." He allowed a pleased smile to extend over his face.

Makayla pitched forward, almost knocking over her wine glass. "His name is Rufus."

"What?"

"His real name is Rufus. Hosea is his middle name." She burst into laughter.

Travis winced with an intake of air. "Rufus and Makayla?"

She dabbed her eyes, which had started to shed tears from laughter. "Do you think I can ask him to change it, legally?"

"I would definitely ask," he said, tilting his head back with a hoot.

Makayla had not planned on mentioning Hosea, but if the thought of Hosea and her caused him the slightest distress, she was here for it.

Tilting his head to the side, he examined her face. "What made you decide to work with me and stop fighting against me?"

She rolled a shoulder. "I realized that my success and failure was kinda tied to you, which, for the record, I hate."

"Ah, so self-preservation. That can be a hell of a motivator." He swirled the wine in his glass.

Makayla pushed her shoulders back, sitting tall in her chair. "Look, I stand by everything I said about working with you."

Leaning forward, he presented a defiant snarl. "You said I didn't deserve to lead."

"Did I say that?" Makayla's voice squeaked as she looked around the nearly empty restaurant.

"Yeah, yeah, you did." He tapped the table for emphasis.

"OK, well then, I stand by *most* of what I said." She gave him an apologetic smile. "Everyone knows you're a great leader. But when you're leading with someone else, that isn't always enough."

"Luckily for us, it is." His penetrating gaze probed her face as he licked his dessert spoon clean.

"Lucky." Makayla tipped her glass, taking another sip.

Travis Holmes needed to be thrown in jail, it had to be a crime in one of these counties for one man to be this damn fine. Averting her eyes, she focused her attention on her half-eaten dessert. His gaze was like heat-seeking missiles, always searching for something. She feared that eventually her eyes would betray her, and he'd discover exactly what he was searching for.

Dropping his glare, he looked down at the tablecloth, wiping away scattered crumbs. "Well, I'm thankful we're on better terms."

Makayla agreed. "I never thought I would see the day when we could be cordial. Looks like Satan is ice-skating to work."

Pursing his lips, his next words were slow and deliberate. "I'm hopeful we can get to a place where we can be more than cordial. Perhaps friends, even."

Makayla covered her mouth to conceal her laughter. The last thing she was looking for was more friends. It was already difficult working with him every day, watching him move on with his life without her.

Frown lines creased the corners of his mouth. "Is it really that far-fetched? There was a time when you were my best friend."

"That was a long time ago." She was an all-or-nothing type of woman. How do you go from having all of someone to only having access to a piece of them? Makayla was greedy and never liked to share.

"Doesn't mean we can't find our way back."

"Are you insane?" Makayla raised a snarky eyebrow. "Your fiancée is not gonna let you have extracurricular friendships, especially not with me."

Clicking his tongue, Travis said, "Hm, maybe you're right."

The dim lights from the restaurant reflected off the floor-to-ceiling windows, making it difficult to make out anything beyond the glass. Of course, she was right. They could never be friends, not while he was with that woman. What ifs and hypotheticals were fine when it was late at night and she was alone, but she didn't want to entertain those fantasies with him. Travis's hand rested on top of hers, pulling her from her thoughts. Because she was tipsy and her defenses were nonexistent she didn't object. She closed her eyes, giving herself permission to indulge as his hand massaged hers. His touch was still intoxicating after all this time, and she was ready to drown in it.

"Makayla . . . I wish . . . I wish we could . . ." Travis jerked his head, releasing her hand.

Her heart tumbled to her stomach. She straightened her back, exhaling a stuttering breath. *He's not yours anymore*, she reminded herself. It seemed like their lives were just a series of unspoken words. At one point, the man across from her was her moon and stars, and now, he was Mars—cold, dark, and unfamiliar. She missed his brilliant and magical glow. The twinkle from his smile that shined just for her. Makayla was tired of biting her tongue and swallowing the blood.

"If I could go back in time and change things I would," she offered, looking down at the fading light from the nearly burnt-out candles.

Travis guzzled the last of his wine. "Let's get out of here," he said, flashing a perfect set of teeth.

When he smiled, it was as though he was auditioning for a Colgate commercial. His smile lit up his entire face, and his hazel eyes twinkled. Those pearly whites had gotten her in a lot of trouble.

That man's smile had her make promises she could never keep and give away things she could never get back.

"OK," she whispered breathlessly.

His hand brushed against Makayla's back as they walked from the restaurant, the contact shooting tingling shockwaves through his entire body. As they walked through the hotel, the distinctive rings, horns, and chimes of reggae music could be heard from the hotel bar and lounge.

"Should we check it out?" Travis said, pointing to the lounge. He wasn't ready for the night to end. He feared once they returned to the room, his carriage would turn into a pumpkin and the magic would be over.

"It's kinda late." Makayla bit down on her lip.

"It's never too late for a night cap." A mischievous smile grew on his face.

With a rueful shrug, she agreed. "OK, just for a little bit." She wagged a finger at him.

The lounge was dimly lit in green and red lights. It was a little past midnight, and the space was more than half full. Travis went to the bar to order drinks. Checking his phone, he saw three missed calls from Regina. Should he end the night? Of course he should, but Makayla had let the drawbridge down, allowing him to cross and get closer. For a long time, being with Makayla was his favorite place to be, with their late-night conversations, riddled with inside jokes and shared memories that would leave outsiders flummoxed. Or her big smile that would switch from angelic to devilish, depending on her mood or the placement of his hands on her body. He just wanted to satiate the void, filling his data banks with new memories of her that he could use to plug the gaping hole she'd left in his heart.

At the restaurant, hearing Makayla admitting her regret was like a salve healing old scars. Makayla never admitted when she was wrong. And when it came to the end of their relationship, everything was his fault; she took responsibility for none of it. He was willing to accept most of the blame, but she was blameworthy too, even if that blame was minuscule in comparison to his. They broke apart because of him; they stayed apart because of her.

Travis found Makayla at one of the last remaining tables in the corner of the crowded lounge with two beers and two shots in hand.

Makayla turned up her nose. "Is that Fireball?" She pointed to the shot glasses.

"Yep," Travis said, taking a seat. Fireball was a call back to their college days of cheap liquor and nights out that rolled straight into the morning. "We should toast."

"To?"

Squinting his eyes for a few seconds, he seriously considered her question. "To the possibilities." Grabbing his glass, he raised his hand.

The side of her lip curved into a smile. "To the possibilities."

"Cheers."

"Salud," Makayla said as she clinked her glass into his.

If Travis didn't do anything else with his day, it was guaranteed that he would find the time to stare at Makayla. Her skin, smooth like a chocolate confection, her doe-like eyes, her glossy peach-hued lips, inviting him in like a moth to a flame. This wasn't the worst idea he'd ever had, but it was close, ignoring his fiancée's numerous calls, as he was drawn in by Makayla's siren song, completely enthralled, not interested in an escape. Since their breakup, Makayla had spent much of her time erasing him from her life. As the years passed, it was like their love was an urban legend, and he was the only one who still believed in it. But hearing her words, he knew he wasn't the only one who remembered.

His eyes darted toward the couples whose bodies swirled to the music. "Do you wanna dance?"

Makayla's eyes shifted to the dance floor. "Uh...yeah, we could," she said, fidgeting with the straps of her dress.

Travis led the way to the dance floor, a mid-tempo reggae song playing. Putting his hands on Makayla's waist, their bodies swayed. She flung her arms around his neck and allowed her hips to roll back and forth. He pulled her closer, moving his hips in time with hers, feeling her body relax into his. As she nestled her face into the crook of his neck, her warm breath tickled his skin. Turning around, Makayla tossed her hands in the air and gyrated her backside against him.

Travis's body rocked when she rolled and shook when she shimmied, his arm around her, clutching her waist. Burying his face in her hair, he inhaled deeply, breathing the fragrance of jasmine that clung to her sleek locks. He pushed her hair to one side so he could feel her skin against his face. Makayla twirled back, gazing deep into his eyes, a soft smile inching across her face. Rubbing the back of his head, she continued to sway from side to side. He pressed her body into his, and for him, she still wasn't close enough.

After several songs, Travis reluctantly accepted that it was time for the fairy tale to come to an end. If he had his way, he would never let her go, holding her hostage in his embrace.

"You look tired," he whispered in her ear.

Makayla cringed, leaning back. "Geez, thanks."

"I didn't mean it like that." He grinned, letting his hands slip from her waist. "We should head up."

Makayla nodded in agreement.

Back at the room, Travis held the door open for Makayla. She strolled into the dark, tossing her purse on the bed, still humming the reggae tune from the lounge. Pulling back the curtains, Travis allowed the moonlight to illuminate her body, undulating to the rhythm in her head. Sinking onto the bed, she unclasped her strappy high heel shoes.

It had been a long time since she'd allowed herself to let loose. She loved to dance, but since her social life was lacking, she mostly danced alone around the kitchen island. It was a nice change of pace to have a dance partner who knew her body. Powered by the giddy excitement that coursed through her veins, she tried to regain her composure. She was tipsy in a hotel room with her ex and was seriously wondering if Travis still did that thing with his tongue.

"That was fun." She smiled as she walked toward Travis, who had angled his body on to the dresser. "Could you?" Makayla pointed at her solitaire two-karat necklace.

"Yeah, sure. Turn around." Travis swept her hair across her left shoulder.

Wiping his hands on his pants, he fumbled with the clasp of her necklace, trying to unhook it. As his hands brushed against her neck, her skin tingled as a slow but steady seismic wave made its way through her body. A soft shiver tickled her spine in response to his breath against her skin. Undoing the chain, he allowed his hand to run down the length of her arm. Makayla let out an audible moan, which made him grab her hips and pull her backside against him.

Holding her breath, her body stiffened before softening into his, she could feel him come to life as she rested her butt onto his lap, leaving no doubt about what he wanted. Travis's right hand moved slowly and deliberately from her hip, traveling across her stomach, between her breasts—which ebbed and flowed with each increasing breath—and around her neck. Planting a single kiss on her shoulder blade, he ran his tongue across her shoulder up to her neck. Makayla tossed her head back, her body trembling from his touch, as he laid a series of kisses on the nape of her neck before turning her around.

Her almond-shaped eyes were filled with longing. Swaying side to side as if in a trance, Makayla traced her finger across his mouth. Searching his eyes for a reason to stop, she moved closer, gazing up at him, her mouth agape and breathing softly. Raising to her tiptoes, she laid a soft peck on his mouth with her full lips. Travis grabbed Makayla's face, kissing her deeply, the frantic, kinetic energy of his body threatening to overtake her. Inching away, she cupped his face, slowly brushing her lips against his. She needed him to slow down, she wanted to savor every second with him. When he kissed her again, his tongue was delicate, his long, deep kisses shutting off the rational part of her brain. Makayla's body responded to his touch, as she wrapped her arms around him, caressing his neck as their tongues explored one another as if for the first time. His kisses gained intensity as his hands explored the curves of her body.

Makayla tried to pull him closer, but there was no room between them. He couldn't get closer, at least not with them both fully clothed. A sigh escaped her lips as she whispered his name. He responded by sweeping her off her feet, grabbing hold of her thighs to help lock her in place. Hooking her hands around his neck, Makayla leaned back, slightly gyrating her hips against his, giving him a preview of what she would do if they were naked. His hand found her ass as he played with the string of her thong.

Makayla's head was spinning, his touch making it difficult to think. Travis had a girlfriend and, although he didn't seem too concerned with that major detail in this moment, it was nagging at her. But didn't she deserve to be happy? And Travis and the growing appendage in his pants would make her very happy. As if he could hear her thoughts, his energy shifted as his warm, pliable grip on her body became cold and inflexible. He released his hold of her waist, her thighs loosening their grip, she planted her feet on the carpet.

Stepping back, he yelled, "Damnit!" With unfocused steps, he paced the width of the room. "I can't ... I have a girlfriend ... I can't."

"Fiancée, actually," she breathlessly corrected him. Escaping to the other side of the room, she tugged at her dress, adjusting the fabric so she was no longer exposed. She couldn't help but think it would've been nice if he'd afforded her the same consideration before cheating on her all those years ago.

"Yeah, which makes this even worse."

"I'm sorry ... sorry ... I'm so sorry," she repeated over and over. A sudden flash of icicles rippled through her body. Her hands were numb. She scratched at her palms, trying to feel something other than shock. Makayla bent over, leaning her hands on her knees, trying to find some oxygen to help clear her head. "I just couldn't control myself."

He was slowly advancing toward her. She took two steps back for each step he moved forward. Her back drawn against the hotel wall, she was all out of moves. With her face in his hands, they searched one another's eyes, both calculating the cost of just one more kiss. Running his thumb across her lips he parted her mouth, sliding his finger inside. Makayla's tongue moved over his thumb as he slowly eased it in then out.

"Fuck ... fuck ... fuck!" He retreated.

Rushing past him, Makayla headed for the balcony in desperate need of fresh air. Eyes cast over the railing, she considered the possibility of survival if she jumped from the eighth floor. After a quick analysis, she determined death was the only likely outcome. If they had been on the third floor, she would've made a go at it. She would have gladly taken a broken leg if it meant she didn't have to explain why she had just kissed him.

When she re-entered the room, Travis wasted no time. "Look, Makayla . . . I apologize. That should never have happened."

"I totally agree," she said, sitting on the edge of the bed before jumping back up, unable to contain her energy.

"Honestly, we were drinking and reminiscing, and I think both of those things just got the best of us."

"Yeah . . . no . . . totally. Exactly that," Makayla agreed, flailing her arms like she was playing a round of charades.

"It was an accident, and we shouldn't read any more into it."

"Yep. We don't need to read, skim, or scan this any further." She was relieved that he'd made the difficult conversation less awkward.

"OK, great." He wiped incessantly at his lips.

"I'm gonna get ready for bed." Grabbing items out of her bag, Makayla hurried to the bathroom. She stood silently behind the bathroom door, listening to Travis's movements on the other side. She thought she heard what sounded like him kicking or punching something. After setting her things on the bathroom counter, she pulled down her lace thong and sat on the toilet seat. Hunching over, she felt drained, like she had just completed a strongman competition. With a touch of her lips, she closed her eyes. She could still feel his mouth hunger for hers. She licked her lips, hoping she could still taste him. A knock on the door popped her daydream bubble.

"Makayla?" Travis's voice called from the other side of the door.

"I'm peeing," she said cautiously.

"I'll wait."

She forced the last trickle to release. Standing, she thoroughly washed her hands. She wasn't sure she wanted to hear what he had to say.

"Yes," she called through the door, not ready to look at his face.

"I think . . . I think I'm gonna go sleep in the car." Travis's voice sounded somber on the other side.

"You don't have to; it's fine." Makayla shook her head like he could see her through the door.

"Nah, I think it's just best," he yelled. And in a much lower voice, he followed with, "I don't trust myself around you," which she knew was clearly not intended for her ears.

"OK. Take a key in case you change your mind." She remained still, listening as he moved around the room. She guessed he was probably grabbing his phone or maybe a pillow.

"Good night." Hearing his voice so close to the bathroom door caused her to jump.

"Night . . ."

The hotel door opened and slammed shut behind him. Makayla was completely alone.

Chapter 24

"Do you want some wine?" Porsha asked, pouring them both a glass.

"Girl, it's three in the afternoon," Makayla objected.

"I know, but for this conversation, wine is the only acceptable option. I mean, real talk, it should be Henny, but it's three in the afternoon, so wine it is." Porsha plopped on the sofa in her spacious family room.

"I think I've had enough wine to last me a lifetime." Makayla pushed the glass away. After Travis dropped her off at her townhouse, she got in her car and drove straight to Porsha, who worked from home on Fridays.

"I want to know everything. Start with the kissing and groping first." A wide smile eased across her face.

"This isn't funny. We work together. I have to work with him."

"You should've probably thought about that before you two started swapping saliva," Porsha teased between sips.

Makayla closed her eyes. "Oh, my God! What am I gonna do?"

Porsha set her wine glass down, crossing her arms over her chest. "Answer me this. Why did you kiss him?"

That is a good question, Makayla thought, one she'd been asking herself for the last several hours. Yes, she'd been drinking, so she guessed she could blame fifty percent of it on the alcohol. But that other fifty percent was all her. Spending the day with Travis exposed holes in the impenetrable force field she'd built around her heart.

"I just wish it never happened," she said, not even trying to explain herself.

"You know what I wish? I wish you'd stop acting so surprised. Travis never got over you."

"He's engaged."

"Yeah, he can be engaged to Regina and still be madly in love with you." Porsha shook her head.

"He's mad, all right, but in love? Not so much."

Porsha sucked her teeth. "Travis is your man . . . Regina just has temporary custody."

Women with temporary custody don't sport diamonds on their ring finger, Makayla thought. *If Travis does still love me, he has a funny way of showing it, saving dates and reserving wedding venues. I knew in college this light-skinned, hazel-eyed bookworm was going to be the death of me. I gave him six years of my life . . . actually, more than that if you count all the years I've spent obsessing and comparing every man to him. Love is overrated. I don't need a man in my bed to make me happy; all I need is good food, good friends, and a good vibrator.*

"You still haven't answered my question. Why did you kiss him?"

"I was drunk." Makayla didn't want to explain her actions.

"I'm calling BS. You don't get yourself locked in a passionate kiss off of some cabernet. You can lie to me if you want, but deep down inside, I think you know you're still in love with him."

Makayla scoffed a laugh, slapping her knee. She wanted Porsha to understand how ludicrous her statement was. *I am not in love with Travis Holmes,* she thought.

"The trip just brought ancient feelings to the surface. I was caught slipping, but I'm fine now," she protested.

"M-Kay, Travis is gonna marry Regina, and when he does, there is no turning back. Marriage, kids . . . forever."

Makayla jumped up from the sofa. "You don't think I know. I know that! What do you want me to do? Go up to him and say, 'I know this is bad timing, but don't marry Regina . . . marry me'?"

"Yes, that. Exactly that." Porsha snapped her fingers.

"He doesn't love me anymore, Porsha," Makayla said softly as she slumped backward on the sofa.

"I don't believe that, and neither do you."

"So, what? Just fuck Regina? I should just ruin her life?" Makayla threw her hands in the air. She wasn't going to be the woman who destroyed someone else's happy home. However, last night made it clear that it wasn't as happy as she once thought.

"Pretty much. You don't owe her anything. This is about a once-in-a-lifetime love."

"No, it's a love that was a lifetime ago. We've both moved on."

Porsha curled her lip. "You haven't moved on."

Makayla stared straight ahead toward the pool in the backyard. This wasn't a rom-com, and she wasn't Julia Roberts. She wasn't going to steal the guy from the girl and live happily ever after.

Porsha softened her tone. "I just don't want you to have any regrets."

Pulling her knees close to her body, Makayla said, "The only regret I have is about what happened in the hotel. How do I deal with that?"

Porsha drove out a harsh sigh. "You could tell him you were under alien mind control."

Grabbing her purse, Makayla screwed her face into a scowl and headed for the door.

"Come back. I'm sorry." Porsha jumped up and ran toward the open door, but Makayla was already halfway to her car. "Really, Makayla?" she shouted, throwing her hands in the air. Makayla ignored her as she jumped into her car, revved the engine, and pulled off.

Calvin watched as Travis fussed over his turkey burger, removing the pickles and smearing mustard across the bun with a butter knife.

"Why do you ask for pickles if you're just gonna take them off?" Calvin mumbled, his mouth full of sweet potato fries.

"Because I like my pickles on the side." He used his knife to cut his burger in half.

"Then why not just get them on the side?"

"Why do you care?"

"You're right." Calvin waved his hand in the air. "Finish your story. You and Makayla head back to the room and . . .?"

Travis cringed, "And . . ."

"Wait a sec, choir boy . . . you two had sex?!" Calvin shouted, snapping his fingers and pointing in Travis's direction.

"No." Travis turned to the table next to them, hoping the couple wasn't eavesdropping. "No. There was no sex," he whispered. "Why are you talking so loud?"

"My bad. So . . . what?" He leaned in, ready for all the details.

"We kissed." Travis used his napkin to clean his spotted fork.

"Pfft. That's it? A kiss?" He leaned back in his chair, visibly disappointed.

Shaking his head, Travis reminded Calvin, "I'm engaged. The only woman I should be kissing is Regina."

Rolling his eyes, Calvin held his hand up. "OK, chill. You're barely engaged."

"She is already pissed that I ignored her calls and text messages for hours. So when I tell her I kissed M-Kay, she might kill me."

"Then don't tell her!" Calvin yelled, banging the table. Lowering his voice, he continued. "Look, T, if you're trying to stay with Regina, you're gonna have to take that little kiss to the grave."

Travis shook his head. "I can't just lie."

"Yeah, you can." Looking at him like he'd grown a second head, Calvin continued. "Who are you, George Washington? You most definitely can lie."

"Cal, lying always makes things worse. It didn't work with Makayla five years ago, and it's not going to work with Regina now."

Calvin tugged at his chin. "How can you be so smart and so

dumb at the same damn time? Regina will leave you, or worse, she'll make you quit your job."

Sucking his teeth, Travis disagreed. "Not necessarily. If I explain it was an accident."

"Bullshit. There ain't no accidental kissing. You wanted it, M-Kay wanted it, and it happened."

Travis couldn't admit it but Calvin was right. He did want Makayla that night in the hotel room. Part of him still craved her right now. "Maybe if . . ."

"No maybe." Reaching for his beer, Calvin's eyes lit up as he had an idea. "Look, pretend I'm Regina. What would you say?"

"OK." It probably was a good idea to practice what he planned to say. Travis rubbed his hands together as he let out a sigh. "Regina, I have to tell you something."

"What is it, babe?" Calvin batted his eyes, raising the pitch of his voice.

"What is that? What are you doing?"

"I'm Regina. I'm getting into character." He pretended to brush hair from his eyes like he'd seen Regina do the few times Travis had forced them all to hang out together.

"She doesn't even sound like that," he said with a wave of his hands.

"She sounds like that to me." He scrunched his shoulders against his neck. "Go on."

Clearing his throat, Travis now doubted the benefits of this exercise. "I kissed Makayla."

Calvin's eyelids stretched wide as he pointed at Travis and covered his mouth at the same time. "You kissed your ex-girlfriend?" Calvin said, once again putting on his best Regina imitation. "How could you? I thought you loved me. I thought we were forever. You dirty bastard." He dabbed at fake tears with his napkin.

Holding up his hand, Travis interrupted the show. "OK, thank you," he said, looking around the restaurant at the heads that had turned in their direction. "I think we're good here. I won't tell her."

He hated to admit it, but telling Regina would just open a whole new can of worms.

"That's my boy. You know you don't handle crying well." Calvin squirted more ketchup on his plate.

Frowning, Travis sipped the last of his root beer. "It makes me uncomfortable."

"What are you gonna do with M-Kay?"

Looking down at his half-eaten burger, he could think of several things he wanted to do with Makayla. A twist to his lips, he said, "I think I'm gonna go with 'pretend it never happened' for five hundred, Alex."

"Hmm." Calvin wiped his hands on his napkin. Travis had known his friend long enough to know there was more on his mind. "Might I suggest that you figure out why you were so willing to risk it all for M-Kay? And maybe, hear me out now, just maybe Regina ain't the one."

Travis gave his shoulders a twitch. "Alcohol is a helluva drug."

"Yeah, and denial ain't just a river in Egypt."

Popping a cold fry in his mouth, he chose to ignore Calvin's last remark. He'd already spent way too much time thinking about this ordeal. It was just a kiss, and both he and Makayla agreed it was a mistake. It was time to move on; nothing to see here.

Chapter 25

Glancing at her phone, Makayla yawned. It had been another long day of meetings, and she was anxious for the weekend to begin. Luckily, the budget meeting was the last of an already long day. She tried to be attentive as Dro and Amanda, the teen ministry leaders, droned on about their projected budget. The singles ministry was up next. They had gone over the budget several times over the past month and were more than prepared to present their numbers. She peeked over at Travis, who was seated on the other side of the large U-shaped conference table. He appeared thoughtful as he listened to the various facts and figures. Numbers were where he was most comfortable, so she wasn't surprised to find him taking notes and even asking questions.

A week had passed since the Savannah trip, and although she had done her best to block the incident from her mind, there was a part of her that wanted to remember . . . cherish the memory. That didn't mean the past week hadn't been awkward. When they were both in the office, she would take her laptop and work in the court-yard or one of the small meeting rooms, and it seemed like Travis was operating from the same playbook because he had been M.I.A. for much of the week as well. Any excuse to be away from that small office and avoid facing their lapse in judgment. It was like all the progress they'd made the past few months had vanished, making it even more far-fetched that they could ever be friends again. They couldn't even maintain a cordial relationship, so she highly doubted they'd be exchanging BFF bracelets any time soon.

"Thank you." Pastor Randolph's booming voice seemed to echo in the large space. "Up next, we have the singles ministry."

Sliding her chair back, Makayla made her way to the front near the flat screen to start their presentation. "The singles ministry has some ambitious goals for the remaining year. Despite these lofty goals, we project that our fourth quarter budget will be ten percent less than last year's."

Travis and Makayla reached for the slide clicker at the same time, causing both to retreat.

"My bad. You got it." He stepped back, plunging his hands into his pockets.

"No, no, you go ahead. You reached first." She shook her head.

Scooping up the clicker, he moved to the first slide. "While our budget is reduced, you will see that the quality of the services and activities we plan to offer has not been compromised."

Makayla looked on as Travis ran through the first few slides. This was probably the closest she'd been to him since returning from Savannah. *What if we hadn't stopped in the hotel? Would we've had sex?* Sex with Travis was like eating a Pringles chip, once you popped, you can't stop. God knows it took all her will power not to give him the green light. Her body craved him, and not because she hadn't been properly fucked in months. It was almost like muscle memory, and even though it had been five years, she remembered exactly what to do and was ready to please him.

"Makayla," Travis whispered. The room was silent, and all eyes were on her. Nudging her, he interrupted her thoughts. "You're up."

"Oh, me? Already? Sorry about that," Makayla said as she shuffled through her note cards, dropping them to the floor. She and Travis bumped heads as they both bent to pick them up. Rubbing her forehead from the impact, she felt the beads of sweat forming on her brow. She hated being the center of attention. Why did she insist on sharing the presentation when Travis could have knocked this out with his eyes closed and one hand tied behind his back.

Passing her a handful of stray note cards, Travis whispered, "Just wing it. You know this stuff back and forth."

Standing, she smoothed her skirt. Glancing at the slide, she took a deep breath and jumped in. "Every year, the church holds its annual picnic, and we've decided to piggyback off of that and host a singles ministry after-party. One of the top requests from our singles is engagement and fellowship events."

Travis nodded in agreement as she ran through their planned activities, after which he outlined the associated cost for each.

After the meeting, Makayla was collecting her items when Travis approached.

"Well, it wasn't pretty, but we got the job done." He gave a sideways smile. "Good job."

"Uh huh," Makayla said, not looking up from her bag. "Have a good weekend, Holmes." She threw her tote over her shoulder. As she headed toward the exit, she flashed one last look in his direction. She wanted to make things right between them, but she didn't know how. One thing she knew for sure was that she would have to be careful around him because all she could think about was their kiss and falling back into his arms.

After the budget meeting, Travis rushed home. He was in the second bathroom of his apartment, wiping down the sink and counter. He added a new roll of toilet paper to the holder and adjusted the shower curtain. It had been a week, and the passage of time hadn't made anything between him and Makayla better. As Calvin had predicted, Travis's plan to ignore the obvious wasn't working. He could hear Calvin now: *What did I tell your ass? That's those unresolved issues coming back at you like a boomerang.* The last thing Travis needed right now was an "I told you so."

Then, there was Regina. Taking Calvin's advice, he hadn't

told her about the kiss, but he might as well have because she was still mad at him for ghosting her for close to eight hours while in Savannah. She had even gone so far as to ask him out right if he had slept with Makayla. His response was an unequivocal no, but the damage was already done. She knew him well enough to know he was holding something back. With fresh linens from the hall closet, he entered the second bedroom. Pulling the old sheets and pillows from the bed, he unflared the fitted sheet and tucked in the corners.

Casting a glance at his watch, he picked up his pace, tucking in the last corner of the fitted sheet. Regina would be there any minute. Because he was stuck in meetings most of the day, she had volunteered to drive to the airport. Thinking about it made his stomach twinge with guilt. Even though she was mad at him—silent-treatment, no-sex kind of mad—she still agreed to this huge favor. Grabbing the purple comforter from the chair, he spread it across the bed, smoothing his hand over the black ballerinas in their pink tutus. Travis heard the front door open and hurried out to the living room to greet his special guest.

"Daddy!" a young girl with curly pigtails yelled as she leaped into his arms.

"Baby girl!" He scooped Daisy, his four-year-old daughter, into his arms, giving her a tight squeeze. "Let me look at you," he said as he stepped back. "I think you got taller since I saw you last month." Travis pretended to measure her height with his hands.

Daisy had visited every summer since the age of one, when she was old enough to not rely solely on her mother's breast milk. Aside from the summers, Travis saw Daisy often, traveling to Oakland at least twice a month to spend time with her along with his mom and sister. He shared custody with Daisy's mother, Bianca, who lived in Oakland. Bianca was a one-night stand that turned into a lifelong connection. One rash decision at a bachelor party had changed the trajectory of his entire life. Together, they created the most special person in his world: Daisy Holmes. Luckily for Travis, he and Bianca were able to co-parent with little to no drama.

He turned to Regina. "What do you think?"

"She definitely looks taller," she agreed, setting down Daisy's pink suitcase.

"I knew it," he whispered, tickling Daisy to excited squeals. "OK, check your watches."

"I don't have a watch." Daisy's lower lip shot out.

"That's OK; just look at mine." Travis knelt so Daisy could get a better look. Pointing to Regina, he asked, "Are you looking at your watch?"

"Uh huh." She leaned against the couch with crossed arms.

"OK, the summer of fantastic, spectacular, crazy fun starts . . ." he paused for dramatic effect, "right now with froyo!"

"Yay!" Daisy shouted, refusing to release her father's hand.

"You know, the place where you can load your yogurt with anything you want." Kissing her forehead, he stood. "All right, go potty and wash your hands, then we're out."

Daisy ran to the bathroom, leaving Travis and Regina alone.

"Thanks for picking her up." Leaning in, he gave her a peck on the cheek.

"Yep," Regina said with a pat to his back.

"How was Alfonso?" Alfonso was Bianca's brother, Daisy's uncle, and he agreed to fly down with Daisy because she was too young to fly unaccompanied. Apparently, Alfonso had met a woman in Atlanta and required very little arm twisting before agreeing to make the trip.

She turned up her nose. "He was all right. He had on a ton of cologne."

Reaching for her hands, he danced from side to side while singing an upbeat tune.

"You're super excited."

"Sure am. I have my two favorite people in the same city."

Pointing to herself, Regina asked, "Am I one of those favorite people?"

"Yeah. Who else would it be?" Irritation shadowed his smile.

The two stared at one another in silence for a moment before she shrugged. "Just checking."

Travis swallowed hard, releasing her hands as he picked up Daisy's suitcase and walked it to her room. Lying wasn't working. Pretending everything was OK wasn't working. The past few weeks made it harder for him to believe there was a happy in their happily ever after. If this was gonna work, they needed to have an honest conversation to clear the air. But that discussion would have to wait; right now, his focus was on spending time with his baby girl.

"Froyo, froyo, froyo!" Daisy yelled, as she entered the living room.

Travis joined in the chorus. "Froyo, froyo, froyo," he sang with Daisy, grabbing her hand. The two circled Regina, yelling the refrain. "Froyo, froyo, froyo."

Regina's serious expression faltered as she began to laugh. "OK, let's go."

Travis grabbed the keys from the bowl near the front door and handed them to Daisy. "You drive," he teased.

Chapter 26

The weekend had not been long enough, but Makayla was in the office early, hoping to catch up on some outstanding tasks before attending the Women in Leadership luncheon downtown. She had been distracted much of last week, and her workload had suffered because of it. Having to work in the same space as Travis was disconcerting, but she had made it through, and she planned to keep doing what she had been doing: ignoring the humongous gray elephant in the room.

"Good morning." Travis hurriedly walked into their office.

Makayla remained focused on her documents, offering up a murmured response. "Morning."

"Say hello to Ms. Makayla, sweetie," Travis said, dropping his backpack on his desk.

"Hello," Makayla heard a tiny voice respond. Slowly peering up from her papers, she stared into the caramel face of a little four-year-old girl who, except for the gray eyes, looked just like her father.

Swallowing hard to clear the rush of emotions, Makayla forced a wide smile. "Hello, cutie. How are you?"

Daisy stared back with a crooked grin.

"Sorry about this. Had a little hitch with childcare this morning." Travis removed Daisy's pink and baby blue Doc McStuffins backpack from her back.

"No worries." Makayla was unable to take her eyes off Daisy.

Every summer and several times throughout the year, Daisy Holmes would come to visit her father. Makayla had seen them walking to and from church or at church-sponsored events, like the annual picnic, but this was the closest she'd been and the first time the two had exchanged words.

"Don't worry, she won't be here long. Uncle Cal is gonna swing by in a bit and swoop her up." He unzipped Daisy's backpack and pulled out a coloring book and a package of crayons.

"Uncle Cal? Well, she'll get an education today, no doubt." She let out a laugh that turned into a sputter.

Directing Daisy to a chair in front of his desk, he agreed. "I'll probably pick my baby up, and Cal will have shown her how to play dominoes and mix a whiskey sour . . . neat."

"All useful skills." She smiled thinly.

Travis cleared his throat. "Could you do me a favor?" He leaned on Makayla's desk. "I have a meeting with your dad in a few minutes. Do you think you could watch her for a bit? She won't be any trouble. She'll probably color the entire time."

"Uh mmm . . ." She looked from Travis to Daisy, who was whispering in her stuffed bunny's floppy ear.

He twisted his hands together. "You know what? My bad. I'll just ask Tami."

"No . . . no, it's fine. Of course, I can watch her." She bounced her shoulders. Kids weren't her forte, but how hard could it be to entertain a four-year-old girl?

A breath eased from his lungs. "Thank you. I shouldn't be gone longer than thirty minutes."

"With my long-winded father, it'll probably be more like an hour." Makayla smirked. "Go. We'll be fine."

"I owe you one." Kissing Daisy on the head, he walked out, notepad in hand.

More than one, she thought. She sized up Daisy, who was swinging her legs in the chair and humming to herself while focusing intently on her coloring. It was hard to believe this adorable little girl, in her denim ruffled romper, was the cause of her breakup with Travis. Makayla shook her head, trying to remove the memories from her mind. *You have work that needs doing*, she reminded herself. If she didn't focus, she would sit there and gawk at Daisy all morning. Makayla cracked open her Bible, looking for a scripture on the topic of hope to add to the singles ministry newsletter.

As she absentmindedly flipped through the pages, the words passed by in a blur. She glanced over at Daisy, stealing another quick peek. Squeezing her eyes shut, Makayla wondered if she'd made the right decision leaving Travis. This wasn't the first time she'd second-guessed the choice she made five years ago.

"Will you color with me?" Daisy asked bashfully.

Makayla turned, opening her eyes to find Daisy standing next to her, coloring book in her tiny hands.

"Uh, yeah . . . sure. What do you wanna color?"

Makayla watched as Daisy flipped through a *Hair Like Mine* coloring book, picking a page with two little girls with bows and barrettes in their hair.

"This one," Daisy said, smiling.

"Good choice." Makayla reached for a black crayon to color in the hair. Daisy stood alongside her, coloring in a Disney princess activity book, taking special care to stay inside the lines. She was definitely her father's child. Who knew a four-year-old could be so meticulous?

"Do you have a favorite Disney princess?" Daisy asked, looking up at Makayla as she placed one foot on top of the other.

"Tough question, but I've always loved Mulan." Makayla grabbed a green crayon. "What about you?"

"Tiana." Daisy leaned in. "You look like her." Daisy hooked her miniature arm around Makayla's arm.

A slight lump welled in Makayla's throat. Grabbing her water bottle, she tried to push it down. The last thing she wanted to do was burst into tears in front of a preschooler for no logical reason. "Are you having fun visiting your daddy?"

"Yes! Daddy took me to a bouncy place this weekend."

"Those places are the best. I bet you had a lot of fun."

Daisy nodded. "After, we made pizza."

"You and your daddy made pizza? Sounds yummy."

"Miss Regina helped too." Daisy neatly placed her orange crayon back in the pack.

All Makayla could do was smile. Of course, Regina was there, playing the stepmommy role. Travis had a new life she knew nothing about. He'd created a new family. When he'd confessed to getting a woman pregnant after a drunken one-night stand, Makayla couldn't get away fast enough. Cheating was one thing; maybe they could have moved past that. But an entire baby was a burden she wasn't looking to bear. Although the sting of that day had faded, she still bore the scars like an Omega Psi Phi fraternity brother after being initiated. She remembered that painful night as though it was yesterday.

"So, do you really think this chick is the one for Calvin?" Makayla asked, dumping the clean towels on the bed she shared with Travis.

"He seems to think so." Bouncing his shoulders with indifference, Travis reached for a towel.

"Well, I hope so because then we can go on double dates and couples' vacations."

His hands trembled as he tried to fold the oversized bath towel. "Uh huh."

"Or not." She flung a towel at him. "Earth to Travis. Where'd you go?"

"Uh, nowhere. I'm right here." He tossed the towel back on the bed.

Throwing her arms around his neck, she kissed his lips before pulling away. "Are you gonna kiss me back or nah?"

"What? No . . . yeah." Leaning in, he parted her lips with his.

Lifting to her tiptoes, she licked the side of his neck. "The towels can wait," she said breathlessly.

"Makayla, I need to tell you something," he whispered.

"Later." She reached for the waistband of his shorts.

Travis grabbed her hands, pushing her away. "No, now."

"OK, Mr. Serious."

"I don't really know how to say this." He moved to the other side of the bed to allow for some distance.

Makayla picked up her phone, scrolling through her recent notifications. "Just say it," she offered absentmindedly.

"Makayla . . ."

"Hmm." She opened a text message from Summer.

"Remember when I went to Greg's bachelor party a few months ago?" His voice sounded robotic from practicing that sentence over and over again in his head.

"Yeah, when you got shit-faced drunk and I had to listen to you cough up a lung the next morning over the phone," she said, texting Summer back.

"Yeah, well—"

"You're such a lightweight," Makayla joked.

Clearing his throat, he continued. "Anyway, all that drinking . . . and I was kinda out of it, and I met this woman."

"OK." She tossed her phone onto the bed. He had her full attention.

He scratched at his goatee. "She invited me to come back to her place."

Makayla leaned forward, cocking her head to the side. "And you declined and went back to your mom's house alone . . . right?"

"I wish to God that's what I'd done." He looked down at his bare feet, unable to look her in the eye.

Jumping from the bed, Makayla screamed, "Are you joking right now?" She let out a nervous chuckle. "You're joking, right?"

"Makayla, could you just—"

"Could I just what? What the hell are you saying?"

"We had sex. I had sex with her," Travis blurted out.

"No, you didn't. No." Makayla's eyes darted around the room, trying to comprehend his words. "I don't understand." She let out a quick, high-pitched laugh. "Why are you telling me this now?"

"What?"

"It's been, what, three months? So, why are you telling me this now?" Her speech was slowed, emphasizing every word.

"I'm telling you because it's eaten at me ever since, and I feel horrible about it. It was a huge mistake, a drunken mistake." Travis shifted from one foot to the other, balling his hands into fists. "Also, she's pregnant. She says it's mine."

Makayla's pulse quickened, and her ears began to ring as if a stick of dynamite had just blown up in her face. "How does she know that?" she asked, still hoping there was some way this was all a big misunderstanding.

Travis bit his lip. "She said she hasn't been with anyone since me."

"Pfft, oh yeah, I'm so sure." She rolled her eyes.

Wiping his sweaty palms on his basketball shorts, he continued. "I took a paternity test. I needed to be sure before I told you." He paced on his side of the bed.

Makayla snorted with a shake of her head. "No. No. You wouldn't... you wouldn't do that."

"Makayla, I—"

"Travis, what the fuck are you talking about?" She shook her hands as though she was strangling him. She'd heard the words, but she still couldn't believe they were coming from her man's mouth. Her balled fist tingled with the urge to hit something. Makayla sucked in rapid, stuttered breaths, trying hard to resist the impulse to jump across the bed and punch him square in his throat.

Holding his hands up, Travis pleaded, "Can you just calm down?"

With a tilt of her head, she scrunched her face. "Calm down? Calm down?!" she screamed. The wheels in her head were turning as she did some quick calculations. "Wait a second ... How long have you known she was pregnant?"

"Huh?"

"You said you took a test. So, if the baby wasn't yours, would you even be telling me?"

His shoulder hunched forward. "What do you want me to say?"

"Oh, so you cheated on me and got another bitch pregnant, and *you want me to tell you what to say to fix it?"* Makayla grabbed a bed pillow, throwing it at him.

He ducked as the pillow sailed over his head. Raising his trembling hands, he begged, *"I just need you to listen to me."*

"Who is she?" Makayla shouted, the vein in her forehead bulging.

"You don't know her."

Through gritted teeth, she sneered. *"Now, see, that ain't what the fuck I asked you."*

He shook his head, swallowing the ball of sawdust to make way for words. *"She's from Oakland. It was one time."*

Makayla felt lethargic, the base of her skull vibrating painfully like she had just been cold clocked. *"Hmm, first time's the charm,"* she mumbled, rubbing her temple.

"M-Kay, please . . ."

"Stop talking." Pacing her side of the room, she tried to figure out her next move. How was she going to explain this to people? What would her parents say? The busy bodies at the church would have a field day with this one. Maybe there was a chance this could just all go away. *"Is she keeping it?"* Makayla eyed him.

Travis meekly nodded.

Hanging her head, Makayla allowed the tears to fall from her eyes. It felt like he had just pushed her down an endless hole, and no matter how hard she struggled, she couldn't grab ahold of anything to stop this free fall. She clutched her stomach as she choked on her tears. Breathing was becoming difficult as she cried out.

Grabbing her wrist, he tried to pull her close. *"Baby, please let me explain."*

"No," she sobbed. She had never felt this level of pain. Travis was the love of her life. He was her best friend. She was so lost in him, she didn't know where she began and he ended. What do you do when your whole world betrays you?

The color drained from his face, leaving it ashen and haggard. *"It was one time, baby. I'm so sorry. Please."* He attempted to pull her into his arms, but she pushed him away.

"No, don't touch me," Makayla screeched, her voice cracking. Stumbling back, she fell to the floor. She sat in a crumpled pile like the discarded bed sheets in the corner of the room as her phone dinged with notifications. Outside their bedroom, it appeared the world was still revolving.

"Do you love her?"

"No." He cringed. "I don't even know her."

"Is that supposed to make it better somehow? You threw us away for some chick you don't even know."

"No, I love you. I wanna be with you." Placing a hand on her knee, he squeezed.

Makayla pushed his hand away and sneered. "Yeah, you want me? Well, I want a man who's not gonna cheat."

Beads of sweat formed on his forehead. "I promise on my life I will never do this again. Ever."

"I don't believe you." Her entire body shook as she used every muscle to suppress a whimper.

His chin dipped in concession. "I'll show you. I'll prove it." His voice cracked, dry and guttural.

"What exactly would you have me do? You think I'm looking to play stepmommy to your bastard kid?"

The corners of his mouth turned down as he leaned away from her. "Whoa, really?"

Makayla pulled at the fibers in the carpet. "Yeah," she whispered. She knew it was harsh, but what did he expect? She always assumed they would share this special moment together like all the others, but now, some other woman was walking around with a piece of him, his first child, something she would never be able to give him.

Nodding, Travis asked, "Is that how it is?

Makayla let out a sullen chuckle. "This is how you made it."

"I know you're mad, but—"

"Damn right I am!" Her breath was labored as fresh tears filled her eyes and threatened to tumble down her cheeks.

"And you have every right to be." His tone was hushed. "But you know me." He tapped his hand against his chest.

"No, no, I don't. Because my Travis would never . . ." Dissolving into tears, she was unable to finish her sentence. Her head spinning, she swayed side to side as the tears flowed. Clawing at her flesh, she pinched her arm repeatedly, waiting to wake up like Sleeping Beauty from this cruel dream. Travis's hands grabbed for her, pulling her into his arms. She was too tired to fight, and in that moment, she longed to be locked in his embrace.

He whispered in her ear, "I'm sorry."

Burying her wet face into the crook of his neck, she breathed deep. She ran her hand across the back of his head, listening to the whisper of his breath against her skin as he exhaled. As his hold on her tightened, Makayla sobbed in his arms.

"I can fix it."

"You can't." She gasped for air.

Rubbing his hands up and down her back, he whispered in her ear, "I can. I will."

Pulling back, Makayla looked into his beautiful eyes. "Tell me you love me."

His face bore a pained expression as his eyes filled with tears. "I love you so much, M-Kay." Cupping her face in his hands, his lips found hers. Makayla greedily took his kisses, wishing she could press pause on the world so she could languish in his grasp a bit longer.

Running her lips against his, she realized she could no longer pretend. "Why did you do this to us?" she asked, not really expecting an answer. He'd made a choice, and choices always came with consequences. "I can't stay, Travis. I can't stay."

"No, no, no, wait. Just wait," he begged, wiping at his tears with his shoulder.

"I need to think. I need to think away from you."

"I'm not letting you go." He shook his head, holding tight to her waist.

"You don't get to have a say in this."

His limbs fell limp to his sides, and tears stained his face. "What am I gonna do?" he asked.

Makayla looked down at her coloring page, only to find her hand trembling as she clutched the purple crayon between her fingers. She felt a tap on her shoulder followed by a small voice.

"What are we gonna do now?" Daisy asked, closing her coloring book.

Clearing her throat, Makayla shut her eyes, pushing the painful thoughts deep down inside where she housed a lifetime of hurt, fear, and sadness. She looked at the clock; Travis had been gone for over forty minutes.

"How about we head over to the café and get a sweet treat?"

"Yay!" Daisy raised her arms in the air, dancing from side to side.

Makayla locked her laptop and grabbed her wallet from her bag. Pushing in her chair, she ushered Daisy out the door. As they walked through the administrative offices, Daisy fluttered next to her, spinning, skipping, and jumping.

"Did you see me?" Daisy laughed. "Look at me, Miss Kayla." Daisy attempted a half-flip with the bottom half of her body.

"Whoa, very impressive." Makayla clapped. "You almost flipped all the way over."

Daisy's face beamed with a huge, prideful smile. "Watch me hop on one leg." She hopped from one carpet tile to the other.

"I can do that," Makayla said playfully, lifting her left leg and hopping on her right. She had a bit of difficulty keeping up, hopping on a five-inch heel. As she and Daisy rounded the corner, Makayla bumped into Travis, who reached out to steady her.

"Oh, my God. I'm so sorry." She grabbed his waist.

"You OK there, One-Leg Willie?" he joked as Daisy ran up to him.

"Yeah, just a friendly race," Makayla explained. "Clearly, Daisy won."

He looked down at Daisy. "Did you have fun with Ms. Makayla?"

"Um hm. I like her. She's funny." Daisy reached for Makayla's hand.

Squatting, he touched the tip of Daisy's nose. "You're a good judge of character."

Smiling at Makayla, he continued. "Thanks again. To show my appreciation, let me treat you ladies to a drink from the café."

"Great minds think alike. We were just headed in that direction."

"You two grab a table, and I'll order the drinks," he said as they headed to the café.

"Do you know what I want?" Makayla asked as she pulled out a chair for Daisy.

"Of course, I do." He winked and walked over to the register with a smile.

Taking a seat next to Daisy, Makayla listened while she talked about her favorite color: blue. As Daisy wrinkled her nose and talked excitedly with her hands, Makayla was struck by how similar her mannerisms were to her father's. She appeared to be a mini-Travis. Her lips curved into a smile at the thought of him raising this little girl. There was no doubt that Daisy had her daddy wrapped around her little finger. A sudden chill overtook her with the realization that any relationship with Travis would include one with his daughter. Porsha made it seem so simple, like all she had to do was bat her eyes, flip her hair, and get her man back. Whatever this was, was bigger than her and Travis. She was longing for that old flame back but had never stopped to consider that the intensity of that flame may be different.

"What's blue and isn't heavy?" Daisy tried to contain the smile that was creeping up her face.

"Hm, I don't know. What is it?"

"Light blue." Daisy giggled loudly.

Makayla threw her head back, laughing. Travis was clearly passing on his unique sense of humor to his offspring. "That was funny."

"Here we are." He returned to the table, placing Daisy and Makayla's cups in front of them before taking a seat.

Makayla watched as Daisy took a napkin and opened it,

spreading it on her lap. Glancing over at Travis, she raised her eyebrow with a smile.

"Yeah, she's into fancy stuff right now. Napkin in lap, pinky up when she drinks. I have no idea where she got it from." He removed the lid from his cup, adding sugar to his coffee.

"It's crazy how much she reminds me of you."

"Yeah, no *Maury* for me. Travis, you are the father," he joked.

"Uh huh," Makayla said, running her finger over the condensation on her cup.

"I'm sorry. I didn't mean to joke about that." He cringed.

"No, it's fine." When she said it was fine, she meant it. She'd spent far too long holding on to anger, an anger that didn't protect her or make her stronger. All it did was keep her stuck, unable to move forward and unwilling to let shit go. Sitting here now with Travis and his daughter, she realized that may have been a mistake. "So, did my father let you get a word in?" Makayla asked.

"One or two."

After taking a sip of her chocolate milk, Daisy set the cup on the table and declared, "This is delightful."

They both looked at Daisy then at one another and began to laugh.

Chapter 27

"Can you say zucchini?"

"Zoo-teeny," Daisy responded enthusiastically.

"Not quite. Zoo-key-nee."

"Zoo-key-nee."

"What's this?" Travis held up a green vegetable."

"Broccoli!"

"And we love broccoli."

"With cheese."

"Should we get some?"

"Yes." She shook her head in vigorous agreement.

Ripping off several plastic bags, Travis also grabbed an onion and bell pepper. "This is gonna be the best spaghetti ever," he said to Daisy, who was distracted by the water misters washing over the produce. Handing her an open plastic bag, he let her place the red bell pepper inside. With his phone in hand, he scanned his shopping list, ticking off items in his head.

"Ms. Kayla!" Daisy shouted as she took off running toward Makayla, who had entered the produce section. Daisy wrapped her arms around Makayla, who set her basket down so she could return the embrace.

"How are you?"

Travis pushed their cart over to where Daisy and Makayla stood. "Hey, funny meeting you here."

"Yes, it is funny meeting you in a Whole Foods. You're more of a Walmart type of guy," Makayla teased.

"At Whole Foods, you're just paying for the name, nothing else."

"Hmm, the meat department would disagree," Makayla said, bending to pick up her basket.

"We're making squashetti." Daisy beamed, slipping her hand inside Makayla's.

"Mmm, sounds meatless."

"We use ground turkey; it's healthier," Travis corrected her. He looked down at Daisy, who was gazing up admiringly toward Makayla. It was hard not to be impressed. *This woman looks like one of Daisy's black Barbie dolls come to life, even in a simple tank top and shorts.*

"You should come over," Daisy said.

"Whoa, slow down, Tickle Me Elmo." He blinked rapidly. Since when was Daisy in charge of their social calendar?

Daisy giggled. "You should come over, and we could eat and play games, and I can show you my room."

"I'm sure Miss Makayla is busy tonight." His eyes dropped to the basket she was clutching with a pint of her favorite ice cream and a bottle of red wine. It looked like her plans included a couch and binge-watching television.

"Daddy, please." Daisy looked up at him with puppy dog eyes, a look he claimed didn't work on him but almost always did.

A resigned breath passed his teeth. "Look, if you're not doing anything, and you're hungry—"

"I don't think that's a good idea." Makayla rubbed her monogram necklace with her fingers.

Daisy started to jump up and down. "Please, please, please, please ..."

Makayla's wide eyes telegraphed her discomfort.

"Oh, she's gonna do that until you say yes," Travis said.

"Please, please, please, please ..." Daisy continued, tugging on Makayla's arm.

"What about Regina?"

A muscle twitched under his eye. "She's in Vermont, visiting family." What he didn't add was that they hadn't spoken since she'd left a week and a half ago.

"Please, please, please, please ..."

"OK, I'll come over ... for a little bit." Air eked from her throat.

"Yay!" Daisy hugged her.

Checking his watch, he suggested, "Thirty minutes?"

"That works."

"Do you need the address?"

"Nope, I got it."

Travis pulled his face in surprise. "Apartment—"

"Twenty forty-one," they said in unison.

"OK, great. I'll see you at my place in thirty minutes."

"It's a date." Daisy beamed.

Travis's heart rattled deep beneath his ribs. This was not a "date" ... This was just two hungry people and a child eating ... in his apartment ... while his girlfriend was out of town.

"Do you want me to bring anything?" Makayla asked.

"Just bring yourself."

"See you in a bit."

Travis watched until Makayla disappeared from view before turning his attention to Daisy. "What was that?"

Daisy ripped out a laugh, completely oblivious to what she had just done.

After dinner, they played the board game Candy Land, and Makayla won the last round.

"In your face," she yelled, doing a happy dance with her shoulders and arms.

"Makayla, she's four," Travis reminded her.

Her body froze in place as she slowly lowered her celebratory arms. "Oh, I mean good game."

Daisy giggled. "You're funny. She's funny, Daddy."

Travis clapped his hands. "OK, that's enough games for tonight. Let's brush your teeth and wash your face."

"Can't I just stay up a little longer?"

"Nope. You know the drill; bedtime is at seven thirty."

Daisy pouted. "Good night, Miss Kayla," she said before heading for her bathroom.

Travis looked at Makayla. "Can you stay a little longer?"

"Uhm?" Her voice was strained as her eyes darted across the room. She had already been here too long. The plan was to stay for an hour, but that hour had turned into two.

"I'll be like ten minutes and then we can brainstorm topics for our workshop."

"OK, sure."

Travis disappeared to the bedroom, leaving Makayla alone. Reaching for the open wine bottle, she stopped short, remembering what happened the last time she'd had too much wine. She replaced the stopper and put the red wine back in the refrigerator. Tidying up the kitchen, she packed up the leftover squashetti in a container and wiped down the counters. Walking around aimlessly, she stopped at a picture of Travis, all smiles, standing next to a horse.

"Where was this taken?" She lifted the picture as Travis reentered the room.

"In Vermont," Travis said, coming to stand next to her.

"And the horse?"

"Oh that's Clive. Regina's family has a farm, chickens, goats, cows, and Clive."

"Wow, I didn't know you knew any horses."

Replacing the picture frame, Makayla turned on her heels. "It's late, so if you want me to go, I totally get it."

"I don't want you to go." His eyes gave her a once over.

Walking over to the couch, she took a seat. "So what should our first workshop be about?"

"I hate to say it, but probably relationships." He joined her on the couch.

"Like dating?" She felt at a bit of a disadvantage, finding it difficult to focus with his knee brushing against hers.

"Dating with a purpose?"

"I don't hate it."

Jumping up from the couch, Travis said, "Let me get a pen and paper so we can jot this all down."

The list of potential workshop topics was long after their thirty-minute brainstorming session. Makayla propped her bare feet on the edge of his coffee table, leaning back into the couch. Following suit, Travis eased back, his shoulder butting hers. Tilting her head, she met his eyes with a smile.

"Do you still want to go?" he whispered, his eyes now locked on her plump lips.

"I don't know. I'm comfortable. I think the itis is setting in. I stand corrected; squash noodles actually aren't that bad. Mind blown—"

He descended on her lips, his perfect mouth pressing against hers caused her head to spin, his tongue rendering her speechless. She wrapped her arm around his neck, needing to be closer. She needed all of him. His strong hands found her bare thigh, his skin against hers, sending shivers tripping through her body. Cupping his face, she fought the sense of urgency that swirled inside of her. She wanted to revel in his touch, preferring to pretend they had all the time in the world.

His lips fell from hers to explore her jaw and neck. This man knew all the places to kiss to make her feel soft and gushy. Makayla raised her hands so he could remove her tank top, pressing her lips to his once he'd tossed her top aside. Travis smiled against her lips, plunging his hands in her curls, leaving trails of kisses down her chest. Settling in on her breasts, he pulled her bra down, not wanting to waste any time. His tongue circled her nipple before planting a soft bite on the meaty part of her breast. Makayla felt like a contortionist, her body twisted as her head slipped from the couch.

Wrapping his arm around her waist, he pulled her upward, setting her on top of his lap, her back facing him.

"Oh shit," Makayla whispered, feeling all that Travis had to offer against her backside. As he unhooked her bra, his mouth went to work on her back as his hands caressed her breast. Makayla's hips were already sliding back and forth in anticipation of what was to come. Melting backward into his chest, she parted his lips with hers, kissing him deeply. Oxygen was overrated, she told herself, not wanting to stop searching his mouth for a much-needed breath.

Travis froze. Why wasn't he kissing her back? "What's wrong?" she breathed out.

"I think I hear Daisy in her room." He shifted his weight, pulling her from on top of him.

Makayla covered her breasts with one hand and reached for her bra with the other.

Standing, he walked to Daisy's room, calling over his shoulder, "Do not put your clothes back on."

Now that he was no longer kissing her, her head was clear. She was alone and half naked in her engaged ex-boyfriend's apartment. This was a mistake. All of it was a mistake. A few hours of pretend had severely clouded her judgement. He wasn't her man; this wasn't her family. Was she really that hard up? There were well over 250,000 men in Atlanta, and her lips kept finding his. Pulling on her tank top, she grabbed her purse and shoes and tried her best not to slam the door behind her.

Chapter 28

"Hello," Makayla answered, smiling from ear to ear.

"What are you doing?" Hosea asked in his usual smooth-sounding voice.

"Packing." She neatly tucked a pair of yoga pants into her suitcase.

"Oh, that reminds me, you might wanna pack a swimsuit. We may get wet while you're here."

Makayla touched her perfectly styled coif. The last thing she wanted to do was ruin it. "Just what do you have planned?" she asked as she walked over to her dresser to retrieve her favorite two-piece.

"It's a surprise. Just make sure you bring a swimsuit."

"Oh, a surprise, huh? Is that why you wanted to book my flight for the crack of dawn?"

Hosea let out a slow, deep laugh. If he'd had his way, he would have booked Makayla on a 6:00 a.m. flight. But since Makayla wasn't a morning person and her issue with promptness was no secret, including to Hosea, a 9:00 a.m. flight was more fitting.

"I can't wait to see you. I think my friends are starting to think I made you up."

"Well, in a few hours, you'll be able to show them that I am very much real."

"You're not nervous or anything?"

"No," she lied. This trip to Houston was make-or-break time.

She'd allowed Hosea to wriggle on the line for far too long. When she got to Texas, she was going to pull out every last trick in her sexual arsenal. The plan was to come home with a boyfriend. Jump starting this relationship with Hosea was exactly what she needed to completely close the door with Travis, which was something she was finding difficult to do. Maybe because her foot was blocking the way.

"Liar," Hosea teased.

"OK, maybe I'm a little nervous, but I just want to make a good impression."

"I have no doubts that my friends and family will be very impressed by you," Hosea encouraged her.

Did he just say family? Makayla's chest grew tight. "Look, let me go on ahead and finish this packing. We'll have plenty of time to talk when I see you tomorrow."

"I can't wait. Text me when you board the plane."

"Will do. Good night." She tossed her phone on the bed, covering her face in her hands. He could quite literally be the perfect man. Smart, funny, and fine as hell, with his flawless brown skin and chiseled physique. Despite all that, her brain was flooded with thoughts of Travis. Running her fingers across her lips, she reminisced on their less-than-platonic dinner. His touch resuscitated hopes and dreams she thought were long dead.

Makayla was a smart woman—graduated magna cum laude from Clark Atlanta University—and she was just as good a liar. She had lied so hard for so long about her dislike for Travis that she started to believe it. But his kiss, the taste of his mouth, the grip of his hands, the burning desire in the pit of her stomach ... His kiss had called her bluff. Hosea was a sure thing. Travis, on the other hand, was a confused groom-to-be who was experiencing cold feet. The smart bet was on the good Pastor Wright. It was time for her to move on, and Hosea was just the man for the job.

Travis was looking forward to a quiet Thursday night at home alone. Daisy was attending a sleep over, and Regina was still in Vermont, no calls, no texts, and no replies. If she was breaking up with him, she could at least have the balls to let him know.

Biting into his pastrami sandwich with all the fixings, he turned on the television to watch the basketball playoffs when his phone rang. A picture of his sister Aisha popped up on his screen. *She's probably calling to trash talk my team.*

"Hey, foolio. What's up?" He laughed at the nickname he and his sister had used for one another for years.

Aisha coughed and sputtered on the other line. There was a lot of background noise, which made it taxing to hear her. He muted the television, hoping it would help.

"What's wrong?" He could barely comprehend his sister, who was crying on the other line. "Wait, slow down. I can't understand you." Leaning forward on the couch, Travis closed his eyes, hoping he could catch a word through the commotion on the other end. It didn't help that his pulse was beating in his ears, making it difficult to hear anything else. Aisha wasn't an emotional person, so if she was crying, something was wrong.

Aisha screamed and sobbed in his ear as she spoke with choppy utterances.

"What are you talking about?" The hairs on the back of his neck and arms rose as a shiver ran down his spine.

Aisha made a second attempt to cough up her words. He could hear a voice whispering in the background.

"Where . . . where are you?" His fingers were ice cold, and he was having difficulty breathing, as if a heavy weight had been placed on his chest.

Aisha just kept repeating the same two words over and over again. "Mom's gone. Mom's gone."

"Pu-put . . . Mom on th-th-the phone," Travis stuttered.

"Mom's gone," Aisha repeated. Her voice was gurgled and almost unrecognizable to his ears.

Jumping up from the sofa, he screamed into his cell phone,

"Damnit, Aisha! Put Mom on the phone!" His knees could no longer support his six-foot-two frame, and he collapsed to the floor, still clutching the phone.

"Mr. Holmes . . . Mr. Holmes," an unfamiliar voice called out on the other end of the line.

"Travis. Call me Travis," he said out of habit, as he gasped for breath, realizing it was a good thing he was on the floor because he was certain he was going to pass out. He could only hear single words and not complete sentences—accident . . . head trauma . . . we did all we could—coming from the unfamiliar voice on the other end, who identified herself as the lead doctor in the trauma unit at Providence Hospital.

"Travis, are you there? Can you hear me?" Aisha said, having intercepted the phone back from the doctor.

He tried to respond, but nothing came out of his mouth. His stomach felt bottomless, and the room began to spin. He closed his eyes and began to weep loudly.

After nearly three hours, he finally peeled himself off the living room floor. The casual summer evening had turned into a dark and ominous night. Stumbling toward the patio door, he pushed it open, stood on the balcony, and listened to the cars driving by and the sound of a couple laughing in the distance. He greedily gobbled up the air, trying to regulate his breath, which was labored and unpredictable like an asthmatic struggling to breathe. What exactly was he supposed to do? He was at a loss; he always knew what to do. Another stream of tears began to cascade down his cheeks as he swayed back and forth, trying to decide on his next move. Grabbing his keys from the bowl next to the door, he headed toward his car. He didn't know where he was going, but he knew he didn't want to be alone.

In her kitchen, Makayla poured herself a glass of Rosé. After taking a long sip, she poured a little more. The doorbell rang, it was 10:48

p.m., entirely too late for unannounced visitors. Making her way to the entry way, she peered out the peephole to see Travis leaning over the door frame. *Shit, is he here to talk about why I left abruptly the other night? Or maybe he's checking in on me because I opted to work from home all week.*

Makayla swung the door open. "I don't know what you're here to yell at me about, but it wasn't me," she half joked. Travis looked up, his eyes red and puffy, splotches of color on his cheeks. "What's wrong?" Makayla searched his face for answers, stepping aside to let him in. Everything about him seemed off, like someone had knocked him off his axis and he was lost at sea with no navigation.

He scanned her living room, eyes narrowed, like he'd just landed on an uncharted planet.

"What's going on?" His silence was making her nervous.

With a jerk of his head, a tear fell from his eye. He wiped it away hurriedly. "I'm sorry. I know it's late." His voice was weak and strained. "I shouldn't have come here," he said, eyeing the door as he shifted from one foot to the other.

"It's OK." Walking over to him, she nestled his face in her hands. "Please tell me what's wrong." Her gaze anchored to his, she could see the pain swimming in his weary eyes.

Travis began to speak but stopped short. He glanced around the room as if he was looking for answers.

"My mom died."

He said the words so matter of fact that she shook her head, certain she'd heard him wrong. "What?"

"My mom . . . was in a car accident. There eh . . . was . . . nothing they could do." His voice cracked.

Covering her mouth with her hands, she backed away. They stood in silence as the weight of his words sunk in. Her stomach became a mass of knotted coils as she pressed her lips together to stop her chin from trembling. Recovering from the initial shock, she reached for Travis, pulling him toward her. She folded her arms around him, squeezing him tight.

"It's OK," he said. Even now, in this moment, he was still trying to comfort her. She should've been reassuring him. But how did you tell someone everything was going to be OK after a loss like this?

Makayla didn't have the words; all she could do was hold him tighter, stroking the back of his head. His body shuddered, and without warning, he began to cry hysterically. His knees buckled as he tumbled to the floor, taking Makayla, who could not support his weight, with him. She crawled over to where he lay in a sobbing heap and rubbed his back. Travis reached for her, wrapping his arms around her waist, burying his face in her lap. He cried for what felt like an eternity, and she was determined to hold him as tight as she could for as long as he needed it.

At some point, Makayla led him upstairs to her bedroom, removing his black Clark Atlanta University hoodie, revealing a plain white V-neck T-shirt underneath. Standing in the middle of the room, Travis swayed slowly back and forth as if it was taking all his effort to remain on his feet.

"You should take your shoes off." Makayla disappeared into the bathroom, returning with a warm face towel and two ibuprofens. She wiped the trail of tears from his face with the warm, damp rag. Handing him the pills, she reached for a half-empty bottle of water on the bedside table. With focused eyes, she watched like an orderly at a medical facility as Travis popped the pills in his mouth and chugged down the rest of the water.

He was thankful for the ibuprofen because it felt like a mariachi band was performing in his head. Sitting on the side of the bed, his eyes followed Makayla as she darted around the room, turning on the ceiling fan, removing the frilly accent pillows from the bed, and turning off the lights. She struggled to remove a suitcase from her bed. He didn't offer to help; he just watched, immobile, as she let out a soft grunt.

"What's the suitcase for?" he asked, hoping he could fill his mind with new thoughts.

With a flinch of her shoulders, she brushed his questions aside. "Nothing." Setting the luggage in a corner, she asked, "Where's Daisy?"

"Sleepover."

"Do you want me to call someone? I could call Regina."

"She's still in Vermont. We're not talking right now."

"Oh ..." she said, walking over to his side of the bed. "You should try to get some sleep. She helped guide his legs under the covers before heading toward the door.

Reaching for her hand, Travis whispered, "Stay." The last thing he wanted was to be alone. His mind was working overtime with visuals replaying of his mother alone in her little blue Toyota Corolla, having to be ripped out by the Jaws of Life.

Tying on her head scarf, Makayla climbed into bed next to him.

He settled into her queen-sized bed, pulling the covers to his chin. Inhaling deeply, he breathed in the soft, fresh scent of her that clung to the sheets. Makayla had always been his safe place. The minute she opened the door, he knew he'd made the right decision coming to her. His throat thickened with emotion, as he exhaled a strangled breath. They lay in complete silence, except for the occasional sniffle. His muscles twitched as he suppressed the urge to reach for her. Directing a heavy-lidded gaze to her side of the bed, he watched as her chest rose and fell, trying to figure out if she was still awake.

"Are you asleep?" he whispered softly.

Makayla released a low sigh. "No."

He listened to the soft whirl of the ceiling fan motor. Focusing his attention on the blades, he counted the rotation. He was on number seventy-four when he asked, "Do you think she was scared?"

Biting her lip, Makayla closed her eyes. "Do you remember the time your mom tried to teach me how to make that 7UP cake you like, and I failed miserably?"

With a weak chuckle, he answered, "Yeah, and she asked me,

'Travis, how in all of Georgia did you find the one woman who can't cook?'"

Makayla clicked her tongue. "What did you say?"

He shifted onto his side to face her. "I told her you had other talents."

"Bullshit, you didn't tell your mom that."

"Nah, I told her you were good at other stuff, like party planning and the piano."

A heaviness settled over him. He knew Makayla was trying to pull him from his morbid thoughts. But any thoughts of his mother were painful right now. Rubbing his hands over his face, he swallowed back tears. "Tell me something I don't know. Anything."

She squinted, searching her memories for something ... anything. "OK. On our first day at Clark Atlanta, I saw you at registration, so I purposely sat next to you at freshman orientation, hoping you'd speak to me."

His eyes twinkled. "Do you remember at that orientation, I asked if I could borrow a pen?"

"Yeah."

"I didn't need a pen. I had tons of pens in my bag ... blue, black, red, highlighters too. I just wanted to get your attention." Absentmindedly, he rubbed his hand across her arm, her body shuddering from the contact.

The moonlight from the window cast shadows over her face. "Well, it worked." Her voice was faint and breathy.

Moving closer, he watched her squirm as his hand moved from her shoulder to her thick thigh, tracing his fingers over her supple brown skin. "Are you OK?"

Her voice high and light, she replied, "You need to stop touching me."

"Yeah, sure, sorry. I'd forgotten how sensitive your skin is." Travis pulled his hands away, resting on his back. In the silence, he could hear her slowly regain control of her breathing.

As a tear slid down his cheek, he asked, "Do you think she knows how much I love her?"

"She knows. She was so proud of you and Aisha. She told me once, she didn't know what she did to end up with a son like you. She called you ... the best part of her, her hope, joy, her fierce love ... all combined."

Newfound tears fell from his eyes as he laid his head on her stomach. As the tears coursed down his face, he clutched her tight. In this moment, he was thankful he didn't have to pretend to have it all together. He could just sob like a baby, protected in her warm embrace.

The next morning, Travis woke up alone in Makayla's bedroom. Squinting to shield his eyes from the morning light, his mouth was dry and his head was pounding. His eyes welled with fresh tears as the realization of his mother's passing washed over him once again. He buried his face in the pillow to muffle his anguished groans. Minutes passed before he was able to finally stand and shuffle to the master bathroom, his feet heavy like they were tangled in rusted chains. Sticking his head under the faucet, Travis gulped the cold water. He splashed water on his tear-stained face and stared at his reflection in the mirror.

"You need to get it together." He tapped the mirror where an exhausted face looked back at him. His sleep had been fitful, and he distinctly remembered waking up and screaming in horror at one point during the early morning. Makayla pulled him back down and held him close, humming in his ear until he drifted back to sleep. He couldn't allow himself to continue to fall apart. Arrangements needed to be made, and he had to be there to support his sister, grandmother, and Daisy.

Mom loved calla lilies. I'll have to order some for the ceremony. When I get to Oakland, the first thing I need to do is go see Grandma. She must be a mess, losing her daughter. I wonder where Mom wants to be buried. We never talked about that. When his grandfather passed, he was devastated, but this felt different. He'd just lost the one person who knew him before he even knew himself. Patting down the pockets of his shorts, he searched for his phone but couldn't find it. He needed to book flights and tell Regina. *What time is it?* He had to pick Daisy up at noon.

"No more tears," he chastised himself.

In the kitchen, Makayla placed a K-Cup in the Keurig machine, setting a large mug underneath. Pulling out the creamer, she let out a big yawn. Her phone display read 7:28 a.m.; she should've been on her way to the airport. She was spent, and she hadn't fully processed the loss, having been so focused on taking care of Travis. Sharon Holmes was like a second mother to her. The last thing Makayla wanted to do was get on a plane to Houston. Unlocking her phone, she decided to text Hosea.

Makayla: Hey, are you up?

Hosea: Yep, just got back from my run.

Makayla: I hate to do this, but I'm not gonna make my flight.

Hosea: What?

Makayla: Family emergency.

Hosea: Is everything OK?

Makayla: IDK.

She covered her mouth with her hand as tears streamed down her face.

Hosea: Is there anything I can do?

Ripping a paper towel from the roll, she blew her nose, reading his text message through blurry eyes.

Makayla: No, I'll call you a little later and explain. I promise.

Hosea: OK.

Makayla: I'm sorry.

Hosea: Don't worry about me. It's OK.

Drying her eyes, she replaced the full mug with an empty one to start another cup. Her phone dinged with a text from her mother. First Lady Randolph would often text her girls with inspirational Bible verses. Today's verse was about perseverance. Makayla shook her head, realizing she needed to tell her parents about Ms. Sharon. A conversation like that was best had in person. She would stop by later to let them know.

"Good morning," Travis said as he entered the kitchen.

"Morning." Makayla bit her lip. "How are you—"

"I'm fine," he interrupted. "Have you seen my phone?"

Tipping her head forward, she handed him his phone from the kitchen counter.

After a quick scan of his phone, he let out a low hiss before sliding it across the white marble countertop.

"I need to book some flights," he said, pulling his hoodie to shield his red eyes.

"I checked. There's a flight headed to Oakland at noon. If that's too soon, I also found one leaving a little after four." Makayla opened her laptop and showed him the saved flight information. "Seats are limited."

"So, I should lock it in?" Travis said, pulling out his wallet and retrieving his credit card for Makayla to book a flight for him and Daisy. Before she could even ask, Travis followed up with, "Don't worry about Regina. She'll fly in from Vermont ... or not."

"Were you able to get any sleep?" she said, changing the subject. Just hearing Regina's name made her feel some kind of way, but she tried her best to disguise it. Each and every time he uttered that woman's name it was like a sharp prick to her heart.

"A little. You know, when you weren't snoring." Travis shook his head with a chuckle, taking a sip of his coffee.

"I don't snore."

"It was like sleeping next to a logger. You were chopping some serious wood," he teased.

She pulled two English muffins from the toaster. "That never happened because I don't snore."

The room fell silent. He took a bite out of the bread, preoccupied by a growing to-do list.

"What am I gonna tell Daisy?" Travis asked, rubbing the stubble on his face.

"You'll find the words. You always do."

"M-Kay, she's four. How do I explain that she's never gonna see her ..." He couldn't bring himself to finish the sentence.

"I believe that the people we love live on through us, in our memories of them and in the retelling of stories." Makayla hoped her words were providing some solace. She wished her father was here; he always knew just what to say in times like these. He had a way of bringing comfort in the midst of unspeakable pain.

"The last time she called, I was too busy. I rushed her off the phone because I was too busy." He punched the countertop, bringing tears to his eyes. Groaning, he clenched his wrist.

Inspecting his hand, Makayla placed some ice in a dishcloth and nursed his injury. It wasn't broken, but he was going to have one hell of a bruise. He wrapped his free arm around her waist, holding her close.

Braving her gaze for the first time that morning, he said, "I love you, M-Kay. I want you to know that."

Makayla pulled back, stepping outside of his reach. Her breathing became shallow as her mouth hung open. Mentally, her brain was churning with thoughts she couldn't grasp.

"Despite everything. You were my best friend, and I'll always have love for you. I need you to know that. I don't wanna leave here not letting you know." He wiped a tear from the corner of his eye. "I have so much regret about us, but your happiness is important to me. And I just honestly want my friend back." Reaching for his cell phone, he stood up, done baring his soul.

Her flesh came alive with a tingle that traveled through her body. She wanted to tell him she loved him too, beyond just a friend. But this wasn't the time or place to make that type of confession. Makayla let out a shaky breath. "If you need anything, just let me know. Anything at all."

He offered a long, ponderous nod.

At the front door, he pulled her in for one last hug, his arms enveloping her. He whispered, "Thanks for booking the tickets for me." He paused. "And thanks for . . . for just being there for me."

With a vacant nod, Makayla drew a breath, taking in one final whiff of his essence. She always loved his natural scent; she wished she could bottle it up and keep a private reserve of Eau de Travis. Pulling away, she shut her eyes, trying to quell the wild thoughts that were filling her head.

"Please text me with the homegoing information. I wanna be there to pay my respects."

Mustering a crooked smile, he stepped outside, giving a thumbs up to her request. She, in turn, gave a half smile. Slowly, he headed down the walkway to his car. Her eyes followed him until he was no longer in sight. Closing the door, all she could do was slide to the floor and let the tears fall. Her tears weren't just because of the loss of his mother; they also symbolized the time lost with the love of her life.

Chapter 29

Standing in his childhood bedroom, Travis pulled the last knot on his tie. The day he had never imagined having to face was a reality. His mother's funeral was to take place in less than two hours. The week leading up to this day had been a blur, from the meetings with Minister Lovegrove, the pastor of his childhood church, to picking out a casket with his grandmother and sister, to sorting through tons of photographs taken over the years for the program. The list went on.

He released a severe breath, running his fingers across the trophies that still stood on display on the shelf in his room. Every track meet, every basketball game, every debate competition, his mother had been there for every single one.

"Hey." Regina stood just outside the bedroom door.

"Yeah?"

Waving her cell phone, she announced, "Aisha's on her way."

"Thanks."

Sadness weighted her lips. "Are you OK?"

"I'm fine."

She ducked her chin in agreement. "I know you're fine, but if you want to talk, you can talk to me."

"Uh huh." Travis checked his watch. "I should do Daisy's hair before I go."

"I can do that," Regina offered.

"Nope, I got it," Travis said, brushing past her. Regina had gotten to Oakland the day before. At the airport, she'd thrown her arms around him, but he couldn't return her hug. He was angry ... angry at Regina for not being there when he needed her. Angry at the world for its capricious nature.

In the bathroom, Travis parted Daisy's thick, curly hair down the middle.

"What do you think Nana is doing in Heaven?" Daisy asked, hugging her stuffed pink-and-white bunny with oversized floppy ears.

Shivers nipped his spine. "Knowing your nana, she's probably rubbing elbows with Aretha and Whitney." Gathering one side of Daisy's hair into a ponytail, he brushed down her soft edges, securing her hair with a hair tie.

"Who?" Daisy tilted her head, now staring up at her father.

"Never mind," he said as he braided the ponytail.

"When will I see her again?"

"Hopefully, not for a long, long time." Twisting each braid into buns, he attached two purple bows.

"She'll forget me." Daisy wrinkled her brow.

"She won't," Travis assured her. He kissed Daisy on the cheek. "Who could forget a face like this, huh?" As he tickled her under her arms, she giggled and squirmed, trying to escape his hold.

"Daddy! Daddy!" she yelled out between giggles.

Lifting her from the bathroom counter and onto her feet, he instructed, "OK, go eat breakfast."

As Daisy ran off to have some sugary cereal, Travis closed the bathroom door behind her. Closing his eyes, he leaned against the door. He let his mind take him back, way back to one of the most important conversations he'd had with his mother right before his college graduation.

"You love her, don't you?" his mother asked, her soft hand holding his.

"More than I thought was possible," Travis said.

"Then it sounds like you know what to do." His mother smiled with a nod of her head.

"Atlanta is a long way from Oakland, far from you and Aisha. The plan was always to come home after college."

"Well, they do have these things call airplanes," his mother teased.

"Georgia?" Travis said, like it was a foreign country.

"If that's where the other half of your heart is, yes," his mother said, giving his hand a squeeze.

A warm smile swept across his face. He could see his mother, her deep dimples folding as she smiled at him, her piercing eyes that could almost see through his soul. Traces of her lingered throughout the house. He could smell her as he stood there and reminisced on that day.

The moment dissipated quickly, pulling him back to reality. His mother was gone, and she was never going to come back. She'd miss him reaching important milestones in his life—his wedding, future children—they'd never know how awesome their nana was. Daisy would have to grow up without her, and she even stood the chance of forgetting her altogether. He walked over to the sink and leaned over it. Tears surfaced from deep inside, coursing down his cheeks. He clutched the sink as gut-wrenching sobs tore through his chest. In an attempt to muffle the sounds of his cries, he turned on the faucet. The tears were falling faster than he could wipe them away.

"Travis! Is everything OK?" Regina called out from the other side of the door. "Aisha's here."

Clearing his throat he, answered, "Yeah, I'm fine. I'm coming." Travis splashed water on his face and spot-dried it with the face towel from the towel rack. When he finished, his entire being drew a breath of courage before swinging the door open.

The organist played the next selection as the choir began to sing "For Your Glory." Opening the program, Travis scanned the pages to see how much longer they had. He was halfway there. After the choir, Pastor Randolph would speak. When Makayla told him the pastor would be in attendance, he asked him to say a few words. Travis sat between Aisha and Regina, who hadn't let go of his hand since they took their seats. Looking back, he smiled at Daisy, who was seated in the row behind him with her mother, Bianca. As the choir continued to hum, Pastor Randolph took to the podium. Clearing his throat, his voice boomed crisp and clear.

"You know why they call this a homegoing? Because Sister Holmes was a good and faithful servant of the Lord. Sharon raised two exceptional children in Travis and Aisha. She touched the lives of so many by being an example of God's unwavering love."

Travis had been to his share of funerals; he knew all the words pastors were trained to say to make the living feel at peace with their loss: so-and-so lived a full life. God doesn't make mistakes. Angels are rejoicing in Heaven. The list could go on. Today, Travis wasn't interested in hearing any of it. His mother was only fifty-five, entirely too young to have lived a "full life." If the angels were in Heaven rejoicing, they were assholes because, in his mind, his mother's death was most definitely a mistake.

"Death is hardest for those who are left behind," the pastor continued. God takes the soul, but we are left with the memories, the laughter, the hugs, and yes, the tears. We must live our lives as a testament to the ones we loved and who loved us." Pastor Randolph exited the podium.

Travis's ears perked up at that last part. Makayla had said something similar a few days before. It was up to him to make sure his mother's life was never forgotten. She lived on through him and Aisha and Daisy; that was her legacy. With a determined nod, he vowed to work hard to ensure that Daisy never forgot her nana.

"That was really nice," Regina whispered in his ear.

He didn't respond. He'd managed to hold himself together this far; only the eulogy by Minister Lovegrove remained. Rubbing his forehead in his hands, he straightened his back. Aisha sniffled next to him, wiping her nose with a crumpled Kleenex. While attempting to keep his breath even, he blocked out Minister Lovegrove's praise of his mother. The cords in this throat protruded as he focused his attention on the beams of the sanctuary.

Flipping through the four-page program, Makayla stopped at a picture of a twenty-something Sharon Holmes holding Travis. He looked to be two or three years old at the time. A warm smile ruffled her lips as she ran her fingers over the black-and-white photo. She focused her attention on the pulpit of the cozy Baptist church as Minister Lovegrove eulogized one of the strongest women she'd met: Sharon Holmes.

Her eyes traveled to the first pew of the church, where Travis was seated straight backed and unmoving. She knew he was an emotional wreck inside. They had exchanged several text messages over the past few days. She was concerned and wanted to check in on him to assure herself he was OK and to let him know she was there for him no matter what. From their late-night conversations, it was clear he was having a difficult time accepting that his mother was gone. He confided in her that he stayed up at night, watching the front door, expecting her to come home and tell him this had all been a huge mix up. She wanted to comfort him, give him permission to let go. Travis believed he needed to be strong for everyone else, but who would be there for him? Makayla blinked, moving her gaze to the woman next to him, realizing that was Regina's job now.

At the close of service, she stood with the others as they waited to express their condolences to the family. She watched as Calvin and his brother, Jaylin, approached Travis, both giving him daps and a hug.

Leaning forward, Makayla assessed the line; her family was up next. She brushed her hair with her hands and fidgeted with the quarter-length sleeves on her purple sheath dress. Her stomach crested and fell like she was on a catamaran in choppy water. She hated funerals. When she was little, her father made her and her sisters attend more homegoings than any one child should have to. He didn't want his girls to fear death, instead considering it a reunion. She still believed in Heaven, but it didn't make death less scary or the loss less painful.

Her father embraced Travis with a few pats on the back. Her eyes crinkled to slits as she tried to make out their words. Before she knew it, Makayla found herself standing in front of Aisha with both a mixture of sadness and guilt. She gave Aisha a shy smile and pulled her into a hug, listening as she sniffled softly in her ear.

There wasn't much time to exchange words; the line needed to keep moving. Aisha released her hold, and Makayla shuffled forward, staring straight into Travis's exhausted eyes. She squeezed his hands tight in her warm palms. Her mouth hung open, hoping to say something reassuring. She stopped short, unable to find the right words. Travis pulled her toward him, wrapping his arms around her. Rubbing his back, she held on tight, feeling his body begin to shudder against hers.

Time slowed as she held him close, allowing him to take all the time he needed to process the moment. Makayla knew he was probably trying to will himself to stop but the tears only fell faster. Abruptly, he reeled back, pushing her away. Makayla reached up and wiped his tear-stained face. He leaned his cheek into her hand, causing a flood of warm sensations to wash over her body.

"Sorry," Travis whispered.

"You don't have to apologize." She gave his hand one last squeeze before moving forward to hug his grandmother.

As the Randolph's walked up to Travis's childhood home, Makayla's head was on a swivel. She'd always loved this house and this block because it was the place where Travis grew up. On one of her first visits to Oakland, he had given her a tour of the neighborhood, showing her the corner store where he and Aisha would get candy and the place where he got the crap beaten out of him by the school bully. Just a few blocks away was the park where he had his first kiss. This neighborhood was important to her because it molded the person she loved most in the world outside of her family.

A line had formed as funeral attendees were flocking in for the repass. At the front door, Travis greeted family and friends as they arrived. Standing stoically, he listened to people tell him what a wonderful woman his mother was. Makayla overheard adults who once had Mrs. Holmes as their teacher tell him how she was an inspiration, and because of her, they were now a nurse, engineer, or graphic designer.

Travis's affectless expression faltered a bit as he saw the Randolph family approach.

"Thank you so much for coming. I feel special. I was blessed with the entire Randolph clan," Travis greeted them.

"Son, your mother was a wonderful woman, and her devotion to God was undeniable." Pastor Randolph shook Travis's hand.

"And her sweet potato pie was the bomb," Summer said. Porsha looked at her, shaking her head in amazement. "What? It's true. It's true." Summer gave Travis a hug. Makayla glanced over at him with an apologetic look on her face. *I can't take Summer anywhere.*

"I'll keep you and your family in my prayers." Porsha squeezed Travis's shoulder as she headed to the kitchen with Colin and Summer.

"If you need anything, anything at all, you reach out to us." First Lady Randolph lifted Travis's chin. "Do you hear me?"

"Yes, ma'am. I appreciate that." He forced a smile.

"We mean that, son," Pastor Randolph said, patting Travis on the back. After grabbing his wife's hand, they walked away to greet Minister Lovegrove.

Makayla and Travis stood alone. She rested her eyes on him. "It was a beautiful homegoing."

"We had to show out for her. Let God know that Heaven was getting a real one." He shoved his hands into the pockets of his slacks. "Thanks for coming."

"Of course. Your mom was family." Her hands fidgeted with the strap of her gray Chanel purse, trying to resist the urge to touch him.

"Your dad's words at the service hit home."

"He has a way of doing that."

"Mom loved your dad's sermons. You don't know what it means to look around and see all you guys here for her."

"Of course, ba . . . I mean, Travis." Her shoulders slumped as she dropped her head, embarrassed by her near slip of the tongue.

A smile flickered across his face.

Someone bear hugged her from behind. "Makayla Randolph, as I live and breathe," Aisha said, imitating a southern accent.

Makayla whirled around. "Oh, my goodness, Aisha!" She wrapped her arms around Aisha's neck. The two swayed side to side in a warm embrace. Makayla pulled away, taking her in. She was still sporting her signature braids, and she appeared to have lost the twenty pounds she'd put on from all the stress-eating during her senior year of college. "It's so good to see you."

"Yeah, it sucks that it has to be because of this." Aisha wiped a tear from her hazel eyes. "But I missed your bougie ass, M-Kay."

"I would prefer it if you guys didn't." Travis playfully pulled the two apart. "Because every time you two get together, y'all team up on me."

"It's 'cause you're such an easy target," Aisha teased.

"Like crabs in a bucket," Makayla agreed, giggling.

"Look, you broke up with that loser." Aisha pushed Travis in the forehead with her finger. "You did not break up with me. Before you leave, I'ma need your cell, work number, email, Instagram, Tinder account, and GPS tracking location. Do you understand me?"

"Yes, it's been too long."

"Too long? Girl, you missed my wedding." Her mouth sank into a sad smile.

Makayla's body appeared to shrink as her head shook in disbelief. Their lives were so intertwined that when they separated, she lost so much more than just her best friend and lover. "I'm sure it was beautiful. Where's Tessa, by the way?"

"You know Tessa stays in the kitchen. She's probably in there right now, loading her plate. Come on." Aisha grabbed her arm, pulling her toward the kitchen.

"See you later," Makayla mouthed, looking back at Travis before following Aisha into the crowded kitchen.

Leaning against the kitchen counter, Travis listened as his family reminisced. Much of the afternoon was spent laughing at inside jokes and stories from past family gatherings.

"It is so good to see you again, Makayla," his aunt commented. "Sharon always spoke so highly of you."

"Thank you." Makayla gave a shy smile.

"She didn't always feel that way about Makayla," Aisha said.

Travis laughed. "The first time my mom met Makayla was in Atlanta."

"We don't need to tell that story." Makayla waved Travis and his sister aside.

"No, we definitely need to tell that story." Aisha stood up, moving to the center of the kitchen. "This one was supposed to meet us for lunch. She was an hour and a half late."

Friends and family in the room groaned.

"In my defense, I overslept," Makayla yelled playfully.

"That is no defense," Travis countered.

"When Makayla finally showed up, we were done eating and getting ready to leave. And Makayla runs in, out of breath and sweaty."

"Not my finest moment, I admit."

"So what happened?" Summer asked.

"She read me for filth," Makayla said.

Travis winced. "It was painful to watch."

"It was far worse being on the receiving end of your mother's stern scolding. With her hands ..." Makayla imitated their mother's quick hand claps when she was emphasizing a point.

"Ohh, when she tapped that palm, you knew your ass was grass," Travis added.

"Granted, I was never late to meet with Ms. Sharon ever again." Light chuckles rolled through the kitchen.

"What's so funny?" Regina asked, entering the room. The guests fell silent as heads turned toward her direction.

Aisha glanced over at her brother, who just shook his head.

"Oh, we were just talking about the first time mom met Makayla," Aisha said.

"Oh yeah?" Regina cleared her throat. "How'd that go?"

"Badly. She wasn't a fan at first," Makayla said.

"Imagine that ... someone who didn't immediately buy into the Makayla Randolph façade." Regina plastered a smile across her face.

"Oh, no she didn't," Summer whispered to Porsha. "Do I need to take my earrings off?"

"Shh," Porsha said.

Travis fixed his eyes on Regina. "Mom was hard on everyone I dated; you know that. But she was actually a big softy in the end." He walked over to her and whispered, "Can you help me in the other room with that thing?"

Regina didn't respond, but she allowed Travis to lead her to his old bedroom. He could barely close the door behind them before she blurted out, "Why is she still here?"

He rolled a thick shoulder. "I suppose she's spending time with family like everyone else."

"Yeah, your family, not hers." Regina pointed toward the kitchen. "Are you serious right now?"

Regina's face softened as she appeared to consider his words. "I just want you to talk to me," she whispered, putting her head down.

"We *are* talking." He knew that wasn't what she meant. She wanted him to open up to her, but he was just trying to make it through this day without having a nervous breakdown.

"You can be vulnerable with *me*. You can lean on *me*," Regina pleaded, tapping his chest with her hands.

Brushing her cheek, he nodded. "I know that, and I appreciate it."

"It just feels like . . ." She took a cleansing breath before continuing. "It just feels like you're pulling Makayla closer while pushing me away."

His hand fell from her cheek as he retreated a few steps. Fire crackled beneath his skin and his cheeks blushed with anger. "My mom just died!" he screamed, tears filling his eyes. Standing in the middle of the room, red-faced, he wiped the hot tears that fell. "This isn't about you!" His voice cracked, his chin quivering. "My mom . . ."

She reached out to embrace him, but he recoiled, leaving Regina to stand there, staring at him as he tried to regain his composure.

"I'm sorry," Regina said, tears dropping from her eyes.

"Could you just not for one day? Could we just not?" She'd abandoned him; of course, he was having a difficult time opening up. "I gotta get outta here. I need to go for a walk," he said, wiping his face with his sleeve, making a hurried exit from the room.

As Travis walked past the family and friends gathered in the kitchen, they all tried to pretend as though they hadn't overheard his exchange in the other room with Regina. Right before the door slammed behind him, he heard Summer say, "Wow, the walls in this house are thin."

Chapter 30

Returning to the house, Travis was greeted by Calvin on the porch. He'd been gone for over an hour, using the time away to clear his head. He'd walked to the high school his mother had taught at for over twenty years, the same school he'd attended, just fifteen minutes from the house.

"Hey, just wanted to give you a heads-up," Calvin said, his jaw clenched.

"What's up?" Travis leaned on the porch railing.

"About thirty minutes ago, Regina dipped, luggage in hand."

"What?" He looked around like he expected to find her walking past. "Did she say where she was going?"

"She said she was going to a hotel. She wanted to give you your space."

"Space? Do I look like I need space?" Walking away to get some distance, he pulled his phone from his pocket and called Regina, but he was sent directly to voicemail. "Where are you? So we have a disagreement, and you just leave me ... again?" He scratched his head, heaving chestfuls of air. "Can you please call me so I know you're OK?" He stared at the face of his phone in disbelief. How did Regina end up making this day about her?

Back on the porch with Calvin, Travis fixed his mouth into something that resembled a smile.

"All good?" Calvin asked.

"No, no, it is not all good." He looked down at his phone, hoping it would ring.

"Well, Makayla's still here."

His stomach turned jittery when he heard her name. "That's not helpful." He shook his head.

Calvin raised his hands. "Don't shoot the messenger." With a shout through the front door, he yelled, "Jay, let's go!" Returning his attention back to Travis, Calvin pulled him into a hug. "You need anything, you let me know."

"Yep."

Calvin slapped Travis playfully on the cheek. "Love you, brother."

"Love you both," he said to Calvin and Jaylin, who had exited the house with a BBQ rib in his hand. As the two headed to their car, Travis shot off a quick text to Regina, asking her to call him before walking inside.

The hum of conversation led him to the kitchen. Stopping at the archway, he looked around at Aisha, Tessa, and Makayla, sitting around the kitchen table, laughing. The house had cleared out, and it appeared to just be them remaining. He hoped he'd get a chance to speak with Makayla again before the day was over.

"What are you ladies in here talking about?" he asked, desperately searching for something to distract him.

"Ah, there he is," Tessa said.

"I was just telling Makayla about the time you stayed out past curfew, and when you got home, there was a trash bag filled with your clothes waiting for you at the front door." Aisha laughed.

"That wasn't funny." Travis pulled out a chair, sitting with them. "I had to sleep at a friend's house for three days before she let me back in."

"And you never missed curfew again," Aisha reminded him.

"No, I did not. I learned my lesson quick, fast, and in a hurry."

"Ms. Sharon did not play," Makayla said.

"No, she did not." Turning to Aisha, he asked, "Where's Daisy?"

"I put her to bed about twenty minutes ago. She refused to go to sleep until Makayla read her not one, not two, but three books." Aisha smiled as she looked in Makayla's direction.

Placing his hand over his heart, he said, "Thank you for indulging my little monster."

"It was actually really cute. And one of the books, she read to me."

"By memory?" He dipped a clean spoon in a pan of pecan pie.

"No, she made it up based on the pictures. It was adorable."

Tessa released a big, exaggerated yawn. "I'm wiped. And my head is pounding. Is it OK if we head out?"

Aisha looked at Travis and Makayla. "Do you need us to help you finish cleaning up?"

"Don't be silly. I can do that," Makayla offered, patting Aisha's hand. "You two go home and rest."

After a protracted goodbye, in which Aisha once again chastised Makayla for not keeping in touch, she and Tessa left, leaving Travis and Makayla alone. Makayla assessed the various plastic containers and casserole dishes. Pulling on rubber gloves, she looked at him. "I wash, you dry?"

"Sounds like a plan."

They got to work, and other than the stream of the warm water and the banging of dishes, they remained silent. Travis stood next to her, drying items as she passed them to him. He walked to one of the counters to stack serveware that was to be collected by church members and friends later in the week. Having Makayla next to him, even in silence, put him at ease.

"Are you leaving tomorrow?" he asked.

"Yes. I head out with my parents and Summer in the morning. Porsha and Colin are gonna go to Napa to visit friends." She handed him the last dish, ringing out the sponge and removing her gloves. Wiping down the kitchen table, she pushed in the chairs.

She tilted her head as she approached him. "Are you OK?"

Travis's eyes focused in on her. "I can't complain; no one would listen." He imitated her father's voice, a sly smile on his face.

"You're not funny."

"Thanks again for coming." He gently tapped her arm.

"Of course. That's what friends are for."

"Oh, OK Dionne Warwick, so we're friends now?"

"We've always been friends. You were just so darn pigheaded," she teased, placing the dried serving utensils in the drawer.

"Me?" He shook his head with a blink of his eyes.

"Yeah. I'm glad to see you came to your senses."

Licking his lips, he flashed a smile. "I know, right? What was I thinking?"

The two burst into an awkward moment of uncontrollable laughter. As his body shook, his heart still ached, his mind still wandered, and his body felt like it was running on fumes and desperation.

Travis wiped a rascal tear that escaped from his eye. "Sit on the porch with me. Let's have a drink." He wasn't ready to be alone. He didn't want her to go.

"I don't wanna overstay my welcome."

"How would you do that when I asked you to stay?"

Makayla nodded in agreement.

Opening the fridge, he pulled out two Sapporo beers, handing them to her. "I'll meet you out front; I'm just gonna check on Daisy really quick."

Makayla made her way to the swing on the front porch. It looked like it had recently been repainted. Sharon was crafty, and she always had a project or two in progress at the house. Looking up the block, she took a deep breath. She had hoped she'd be gone before he returned, but Aisha insisted they catch up, pulling up wedding pictures on her phone.

Travis walked onto the porch. Sitting next to her, he reached for his beer.

"Do you ever miss Oakland?" Makayla asked.

"Oh, yeah. I miss it all the time. I seriously thought about moving back after Bianca got pregnant with Daisy. But then I remembered how expensive it is, and I came to my senses."

Makayla took a swig from her bottle, feeling her jaw tighten at the mention of Bianca.

"What about you? Would you ever leave Atlanta?"

"I don't know." Her shoulders gave a little hop. "I've never lived anywhere else. I think I'd miss my family too much."

"What are you going to do when you move to Houston, Texas?"

"Who said I was moving to Houston, Texas?"

"Well, I don't think Rufus Wright would go for a long-term, long-distance relationship."

Makayla cringed; she'd forgotten she'd told him Hosea's real name. "We broke up ... if you can call it that, seeing how we were never officially together." Makayla threw a covert glance in his direction. "I know that what I want isn't in Houston, Texas." She had made the not-so-difficult decision to cut ties with Hosea, telling him it was complicated and she needed space to figure some things out. Ending things with Hosea was probably one of the stupidest things she'd ever done. She knew it wasn't the stupidest because the stupidest thing she had ever done was get Travis's initials tattooed on her body. It was a small tattoo, but anytime someone asked her what TAH stood for, she had to lie and say, "Tough as hell."

A look of surprise crossed his face. "What do you want?" He leaned back, eyeing her.

Makayla wanted to say, *"You. I want you. I miss us. I want that back."* She said none of those things, choosing a non-committal shoulder shrug instead.

"What about you? What do you want?" She decided to flip the question on him.

"I had all these plans. You know I love a well-crafted plan with tiered phases and goal dates." He paused to take a bite of the slice of pie he had brought out with him.

"Yep, we are very much alike in that way."

"I don't know. I still want to run Life Church one day; that hasn't changed. But the other stuff ... I'm not so sure about. You'd think I'd have learned by now ... the best laid plans often go awry." After a deep sigh, air left his nostrils in a rush. "So, tell me this; did everyone hear my conversation with Regina?"

Makayla clicked her tongue. "Not everyone. I think there were some people in the backyard who didn't hear it."

He rolled his eyes. "Those walls really are paper thin."

"Tissue-paper thin," Makayla agreed. "Is she OK?" She'd watched as Regina left, wheeling her luggage behind her, tossing Makayla a dirty look on her way out.

"Uh, yeah, it's fine. We talked. It's fine."

Makayla knew he was lying when he ran the back of his hand over his cheek, his subtle tell. But she decided not to call him on it. "That's good."

"Yep." His stomach grumbled loudly.

"Is that you?"

"Yeah. I didn't eat much today and this pie isn't helping."

Jumping to her feet, she said, "There's leftovers. I could fix you a plate."

He reached for her wrist. "No, I don't need to eat. I just need you." Color flooded his cheeks. "I just need you ... here ... beside me. That's ... no, that's not better." He dropped his head.

Makayla enjoyed watching him scramble for words as she tried to suppress a smile.

"I didn't mean any of that," Travis blurted out.

"Oh, so you don't like having me around?" she teased, pulling her arm away and crossing them over her chest. Happy to be released from his grasp, she hoped her heart rate would return to its normal eighty beats per minute.

"It's always better when you're around." Tilting his beer bottle in her direction, he took a swig.

Three hours, two beers, and one pint of Cherry Garcia ice cream later, Travis and Makayla had fully caught one another up on the events in their life that they each had missed in the past five years.

Travis retold the story of Daisy's birth and how he almost fainted when her head popped out. Makayla told him about her month-long trip to Spain three summers ago and her unexpected fling with a bullfighter. She hadn't been involved in many serious relationships since she and Travis broke up, but she was far from a nun.

"Wow, so you could have been a matador's girlfriend? I cannot believe you walked away from all that."

"Look, I'm not gonna lie, he was probably the most exciting and sensual man I ever dated."

Travis's smile slid off his face. "I'm literally sitting right here."

"No!" Makayla shouted. "Present company excluded." She patted his knee. "You're great."

"Thank you, appreciate it." Scratching at the label on the empty beer bottle, his face grew serious. Turning to Makayla, he asked, "Why did you kiss me at the hotel?"

Porsha had asked her that same question. She doubted he was ready for this conversation. He'd just buried his mother, and his fiancée was M.I.A.

"I don't really know," Makayla lied. "Why'd you let me?"

"Because . . ." Travis rubbed his brow.

"Because?"

"Because . . . in that moment, it felt right." Collecting the empty beer bottles, he stood. "I'm gonna check on Daisy," he said with a crooked smile, disappearing into the house.

Even though it was dark, the neighborhood was still abuzz with activity—kids playing basketball in the street, little girls jumping rope down the block, rap music blasting from a passing car. The sounds of summer. Looking toward the door, Makayla swung back and forth. She knew she couldn't play this game much longer; her feelings for Travis were too strong. When he returned to Atlanta, she would sit him down and tell him she loved him. Waiting was no longer an option; this conversation was long overdue. Even if he told her he didn't feel the same way, which, though slight, was still a possibility, it was worth the risk.

Makayla's face lit up as he walked back onto the porch. Her burgundy-painted lips turned upward in a bright smile. She felt electricity course through her veins, powered by his kilowatt smile.

"How long are you staying in Oakland?" Makayla asked.

"Probably another week or two." He scratched at his chin. "We have some decisions to make. We need to settle Mom's estate and decide what to do with the house."

Makayla nodded. "Well, I'll miss you."

"Really?"

"Yeah. Don't sound so surprised. I've kinda gotten used to your stupid face."

"This face?" Pointing at himself, he needled her in the ribs, pushing his face close to hers.

"I'm not ticklish," she claimed, trying to block his hands that were reaching for her sides and stomach. She couldn't control her laughter as Travis found all her sensitive spots. A warmth washed over her like a wave as he playfully tugged at her.

"I kissed you because I'm still in love with you, and I think you're still in love with me," she blurted out, catching them both by surprise.

Travis retreated, bumping into the patio railing as he tried to distance himself from her.

Makayla's chest heaved in anticipation of his next words.

"I'm engaged, M-Kay," he whispered, looking down at his Oxfords.

"I'm aware." *Painfully aware.* "And I know it's bad timing." She stood, immediately wishing she hadn't because her knees felt hollow.

"Bad timing?" His brows curled down.

"If I don't say anything now and you married ... her. I'd never be able to forgive myself. You don't have to feel what I feel, but you need to know how I feel. How I've always felt." She tossed her hand in the air helplessly. "I love you." Her eyes turned foggy as she pushed back tears. "I always have. I never stopped."

His eyes twitched, blinking rapidly. "I can't," he whispered, pushing his hands outward as if he wanted her words that were now hovering between them to dissipate.

Nodding vigorously, she said, "It's fine. That's fine." Her heart lost all rhythm, becoming frantic and wild as she looked into his eyes.

"Makayla ..." He reached for her.

"No, I get it; I'm too late. It's OK," she said, backing away.

"It's not that ..."

"I should go. I need to go. I'ma call an Uber." Rummaging through her purse, she found her phone.

"I can put Daisy in the car and take you to your hotel."

"No, it's OK; I can just call an Uber." Rejection was a noun she was very familiar with. She could feel her underarms dampen, the first signal that it was just a matter of time before pebbles of sweat moistened her face. She tried to etch a smile on her face, hoping to erase the shock and anger that was simmering underneath.

"I don't . . . I don't mind driving you." He shuffled his feet.

"I think it's best I take an Uber." Makayla fumbled with her phone, requesting a sedan as quickly as her fingers could click. She could feel the humiliation washing over her, and she did not want to be standing on this front porch when the tears came to solidify how pathetic she was. "Three minutes away."

When she finally turned back around, it felt like they were worlds apart and not standing just a few feet from one another. The two stood in silence, waiting for the Uber to arrive. She watched as Travis checked his watch every few seconds, like he was anxious to get rid of her. This felt like a slow death. She looked down at her phone, and it said her driver was now one minute away. She collected her purse from the corner of the patio so she could make a quick dash to the car. At this point, the driver didn't even have to stop; she could just get a running start and fling herself through the open passenger window.

I am going to kill Porsha. Makayla decided she was going to have to change her name and relocate to Alaska. That was the only option after this shit show. *Abigail is a pretty name. My new friends could call me Abby for short.* As the car pulled up, they bumped into one another, trying to flee the scene of the crime. Travis followed her, reaching to open the car door.

"Please text me, so I know you got to the hotel OK." Closing the door after she was situated in the back seat, he tapped on the window, signaling for her to roll it down. "Makayla …"

"Could you please drive?" she asked the Uber driver, sniffling. He complied, pulling away from the curb.

"Are you OK, miss?" the driver asked as he turned right at the corner.

"Yes," Makayla choked out before dissolving into tears.

Chapter 31

Walking through the administrative offices, Travis was greeted by sympathetic stares and kind words. It had been three weeks since the passing of his mother, and it was his first day back in the office. He'd spent the time away, tying up his mother's personal affairs. Aisha and he couldn't agree on whether to sell their childhood home, so they chose to list it as a rental until they could make a definite decision. He then scheduled an impromptu road trip with Daisy, Aisha, and Tessa to Legoland in Carlsbad, California. The last few weeks had been filled with sadness, and he just wanted to hear his little girl laugh.

Now, back at work, he was anxious, evidenced by his nonstop sweaty palms. He'd spent a great deal of time preoccupied with Makayla's words and how poorly he'd handled it. Everything was all messed up, and what he wanted more than anything else was to talk to his mother, to ask for her advice. Should he end things with Regina to be with Makayla, who, until very recently, was plotting his downfall? Was he spending too much time admiring the neighbor's grass while neglecting the landscape in need of watering in his own backyard?

Makayla's confession placed him in a difficult spot, despite the fact that hearing her profess her love left his insides vibrating. With all that had been going on, Regina and he had not spoken since their argument on the day of his mother's funeral. She wasn't returning his calls and after the first few days, he stopped trying. The two were overdue for a frank conversation. Makayla's ill-timed confession would just have to wait. Stopping short of the office door, he took a hearty breath, hoping to slow his heart rate. He needed a minute to mentally prepare himself for whatever mood Makayla may be in. Entering the office, he was greeted by a desk that was flooded with flowers and baked goods in colorful tins.

"Whoa, what's all this?" he asked, stopping in his tracks.

"You know the church aunties are always looking for an excuse to bake something," Makayla responded. The fact that she wasn't hurling one of the many vases and baked goods on his desk at his head was a good sign.

Opening a random tin, the aroma of chocolate peanut butter bars hit his nose. "You'll have to help me eat all this 'cause there is no way." Travis rubbed his beard, opening a bag of fresh donut peaches.

"What's happening with your face?" She pointed at him.

"Oh, this?" He stroked the growing hair on his cheek. "I got lazy, then Daisy told me it made me look handsome, so I kept it. What do you think?"

"It makes you look old." Makayla shrugged half-heartedly.

"Distinguished?" he corrected her, pulling at his chin like a wise elder.

"No, just old." This time, a laugh barreled up her throat as she was unable to keep a straight face.

"You just lost your tasting privileges, my friend," he joked, pointing at the abundance of goodies on his desk. His heart was still beating like a homecoming marching band drum solo, not from his nerves but from the smile that lit Makayla's face, angelic and mischievous at the same time.

"Maybe we can come to an agreement." Standing, she grabbed a covered pie dish from a box.

His eyes moved from her long, brown, shimmery legs to the pie dish in her hand. Leaning forward, his mouth started to water. "Is that?"

"Yep," Makayla said, carrying the dish like a sacred offering.

"Your momma's lemon meringue pie?"

She added the dish to his already overflowing desk. "She hopes it helps to cheer you up."

Lifting the ceramic dish cover, he bent down and took a whiff. "Perfection." He replaced the lid, surveying his desk. "It smells like a bakery in here. I don't know if I'll be able to focus." He moved some of the flower vases and baked goods from his desk to Makayla's to make room for his laptop.

"How was your flight home? Did Daisy talk the entire time?" Makayla lifted a bouquet of sunflowers, setting it on her desk.

"Nah, I was solo dolo on the flight back. School starts in two weeks. It didn't make sense to fly home just to turn around in a week and fly her back to Oakland." Taking his seat, he reached for the stack of mail and documents in his inbox. Flipping through, he stopped at a postcard-sized black and gold card. "Are you going to the charity ball next month?" He held the card up with a shake.

"If I didn't, my mother would disown me."

The charity gala was an annual event hosted by Patricia Randolph. The event was a black-tie affair and a who's who of Atlanta's power players, entertainers, athletes, politicians, and business professionals.

"I totally forgot about it. I still need to rent a tux." Travis stuffed the reminder card in his backpack. "Thanks for holding down the fort while I was gone."

She waved him off. "You'd have done the same thing for me."

"Yes, but I still want you to know that I appreciate it. Truly." He swiveled in his chair. "Your dad was right."

"About what?"

"About us being a good team." He grinned. "Don't get me wrong, you gave me hell for a minute there. But after a while, things started to come into focus. I guess old habits are hard to break."

"Once again, Dad was three steps ahead of us."

"Don't you hate it when he does that?" He wrinkled his nose, giving her a wink.

Travis sprayed his kitchen counters with Lysol. Running a sponge under warm water, he wiped down the concrete countertops. He had been cleaning for the last hour. He'd vacuumed the carpets, mopped the floors, and cleared out the dishwasher. Rolling his shoulders, he hoped to release the tension that was gripping them. Regina was on the way over, and he was dreading the meeting. She'd finally reached out with a text that read "We need to talk." He didn't know where her head was regarding their relationship. Maybe she wanted to try and fix things. The last thing he wanted was to ambush her with a breakup conversation if she was hoping for a reconciliation.

Moving around the room, he wiped down doorknobs and light switches. He was hoping to block out the thoughts that swirled in his head. Travis obsessed over the details, and his pending conversation with Regina was no different. He had already ruled out phrases, like "It's not you, it's me" and "I just feel like we are heading in different directions." Even if both statements were true, he didn't feel the same about his relationship with Regina, and he was at a fork in the road, ready to continue his journey alone.

Washing his hands, he surveyed his kitchen. It was spotless, with everything in its place, just the way he liked it. He was hopeful that by the end of his conversation with Regina, his romantic life would also be a little less cluttered. The doorbell rang. He smoothed down his modest beard before walking to the door. Swinging the door open, Travis pasted on a smile.

"Hi," Regina said. Unlike him, she didn't bother mustering a smile.

"Hey." He moved aside, allowing her to come in. "You could've used your key."

"I thought it best not to, considering."

"Can I get you some water or juice?"

"I'll take water. Thank you." Dropping her purse, she looked around his apartment like it was her first time there.

He took his time filling the glasses while he rehearsed what he would say in his head. *Regina, I feel like we are in two different places in life, and maybe it would be best if we took a step back and reevaluated what we want. Apart from one another. No, scratch that ... We should take a step back and reevaluate what we want. We should take the time and space we need to figure things out ... separately.* Travis shook his head, letting out a long sigh. Heading to the living room, he handed Regina a glass.

"Thanks." She held the chilled glass tightly in her hands. "Thank you for agreeing to meet me."

"Mm hm." He placed his glass on a coaster before taking a seat on the opposite end of the couch.

"I know you're mad about how we left things in Oakland," Regina started, shaking her head with a frown.

"I'm not mad. I'm disappointed." He wiped his hands on his jeans, trying to avoid her gaze.

"First, I want to apologize again for leaving. I was hurt and, honestly, a little embarrassed, and I handled it poorly."

"Apology accepted." His jaw tightened. At this point, what had transpired on the day of his mother's funeral was water under the bridge. She couldn't change it, and no matter how sorry she was, she couldn't make it right.

Regina's eyes hollowed out as she stared off into the distance. "The night you asked me to marry you was probably the happiest moment of my life. I didn't sleep that night. Did you know that?"

A quick no jerked his head.

"I couldn't fall asleep. I was so excited, playing images of our future life in my head. Silly, I know, but I could see it all: the house, the kids, the summers at the beach, barbecuing with friends in the backyard. I remember looking over at you as you slept and thinking, 'How did I get so lucky?'" She released a mirthless chuckle. "I thought we were blessed to have found each other. And you seemed happy too."

"I *was* happy."

Regina's forehead wrinkled, sizing him up. "Maybe. These last few months have felt different. Gone are the butterflies when you walk into a room. The butterflies are still there, but they're not from excitement; it's anxiety. My stomach is constantly in knots from the disagreements and me having to walk on eggshells, trying not to say the wrong thing. It wasn't like this before."

"Before what?" he said through clenched teeth.

"Makayla. This all started after you two started working to-gether." She brushed her auburn curls from her eyes.

Travis rubbed his forehead. He couldn't refute her claim. "I don't disagree. But what is happening between us is bigger than her."

"How do I compete with her?" Her eyes pleaded.

"It's not a competition."

"You're right about that. She's already won and is polishing her trophy."

He scratched his beard, searching for the right words. "Can we just keep this to the issues between you and me and not drag in anyone else?"

"No, because she is very much a part of this relationship. For the past few months, we've been a threesome—you, me, and your fan-tasy girl. Do you have any idea what it's been like for me these past few months, hm? Do you even care?"

"Of course, I care."

"I've watched our relationship change. The way you talk to me, the way you look at me, the way you hold me. And every time I voiced concern, you would make me feel like *I* was the crazy one. Like every-thing was normal. All the while, you were playing footsies with your ex-girlfriend." Her chin sat high as her nostrils flared.

He reached for his water glass, drinking slowly so he wouldn't have to respond.

"I can't help but feel like you regret ever asking me to marry you."

Travis choked on his water, coughing to clear his throat. "I made a commitment."

"Is that what I am, a commitment?" she snapped with an indignant fold to her arms.

Rearing his head back, he screwed his face into a grimace. "Come on, Regina. Stop. You know what I mean. Every relationship has cracks."

"Cracks, I can handle. We are broken."

"OK." He bounced his shoulders with indifference. He didn't know whether to defend what they had or let her statement stand. Yes, this relationship wasn't working and it hadn't worked for a long time. The glaring fissures between them couldn't be mended. Travis knew that this meeting with Regina could only end one way, and he was hopeful she would do the dirty work and dump him so he didn't have to be the bad guy.

"OK?" She cringed. "I just told you our relationship is broken, and your response is OK?"

Swaying slowly back and forth in his seat, he racked his brain for better words.

Regina twisted her engagement ring around her finger. "You know what? You don't love me. And I don't think you ever have."

"That . . . um . . ." He wanted to protest, but Regina was right. Of course, he loved her, but not in the all-consuming way he'd loved Makayla. "What are you saying?" He threw his hands in the air.

"I'm saying I see the way you look at her, and I realize that you have never, not once, looked at me in that way."

He opened his mouth to object but was shut down.

"Don't deny it." She pointed a finger at him. "I've seen it, this longing for her and whatever it was you two had."

"It doesn't mean . . ."

"It means everything!" Regina shouted, tears collecting in her eyes. "Do you really want to pretend? Because I don't. You have been going through the motions with me these past few months. When it came to planning the wedding, it was like pulling teeth to get your input on even the simplest detail. I thought it was just because you're a guy, but now I know it was because you never wanted to go through with it."

"That's not true."

"You owe me so much, but right now, I would settle for the truth," she sneered.

"I never wanted to hurt you."

"Answer me this. Do you love her?

He let out an unintentional chuckle. "This isn't helpful."

"What? Honesty? Accountability?"

"It's not that simple."

"Actually, it's not that hard. I'm asking you to be honest with me, something you have been unable or unwilling to do for quite some time now."

Speaking softly, he said, "There's just a lot going on right now. I feel like things with Makayla are unfinished. And I don't even know what that means or what it even looks like."

"So, in the end, it's Makayla Randolph with the steal."

"It's not a steal. It's—"

"No, you're right; it's not a steal. She can't steal something that you are eagerly trying to give away."

"I didn't mean for any of this to happen," he mumbled. Hurting her was never part of the plan.

"But it did." Her chin trembled. "You lied to me for months. You knew, and you pretended everything was fine. All the while, I'm planning *our* wedding and booking venues and trying on dresses. That whole time, you knew you didn't want this. You knew you didn't want me." Regina's chest heaved as she tried to retain her composure. "You sold me a dream you had no intention of fulfilling. Makayla was right; I was just some consolation prize to you. You wanted the brand-new shiny car but settled for what was behind door number two."

"Listen to me; you're making it out to sound like I lied to you this entire time. I loved you and what we had."

"Maybe in the beginning, but now, it just feels like I'm some inconvenience that you're forced to tolerate." She moved closer. "It's just you and me here. You promised you'd always be straight with me, and I'm asking you to be real with me now. I'm not crazy. Why didn't you just break up with me months ago?"

Travis remained silent.

"I'll answer that. You didn't because you wanted a backup plan. Just in case little Miss Perfect wasn't interested in getting the band back together. You asshole."

Travis's chin dipped to his chest. "I didn't want to hurt you."

"And yet, here I am . . . hurt. Can you just, for one second, step outside your pristine bubble and see it from my point of view? You say you didn't mean for this to happen. You say you never meant to hurt me, but you never did anything to stop it. You could have told me you were confused or conflicted or that you had just plain fallen out of love with me. But instead, you chose to string me along. You want to claim to be the good guy so much, but good guys don't do that. Good guys tell the truth, even when it's hard."

"You're right!" Travis yelled. "I'm sorry. You're right, OK?" Standing, he paced the space in front of the couch. If Regina wanted honesty, if that was what she needed to move on, then he would give her that. "You are not the only one who felt lucky. I felt lucky too. I met this amazing woman who loved my kid and made me feel things I hadn't felt in a long time. I asked you to marry me because I loved you, and you made me happy." He reached for his water glass, taking a long sip before continuing. "I didn't want to take the singles ministry job because I didn't wanna work with Makayla. I hated her; I was mad at her. But there was something else there under the surface.

"At the time, I didn't know that I still cared about her. But working with her every day forced me to confront some things. Should I have said months ago, 'Regina, I don't know if I can do this?' Yeah, sure, I guess. Was I being selfish? Maybe." He looked down at his feet, trying to decide how much he was willing to reveal. "Honestly, I was just trying to figure it out, and I wasn't willing to implode our relationship over a feeling. I'm not saying I was this perfect boy-friend. Could I have handled it better? Yeah. But I didn't wanna lose you."

"Were you ever even in love with me?" she asked as new tears slid from her eyes.

"Yes, absolutely, one hundred percent. But did I love you the way you needed me to? No." Travis released a heavy sigh, hoping to get out the words he had bottled up inside. "I wanted this. I wanted us to work. But at some point, things just got so mixed up. It wasn't my intention to lie to you. But I did. It wasn't my intention to belittle your feelings. But I did." His body shook as he tried to hold back tears. He was embarrassed, only now understanding the harm his lies caused. "I thought by not telling you the truth that I was helping to spare your feelings in some way. And I didn't know what I was feeling for Makayla, and I needed you." Chewing on his lower lip, he tried to swallow, but it felt like a ping pong ball was lodged in his throat. He wiped at a tear as it slid down his cheek. "I should have told you once things started to change, but I was afraid and, quite honestly, I didn't want to.

"I never meant to hurt you, but you're right, I never stopped to ask myself how all of this was affecting you. This, you and me, it's my fault. I know you wanna blame Makayla, but it was all me because my responsibility was to you. My obligation was to you. You trusted me, and you gave me all of you, and I wasn't careful with it. You think I don't know I fucked this up? I know I fucked this up. I can't fix this. All I can do is say I'm sorry." Travis wiped his wet face with his hands.

Standing, Regina removed her diamond ring and placed it on the coffee table. The finality felt like a dagger to his heart.

At the door, she turned to face him for one last look, his eyes red and face slack.

"I hope you find what you're looking for," she said before moving over the threshold into her new life without him.

Chapter 32

Calvin dribbled the basketball through his legs. Turning, he body-checked Travis before stepping back and shooting a basket that hit the rim before falling back to the ground.

"You're about to lose this game." Travis broke into a pre-celebratory dance.

Calvin clicked his tongue, tossing the ball to Travis. "Check, motherfucker."

Bouncing the ball before advancing down the fenced-in, outdoor court Travis faked as if he was going to go right. He dribbled the ball behind his back, heading left toward the hoop.

Calvin's foot slid as he tried to recover. He yelled after Travis, "Have you spoken to Makayla?"

The sound of her name had the effect Calvin intended. Travis tripped over his feet. Throwing the ball up in a desperate attempt to save the shot, he stumbled forward while the ball soared through the air before touching down.

"Focus, T," Calvin said with a sly smirk.

"Asshole," he mumbled as he ran to retrieve the ball.

"All is fair in love and basketball, my friend."

"OK, who are you, Omar Epps?"

"Maybe I was just checking on my friend who got dumped two weeks ago." Holding out his arms, he waved his fingers, signaling for Travis to pass him the ball.

"I didn't get dumped; it was a mutual decision." Travis chucked the ball over to Calvin.

"Yeah, a mutual decision that Regina initiated because you were too bitch-ass to end things."

"Bitch-ass, huh?" He stared at Calvin furtively.

"Yeah, and it looks like you're about to continue to be a bitch regarding M-Kay," Calvin teased while attempting to spin the ball on his fingertip.

Walking over to his water bottle, Travis shook his head. *So, now I'm a bitch for taking some time.* After his breakup with Regina, Travis had to deal with some harsh truths. He always thought he was a good guy. People always said he was a catch and any woman would be lucky to have him. But if you polled Regina or Makayla, they wouldn't support that sentiment. His last two serious relationships had both ended badly and he was the common denominator. The fact that Makayla was open to the possibility of a second chance with him was a miracle.

He didn't want to leave a relationship with Regina and walk right into a new one with Makayla, carrying all his mismatched luggage filled with bullshit and toxic behavior. She deserved the best of him, and if she took him back, he would spend the rest of his life being the man she could depend on. When Makayla Randolph was through with you, she burned the bridge behind her so you no longer had access to her energy. So, the fact that she had spent months paving a new access road to her heart was not lost on him.

Turning to Calvin, Travis reassured him he had a plan. "Look, I know what I'm doing. I'm not afraid. I'm just getting all my ducks in a row."

"For what?" Calvin threw his arms in the air. "She loves you; you love her. This is the part where you seal the deal." He stuck his tongue out and thrust his hips back and forth. "If you know what I mean." He winked.

"Look, no one wants to seal the deal more than me."

"But?"

"I have a plan."

Calvin rolled his eyes. "Life isn't about plans; it's about results."

"Let me worry about all that."

His friend's voice took on a somber tone. "Look, all jokes aside, I just want you to be straight. And with Momma Sharon gone, the responsibility falls on me to make sure you're good."

"I get it, and I appreciate it. I do. I just need to move on my time-table." Travis had leaned on Calvin quite a bit these past few weeks, and he'd always picked up the phone, answered the door, and allowed him to vent or cry when needed.

"I also want to mention that I've known for years that Makayla was the one. But you two were too busy acting like dumb and dumber. Straight idiots."

"Thanks, Cal; that was beautiful." Travis scooped the ball up from the blacktop. "Now, you ready for this ass whooping?"

"You wish, choir boy."

Makayla surveyed the large ballroom at the Waldorf Astoria in Buckhead, with its marble floors and coffered ceilings. She was in search of a familiar face she actually wanted to talk to. The ballroom was filled with giddy attendees dressed to the nines. She dreaded these types of events. As an extrovert, she loved being social, but the level of grandiose and not-so-subtle shade thrown around left a bitter taste in her mouth. Atlanta was the type of place where everybody knew everybody.

Makayla did an about-face when she caught a glimpse of Harrison Fields, a writer who always asked her "When are you gonna let me show you a good time?" while looking at her lecherously. Bumping into one of the tables, she had to reach and steady the elaborate floral arrangement for fear it would topple over. Slowly crossing the dance floor, she stopped to adjust her black form-fitting, one-shoulder, floor-length dress.

"Oh my God, is that you, Makayla?" Turning, she found a woman with way too much makeup on.

"Annette? Hey," she responded, recognizing the sour expression Annette seemed to always wear on her face. The two had gone to high school together, and as Makayla remembered it, Annette hated her guts. "It is so good to see you."

"You look as lovely as ever," Annette observed after giving her a long hug.

Makayla searched Annette, her eyes darting from her nails to her clutch to the fake strand of pearls wrapped around her neck, looking for something she could compliment her on. She was unsuccessful, so she settled for, "How have you been?"

"Blessed and highly favored. You know, I have three boys, right?"

"Shut up!" Makayla exclaimed. Of course, she knew; they lived fifteen minutes from one another.

"Yes, Jepson, Jefferson, and Jeremiah." She pulled up pictures on her phone. "They keep me so darned busy. But I couldn't miss the charity gala, not this year. Last year, I was as big as a house with my little Jer Bear. What have you been up to?"

"I'm working at the church, so that keeps me pretty busy."

"Anyone special?" She searched Makayla's naked ring finger.

"No."

"Really, no boyfriend?"

"Nope."

"Oh." Annette placed her hand up to her ample bosom. "Wow, that's surprising. You were so popular in high school."

With a hand to her heart, Makayla replied, "You know, I could have gotten married and had a mess of babies, but I decided to focus on my career and bringing people closer to the Lord, which I think is so important. Don't you?"

"Oh . . . yes, of course. Such important work," Annette agreed.

"I'm gonna get a drink. It was so good seeing you again. I do hope we can catch up more later." Makayla walked away, not giving Annette the opportunity to say another word.

On her way to the bar, she swiped a few stuffed mushrooms from one of the wooden serving trays making its way around the room by waitstaff in black vests and bowties. At one of the two bars, she popped a mushroom in her mouth while waiting in line, admiring the large, detailed ice sculptures in the shape of koi fish.

"This is one swanky event," an all too familiar voice spoke from directly behind her. Whirling around, she saw a clean-shaven Travis in an expertly tailored black tuxedo. *For someone who doesn't dress up often, he's wearing the hell out of that tux*, Makayla thought.

"Funny meeting you here." Makayla smiled.

"At the bar? Not really. I find having a drink in my hand helps to make these types of events more tolerable." He shamelessly let his eyes travel the length of her body, taking her all in.

"Great minds." Makayla flashed a sly smile before ordering a glass of Zinfandel. As she reached into her clutch to leave a tip, Travis stopped her.

"I got you," he whispered, pulling cash from his money clip and tucking it into the tip jar. Grabbing his beer, he asked, "What table are you at?"

She handed him her wine glass so she could retrieve her table card from her purse. "I'm at table thirty-seven, wherever that is." Turning in a circle, she was a bit overwhelmed by the mass of tables scattered throughout the ballroom.

"That's my table." He handed her back her wine glass. "Let me escort you to your destination." Travis's hand rested on the small of her back, and she didn't shrink from his touch, allowing him to lead the way.

As they approached the table, Porsha jumped up. "There you are. I've been calling you." She placed her hands on her hips.

"Sorry, my phone's in my purse." She scanned the place settings to determine her exact seat. Her place card had her seated next to Travis. *I wonder how that happened?* she thought, looking suspiciously at Summer and Porsha. Pulling out her chair, Travis waited for her to sit before taking his place next to her. With a sip of wine,

Makayla turned to Summer, who was seated on her opposite side. "I love the dress. I told you it was gonna work."

"Yes, my fashionista sister is right again." Summer smiled, leaning in to whisper, "Miles liked it too. Girl, he had me bent over the kitchen counter right before we left the house."

Makayla shook her head and cringed. "OK, I've asked you repeatedly not to share that type of information with me." The last image she wanted running around in her head was her big sister taking back shots.

Ignoring her prudish sister, Summer whispered loudly, "Travis looks fine."

"Shh," she hushed her loud-mouthed sister, turning to Travis. Luckily, he was engrossed in a heated conversation about football with Colin and Miles.

"Good enough to eat. Finger lickin' good," Summer continued, licking her lips.

"Enough," she said, fidgeting with the gold ring on her matte white and black finger.

"What? Girl, I'm just saying, a man that fine should not be alone. All his talents just going to waste." Summer smirked, giving her sister a mischievous grin.

"I will stab you with this fork if you don't stop," Makayla threatened through gritted teeth.

"Any word on why they broke up?" Summer leaned closer with a whisper.

"What? I don't know. Why would I know?" She took another long sip from her glass.

The church gossips, her sister included, were working overtime trying to figure out what happened between Regina and Travis. Makayla's name came up in more than a few conversations as the possible cause. He never mentioned the breakup to her. But he had to know that she knew. Everyone knew. Still he'd chosen to remain silent. That appeared to be his new modus operandi of late.

Summer leaned forward. "Travis, how have you been holding up?"

Turning to face Summer, he shrugged. "Honestly, just taking it day by day."

"I can imagine. I know it's hard to believe right now, but it gets better."

"Thanks."

It still didn't feel real to Makayla that his mother was gone. If she was having a hard time coming to terms with it, she could only imagine what Travis was going through.

"Are any of you planning to bid on any of the items up for auction?" Travis addressed the table, deftly shifting the attention away from himself.

"Colin and I have our eyes on that vacation getaway to Mykonos," Porsha said, squeezing Colin's hand. "What about you?"

"Nah, that stuff is entirely too rich for me."

"M-Kay?" Porsha asked.

"I feel like my presence is charity in and of itself," Makayla teased.

"Being able to watch you in that dress is definitely the gift that keeps on giving." He gave her a wily grin.

Catching her breath, Makayla tried unsuccessfully to conceal a smile. Before she could respond, her attention was drawn to her mother, who was standing on the dance floor in the center of the room, microphone in hand.

"Welcome to the nineteenth annual Randolph Charity Gala. Can you believe that Eugene and I have been holding this event for so many years now? Nineteen years, and it only gets better. We want you to fellowship and catch up with old friends. Tonight, is about good food, good music, and generous hearts."

Every year, it was the same thing; they were there to have a good time, but more importantly, her mother wanted the attendees to open their wallets. If anyone could get people to give and thank her while they did so, it was Patricia Randolph. After dinner, the DJ played some classic R&B to get the guests to loosen up. Leaning against the back of her chair, Makayla watched as Porsha and Colin cut a two-step on the dance floor. For a white boy, Colin had a bit of rhythm, but he couldn't keep up with her sister who, after a few glasses of Rosé, was shaking it fast.

"Do you wanna dance?" Travis asked.

"Yeah, sure." She stood, smoothing down the front of her dress. Joining Porsha and Colin on the dance floor, the two danced to SWV's "I'm So Into You," both of them singing the chorus to one another at the top of their lungs. Porsha gave Makayla a look that said, "Get ya man, sis." When they dated, dancing with Travis was one of her favorite pastimes. She loved moving her body in time with his, on and off the dance floor.

After a few fast numbers, the DJ transitioned to a slow song, and Makayla turned to exit the dance floor, but Travis grabbed her arm, pulling her against him. Their bodies swayed back and forth as if locked in a trance. As his hands traveled from her waist to her back, she exhaled, allowing her body to melt into his. Placing her face in the crook of his neck, she breathed him in deep, the scent of him entering her nostrils. Makayla felt tingly goosebumps as he slowly rubbed his fingers up and down her bare arm. Lifting her head, she searched his face for direction.

"Do you wanna get some fresh air?"

"Sure, I love fresh air." She cringed inside as the words came out. *Goofy much?* she thought to herself. Following him, they exited the ballroom through the patio doors, walking the lush grounds.

They walked in silence for a bit, with Travis casting furtive looks in her direction. Walking past a group of partygoers, they turned right down a path that led away from the ballroom.

"I'm sure your mom is raking in the big bucks tonight."

"She had a goal of over a million, and she is not going to leave one stone unturned. You know how she is."

"Yeah, she's like a loan shark looking to collect on a debt. She even got me to pull out my checkbook."

"Whoa, not tightwad Travis opening the purse strings. And she didn't even have to break your legs." Makayla giggled.

"I'm not a tightwad. I just believe in saving for a rainy day." He wagged a finger in her direction.

Nodding with a frown, she replied, "Right, of course. My bad." Her attention was drawn to a gazebo illuminated with strings of white lights and decorated with dozens of bouquets of lilies, hydrangeas, magnolias, iris, and dahlias lining the wooden gazebo floor in assorted vases. "Wow, how beautiful," she gushed, veering from the path to get a closer look. "Do you think it's for a wedding or something?" She looked over her shoulder at Travis, who was lagging behind her.

He hitched his shoulders. "I don't know," he mumbled, attempting to wipe his sweaty palms discreetly onto his tuxedo pants.

Makayla looked around, making sure there wasn't any hotel staff nearby before climbing the stairs and entering the gazebo. Setting her clutch on a bench, she bent down to get a closer look, delicately holding one of the creamy white magnolias in the palm of her hand.

"The space is too small for a wedding. Maybe an engagement?"

The night, although warm, was fresh and comforting, with a velvety softness. The scent from the flowers fragranced the air. Leaning his head back, he allowed the stillness to wash over him. They were far enough away that the loud music and boisterous chatter from the gala were muted. Finally opening his eyes, he looked over at Makayla who was gawking at him.

"What?" Travis snorted. "Why are you staring at me like that?"

"Probably because you've been acting weird since we left the party. What's up, Holmes?"

Chewing the bottom of his lip, his mind raced. There was so much he wanted to say, but now that he had the floor, he didn't know where to begin.

"I was just wondering, why did you agree to date me in college?"

"OK, that's random, but it's an easy answer. I felt sorry for you.

You were this skinny kid who had no game. Zero." Her lips held a loose smile.

He gagged on a fake laugh. "I'm actually being serious. Like I really wanna know."

"Really?"

Travis pointed at himself. "Yes, this is my serious face."

"OK, well, it's still an easy answer." She swayed her body slowly back and forth. "You listened when I talked; most guys didn't. You made me laugh till my sides hurt. You were super smart, always teaching me something new. But most importantly, I liked who I was with you and how I felt even when you weren't around."

He looked down at his feet, attentively nodding his head. "Sometimes I wish I could go back. Things were a hell of a lot simpler then. I'd made fewer mistakes, burned less bridges."

The smile on her face collapsed. "We can't go back."

"No, but maybe we can move forward." He inched closer, pulling an iris from one of the bouquets and offering it to her.

Makayla nervously scanned the area surrounding the gazebo. "You can't just take flowers. What if someone notices?"

With a light laugh, he stepped back a bit. "I think it's OK, seeing how I put these flowers here."

The corners of Makayla's mouth curled. "You hate flowers." Turning in a circle, she reexamined the scene, looking for clues. "You always said flowers were a poor investment because they died before you even had a chance to enjoy them. This is extravagant and over the top and a lot of money."

"Yes," he agreed, attempting to hand her the flower again.

Reluctantly accepting the single iris, she twirled the stem in between her fingers. "Why would you do this?"

"For you." He locked eyes with her, desperately wondering what she was thinking.

"Me?"

"Listen, my feelings about flowers haven't changed, but you love flowers, so I thought I would make up for lost time and get you all the flowers I should have given you when we were together. Makayla, I've made so many mistakes, but losing you was the biggest one." Even though the night offered a gentle breeze, he could feel his temperature rising.

"When we were at my mom's place . . . and you said what you said, I didn't know how to respond." Clearing his throat, he continued. "I had a lot of baggage back then, and in that moment, it didn't seem fair to you or us."

Makayla followed him with her eyes as he paced over the deck flooring of the gazebo, walking in one direction and not really making any progress before he turned and walked back.

"I'm ready to talk now, though, if you're still interested."

"I'm listening."

"I miss you," he blurted out. His heart pounded against his rib cage, threatening to burst out. "You were more than just my girlfriend; you were my best friend. You're the only one who knows that I slept with a teddy bear until I was sixteen."

"Ah, Mr. Cuddlesworth." Makayla's face brightened as she remembered Cuddlesworth, the brown and dingy-white stuffed bear.

"Yeah, good ole Cudds." Travis pitched back on his heels. When he'd practiced this conversation at home, it always ended with him blathering like an idiot. *No one cares about the damn bear. Get it together.* Taking a deep breath, he tried to regroup. "I always wondered what a woman like you saw in a guy like me. If I'm being honest, I think I kinda obsessed about it. I wanted to be able to provide for you and take you on trips and to nice restaurants. I really wanted to be the man you thought I was. And I was terrified that eventually you'd realize that I was just this poor kid from Oakland and you'd run off with a dude named Chadwick. So, I sabotaged us. What I didn't realize was that losing you was like losing one of my senses. I had to figure out how to function again. But the thing is . . . I don't function without you." Tugging at his bowtie, he was feeling a bit claustrophobic.

"After I blew everything to hell, I tried to fix things but then

Bianca ... You were mad and I didn't have any good excuse. And as the months went by, we kept drifting further away from one another until I couldn't reach you, no matter how far I stretched. So, I lost the one person who I could genuinely be myself with. When I was with you, I didn't have to be Sharon's son, the straight-A student who was on the honor roll and taking college courses his junior year. I didn't have to be the role-model brother who protected his sister from bullies. I didn't have to be the inspiring young man on a scholarship who wanted so desperately to fit in. With you, I could be my real self, the person I was when no one was looking. And you loved me in spite of my imperfections and insecurities."

"Travis, don't you know that you were that for me too? All my life, I walked around with the weight of the Randolph name on my shoulders. People expect so much when you're Eugene Randolph's daughter. You were the first person who didn't care about any of that. You just thought I was pretty and smart. I loved the way your face lit up when you looked at me. I didn't care about the money situation, I swear. I just loved you and the way you loved me back."

Travis's heart was beating double time. Why had he allowed all this time to pass with so much left unsaid. "I just feel like I messed everything up. You trusted me and I hurt you. I can't say I regret what happened because it gave me Daisy, and she's my world." Travis tilted his head, hoping his words weren't just incomprehensible ramblings of a desperate man. "Does that make sense? I hope that makes sense."

"I get it. Daisy was meant to be here, and she's a bright, funny, and exceptional little girl."

Swallowing hard, he continued. "For me, it has always been you. Ain't a day gone by that I haven't thought about you, wishing I could make it right. You were the love of my life." He paused, shaking his head. "You *are* the love of my life."

Her chest heaved from the weight of his words, her chin quivering, and he was certain that at any moment, tears would spill from her eyes.

He continued. "I wanna hit the snooze button so I can cuddle with you for five more minutes. I wanna clean the house on Saturday mornings while we dance around to old records. I wanna raise a family with you. I wanna wake up groggy eyed at three in the morning and help feed the babies."

Makayla squinted her eyes while raising a perfectly arched eyebrow.

"Yes, I said babies, so many babies." He chuckled. "I wanna go to soccer practices and ballet recitals. I wanna wash dishes next to you every night. I wanna fight about what television show to watch after dinner. I wanna feel your cold feet rub up against me under the covers. I wanna flood your face with kisses and make your body feel like it's just us two in all the world. I wanna tell you I love you every morning before heading to work, and I wanna whisper, 'I love you' in your ear, so it's the last thing you hear each night. I just wanna love you as hard as I can, for as long as you'll let me."

Tears tumbled down her face. "Can we just skip to the kissing part now?"

Before the words had fully left her mouth, he pulled Makayla against him, his grip firm yet gentle. Every nerve ending in his body was firing, yearning for her touch. Licking his lips, he slowly brought his mouth to hers. The kiss engulfed them, their lips moving in unison as she dropped the flower, wrapping her arms around him. Makayla's mouth tasted like peppermint, cool and refreshing. His lips moved from hers, trailing down her neck, as she arched her back, longing for more.

Pulling back, breathless, her lip trembled as she whispered, "I have a room upstairs."

"Then why are we still down here?" he asked, unwilling to release her from his grasp. He kissed her full lips, walking backward and tipping over a glass vase as he tried to lead her out of the gazebo.

"Wait." She reluctantly pulled away. "I need to check in with Porsha and Summer or they'll come looking for me."

Travis straightened his tuxedo jacket. "OK. How about we meet at your room in twenty minutes. What room are you in?"

"Twelve forty-two." Makayla bit her lip.

He looked at his watch and, caressing her face, kissed her one last time. He begrudgingly stepped back. Rushing from the gazebo, he yelled, "Twelve forty-two in twenty minutes."

Making it back to the room with a few minutes to spare, Makayla tossed her clutch on the chair, heading to the bathroom to examine herself in the mirror. She told her sisters she wasn't feeling well and was headed up to her room to get some sleep, sure to let them know that she was just going to take some ibuprofen and go straight to bed.

Inspecting herself in the mirror, she was thankful for the matte red lipstick because her lips still looked flawless. Removing several bobby pins, she let her hair tumble over her shoulders in soft, loose waves. She rummaged frantically through her toiletry bag, spritzing her wrist, neck, and inner thighs with her signature fragrance. After performing a quick breath test, she opted for several sticks of fruity gum in her purse; she didn't want to smell like toothpaste. She chewed hard, trying to extract all of the artificial strawberry flavor before spitting the wad of gum in the trash can.

Even though she expected it, the knock on the door still startled her. She forced herself to walk slowly toward the door, not wanting to seem too eager.

"OK, be cool," she warned herself before opening the door.

"Hi," Travis said, smiling bright.

"Hey." She leaned awkwardly against the door jam. "What did you do, go shopping for twenty minutes?" She pointed toward the plastic bag he was carrying.

He shook the contents of the bag. "Oh, yeah. I had to stop at the hotel store for . . . supplies."

"Whatcha get?"

Rifling in the bag, he pulled out two bottles of water, a magnet, a candy bar, and a box of condoms.

"Ah . . . good haul." Makayla realized he probably wasn't expecting to have sex tonight and had not come to the gala with a bunch of Magnums in his wallet.

"There were a lot of familiar faces in the store," he said, removing his tuxedo jacket and folding it neatly before placing it over the desk chair. "I almost bought a shirt that said Hotlanta on it. I was just throwing things in my basket, waiting for the crowd to disperse." Inspecting the room, he walked to the floor-to-ceiling windows, admiring the views of the city lights.

Letting out a shaky breath, Makayla said, "Is it weird that I'm nervous?"

"Nervous? It's just me," he said, shifting his weight from side to side.

"That's exactly why I'm nervous ... because it's you. It's finally you."

Travis moved across the room with deliberate steps until he was standing in front of her. Her eyes locked on to him with excited anticipation. "Hi," she whispered with a giggle.

He ran his fingers up her arm, resting his hand on her neck. A thrilling, tingly sensation began a trek through her body. Leaning in, his eyes locked in on her mouth. He brushed his lips against hers before parting her mouth with his tongue to taste her. Grabbing at his crisp, white shirt, she tried to pull herself closer to him, returning his kiss with years of suppressed longing. Their feet shuffled gracelessly toward the king-sized bed, his mouth never losing contact with her lips, neck, or shoulders.

With a gentle push from Travis, her backside hit the bed with a bounce. His hands moved under her floor-length dress and rubbed her thick thighs before grabbing her thong and pulling it down. Tossing her black lace panties aside, he disappeared under her dress skirt, but his presence was very much felt. And just like that, her drought was over. The clouds darkened and the air smelled fresh as he saturated her earth, moist and slick.

It was slow at first, with only a few scattered, plump raindrops. But it was clear a storm was on the horizon as she grabbed ahold of his head, his tongue twisting and wiggling. Glitter-filled magic coursed through her veins as her body seemed to levitate off the bed while shooting sparkles from her fingertips and toes. She clutched the bed cover, squirming but not wanting to be released. After Makayla was finished calling on God, Oshun, and the powers of Grayskull, Travis crawled out, and with her legs still trembling, he pulled her to her feet.

"How do I get you out this dress?" He turned her around, looking for access.

Leaning against him, she planted her feet, fearful her wobbly legs would give out.

"Back . . . hook eye and zipper." She gasped, still trying to regain her composure.

With a quick spin, Travis easily unclasped and unzipped the velvet dress. Shimmying out of her dress, she stepped back. His eyes drank her in, making Makayla feel self-conscious. She was thankful she'd kept her standing appointment with her aesthetician. Reaching for his belt buckle, she decided it was time to level the playing field. Unbuckling his belt, she pulled his shirt from his slacks. Dropping her hands, she watched as he unbuttoned his shirt to reveal his muscular chest. Makayla had always joked that he had muscles on the low because in a shirt, he looked like any other dude, but when he removed it, it was all muscles, abs, and the perfect V shape that ran from his hips to his pelvic region.

Travis stepped out of his pants, and Makayla smiled as her eyes danced from his chest to his strong legs. Lastly, he removed his boxer briefs, standing in front of Makayla in all his glory, causing her to cover her face with her hands. She had forgotten what she was getting herself into or, rather, what was about to get into her. Closing her eyes, she mumbled to herself, "Don't be weird" before turning to find Travis suited up and walking her way. "Oh, wow." Makayla averted her eyes, squealing.

"You all right?"

"Yeah, I'm very excited," Makayla said to the ceiling. "It's been ... so long since I've had sex. Way too long." She shook her head at her pitiful sex life. "And the last time, it was so terrible." She could not stop the words from spilling out of her mouth. "It's sad, really. Orgasm? What's that?"

"M-Kay," Travis interrupted her.

"Hmm?"

"Just breathe."

"OK, just breathe . . . yep." She straightened her back as every muscle went rigid.

He walked forward, gently guiding her back to the bed. His eyes hooded and hazy, he devoured her lips, his kiss instantly taking her breath away. Travis Holmes was a magician, and when he kissed her, all her thoughts disappeared. Any lingering nerves she was holding melted away, she remembered those lips that had kissed her so many times before and the hands that were now submerged between her thighs. A smile danced across her lips as her body thawed into the bed. Her breath stuttered as his touch intensified, causing her vision to blur.

Travis explored her with his tongue and hands, her body constricting before melting underneath him, only to tense up again from the intensity of his touch. Finding her mouth, his lips urgently kissed hers as his hands explored her curves. *Is this really happening?* Her mind was spinning. Makayla's fingernails ran across his back, confirming this was not one of her dreams. Wrapping her legs around his waist, she locked onto his eyes, the depth of his gaze bottomless, as their bodies moved in rhythmic motion.

"Oh, my God," her voice called out slow and heady.

Travis responded, the rich timbre of his voice whispering in her ear. "You feel so good."

Their tongues moved back and forth, desperately trying to

convey what words alone could not. Pulling her toward the edge of the bed, he stood, tightening his grip around her waist. She tapped the mattress like an MMA fighter, throwing in the towel, but she was far from done. Heat rose, traveling from her stomach to her chest. Reaching for him, she pulled him close. She wanted to feel the weight and warmth of his body on top of hers. His mouth was like a portal, transferring his energy to her, causing her toes to curl and leaving her devoid of distinguishable words.

Travis snuck voracious peeks at her face as she bounced from laughter, to squeals, to low, intense moans. She loved the way he invaded all her senses. The scent of him dancing on her nostrils. The feel of his body pulsating and writhing over her. The taste of his tongue as it danced against hers. The sound of his breathing as it built in intensity, gently tickling her face. The sight of his body responding to each swivel of her hips.

Time ceased to exist as Travis whispered in her ear, "I love you, M-Kay."

Her entire being tingled, her brain humming as his body moved over hers, radiating with heat. Smiling against his mouth, she let her eyes float shut. She could no longer feel the firm mattress against her back; all she felt was him and the firing of her nerve endings as he wandered free in her love. A fluttering release of breath escaped her lungs as she arched her back. She only felt him, every thrust, every heartbeat, every dream they'd ever shared.

Epilogue

Travis's alarm chimed. Reaching out, he silenced the urgent buzzing and vibrating. With a shake of his limbs, he let out a big yawn. To his left was the mass of sheets and blankets Makayla had buried herself under. His hands roamed under the covers in search of her body. Once he found her, he wrapped his arm around her waist and pulled her close until he could feel the warmth of her bare skin against his.

"What time is it?" she whispered with a raspy voice, her eyes still half-closed.

"Time to start the day." He kissed the nape of her neck while cupping her breast in his hand.

"Nope, too early." Makayla grabbed the bed covers, pulling them over both their heads.

"We cannot be late again."

Makayla let her hands roam under the covers. "We can be a little late," she said with a devilish grin.

He gasped as Makayla found what she was looking for. "Maybe just a little bit late." Kissing her lips, he pulled her on top of him.

"Good morning. Is it still morning?" Tami asked, checking her computer screen for the time.

"Yeah, you're good. We still have a few minutes before noon." Travis smiled.

"Pastor Randolph wants you to wait in his office. He'll be back in a minute," Tami said as she twirled a strand of her red hair.

"Will do. Thanks." His face lit up as he walked into the office and found Makayla peering out of the large window. "Hey."

"I think someone's car is getting repossessed."

Leaning in over her shoulder, he peered out the window. He tried to contain himself, but the warmth of her body was giving him flashbacks to the start of his day. Travis planted a quick kiss to her neck, causing her to turn around and look toward the door before giving him a stern eye.

It was no secret that the two were back together; they'd been dating exclusively since the charity gala three months ago. But they had agreed to keep their professional and personal lives separate. They shouldn't be stealing kisses at work, and he shouldn't be fantasizing about his hands gripping her backside.

Travis took a seat, flipping through his notebook and stopping at a blank page. Taking a seat next to him, she crossed her golden legs. He was having a difficult time concentrating with her in the room. Since reconnecting, they spent most of their time together. If they weren't at her townhouse, they were hugged up at his apartment. They had so much time to make up for, and he wanted to spend that time talking to her, kissing her, and laying underneath her or on top of her or between . . . his thoughts were interrupted by Pastor Randolph entering the room.

"Hello," Pastor Randolph's voice boomed. Pulling out his chair, the pastor dropped his phone and Bible on the oak desk before taking a seat. "How are we doing?" he asked, smiling from ear to ear.

"Good, great." Makayla shook her head vigorously.

"Thanks for meeting with me. I know we are all very busy, so I'll keep this brief," he said, leaning back in his leather chair. "I just wanted to have a check-in to see how things are going with the singles ministry."

Travis glanced over at Makayla before answering. "I think things are going well. We've held a ton of outreach events that have produced significant engagement. People seem excited about the direction of the ministry."

"And most importantly," Makayla interjected, "we've been able to increase new single member growth at a rate of twenty-seven percent."

"That part." Travis pointed to Makayla with a smile.

"I expected you two to work well together, but I must confess that you both have gone above and beyond my expectations."

She turned to Travis, giving him a bright smile.

"If you two keep this up, you may be running the place in a few years. Mr. and Mrs. Holmes has a nice ring to it." He winked.

Makayla blushed, shaking her head. "Daddy, we talked about this, remember?"

While Travis and Makayla tried to keep the googly eyes to a minimum while at work, the pastor had gotten into the habit of calling Travis his future son-in-law. At staff meetings, yelling it out loud when he bumped into Travis in the halls; he even said something during a Sunday sermon a few weeks ago, claiming he had three strapping son-in-laws, when, at the moment, he only had two.

Pastor Randolph grimaced, showing the palms of his hands. "I know, but I'm just so happy that you two found your way back to one another. Love can be persistent, and it always finds a way."

"Let's move on," Makayla suggested.

"I'm just saying the Bible says when a man finds a wife, he finds a good thing. I think Travis would agree that you are his good thing."

Now it was Travis's turn to blush, his face turning red. "Uh . . . I don't disagree." He opted for the least telling response. They hadn't had conversations regarding their long-term goals; they'd been too busy living in the moment. But Travis knew that a proposal wasn't far off. He meant it when he said they had wasted too much time.

"Can we just get back to discussing the singles ministry. I mean, that is why you called us here, right?" She cast a look of frustration in her father's direction.

"You're right. I get it; you want to keep the professional and personal separate, and that's a good plan. We can put a pin in the marriage conversation for now." Pastor Randolph pretended to wipe his hands as if indicating he was finished with the topic. "The recent singles workshop you put together was well received with record attendance. Would you two be interested in turning that into a series of workshops?"

Travis looked to Makayla, who nodded enthusiastically. "Yes, we would love to put something like that together," he beamed, speaking for both of them.

"Great, then it's settled. I'll be excited to see what you come up with at our pitch meeting next month."

"We won't let you down." His mind was already racing with ideas.

"OK, I'm done," the pastor said, standing alongside Travis and Makayla. "Travis, I hope to see you at dinner on Friday night. Patty is making oven fried chicken and her world-famous red velvet cake for dessert."

"I can never turn down Ms. Patty's cooking."

Casting an eye toward Makayla, Pastor Randolph added, "Don't worry. We'll work on this one's cooking skills."

"Now, *that* I would pay to see," Travis said.

As they walked back to their office, Makayla looked up at Travis. "So, you really had to jump on the 'Makayla can't cook' bandwagon?"

"What? No, I love your cooking. Your Caesar salad right out of the bag is great. And who could forget your dinner rolls? The way you pull them from the packaging and warm them in the oven ... perfection," Travis said with a chef's kiss.

"Keep it up and you can make your own bowl of cereal with extra marshmallows," Makayla teased.

"I'll be good. I promise," he said, throwing his arm around her shoulder.

"Not too good, I hope." She raised an eyebrow, giving him a cagey grin.

"Daisy is excited to see us next weekend," Travis said, spreading face wash over his face.

Spitting a mouthful of toothpaste into the sink, Makayla said, "I can't wait to watch her play."

"Keep your expectations low."

"No, I'm sure she's great."

"She's four." He wiped down his side of the bathroom counter with a hand towel before chucking it in Makayla's hamper. Since they'd started dating, she had made room for him, not only in her life but in her bathroom. She completely cleared out one side of the dual sink vanity so he could make himself at home.

"So? Serena and Venus were four once." Makayla slathered her arms with honey-scented body butter.

"Yeah, and I'm pretty sure they sucked at sports when they were four too," Travis said, standing behind her.

"Well, I'm going to make a sign that says 'Go Daisy' on it with glitter and ribbons."

Wrapping his arms around her, he looked at their reflection in the mirror. "I'm sure she'll like that," he said, brushing his lips against her shoulder.

It was important to her to build a relationship with Daisy. If that meant weekend trips to Oakland and Skype bedtime stories, then that was what they would do. Travis buried his face in her neck, causing her to giggle in delight and turn to face him.

"It's late," he said.

"It's not even ten o'clock," she pointed out.

"Yeah, late. We should go to bed."

"But I'm not even tired. What could we possibly do in bed for hours?" She batted her big brown eyes.

"OK, I don't know about hours, but I could give you a good

forty-five minutes." His hands crept downward, grabbing ahold of her backside.

Trumpeting a laugh, Makayla agreed. "I'll take it."

Looking into his eyes, she sighed. This man made her happy. She wasn't foolish; she knew every day wouldn't be perfect, but as long as she had him by her side, they could weather any storm. Right now, she just wanted to enjoy this man, his smile, his sweet words, and his body.

Gently biting his lip, Makayla whispered with a wicked smile, "Your time starts now."

THANK YOU. LET'S CONNECT.

Thank you so much for reading *Working Through It*. If you liked the book, please help a sister out and leave a review or tell a friend. Your feedback is important to me and will help other readers decide whether to read my book too.

Feel free to connect with me virtually. I would love to engage with you.

Instagram: @authorkashathompson
Website: www.kashathompson.com

Made in the USA
Las Vegas, NV
05 October 2023

78586906R00166